Starkissed

Lanette Curington

A Samhain publishing, Ltd. publication.

Samhain Publishing, Ltd.
577 Mulberry Street, Suite 1520
Macon, GA 31201
www.samhainpublishing.com

Starkissed
Copyright © 2008 by Lanette Curington
Print ISBN: 978-1-59998-747-7
Digital ISBN: 1-59998-721-X

Cover by Christine Clavel

First Samhain Publishing, Ltd. electronic publication: July 2007
First Samhain Publishing, Ltd. print publication: May 2008

Chapter 1

Arreis aka Trader World

March 2308 TST (Terran Standard Time)

A tankard of pale green Hykaisian ale smashed into the wall as Leith McClure stepped into the dimly lit tavern. A few drops splashed onto her leather survival jacket. She started to wipe them away with her bare hand, but the droplets bubbled and ate tiny holes in the sleeve of her favorite jacket.

"Don't touch it, Leith!" Steve Hancock warned. "That stuff is acidic to anybody except Hykaisites."

"So I noticed," she murmured, watching the liquor ruin the black jacket that had been a Christmas present from her parents three Terran Standard years ago.

Two bodies sailed through the air a meter in front of them and crashed into a table in the center of the smoky room. The triangular table, reinforced to take such abuse, remained on its three legs. The two Peridots saved their drinks by holding them to the side. They shoved the bodies to the floor and continued their conversation between snorts.

The victory bellow of a rogue Hykaisite drowned out all other noises as a Numerian dancer drifted by, its holographic costume of interwoven light beams leaving a vapor trail behind.

It halted in front of Steve, fondled his crotch, and whispered in his ear. He smiled and laughed but shook his head. The Numerian floated to Leith and raised its hand. Leith caught the Numerian's wrist before it could touch her breast and indicated no with a quick jerk of her head. The Numerian shrugged and floated away.

The rogue Hykaisite ended his bellow with a coarse growl and beat his chest five times. Just as he settled down, an argument broke out in the corner where a group of Danid Hybrids played Martian poker.

"Explain to me again why we have to meet the buyer *here*," Leith shouted to be heard above the noise.

Steve laughed. "Lighten up, Leith. Arreis is the hot spot of the galaxy. The planet isn't a member of the Galactic Alliance, so anything goes." His laughter died, and he gazed at her with eyes half-closed—a look he often wore when coming on to her. "If you'd let me, I could show you more interesting places than this."

"Not in this dimension," she snapped and turned away from him. She had never considered him as anything other than a friend, and his insinuations made her uncomfortable.

Steve moved around her until he faced her, only centimeters away. A red flush of fury replaced the expression she despised. "Someday you'll regret saying no to me. And the day will come sooner than you think."

Leith shook her head. She was tired of his ineffectual come-ons and sexual innuendos and the look that did not appeal to her at all. "Why don't you call the Numerian? It might be impressed, but I'm not."

Steve's face twisted into a sneer. "At least the Numerian has an interest in sex."

A twinge of uneasiness slipped up her spine. Steve became hostile at the first hint of a negative response to his advances. He knew the family business better than she, but she wondered if putting up with his attitude was worth the aggravation.

Leith didn't like Arreis, more commonly known as Trader World, and its dens of iniquity where she floundered out of her element. She glanced at her Terran Standard watch, another gift from her parents. This one was meant to ease the transition from full-time student to running McClure Shipping. If she were back on Earth right now, she would be enjoying a lecture by a favorite instructor. The university—classes, lectures, and studying—was her world.

"But why *here?*" she persisted. Refusing to acknowledge his insult, which meant not acknowledging *him*, was the best way to get under his skin. "I know there are quieter places on Arreis. I saw several cafes and restaurants where we could meet without all the—the distractions."

A chair flew across the room and disintegrated against the broad, muscular back of the Hykaisite. He turned his shaggy head and, with a war cry, jumped from his seat to charge the brawling Hybrids.

"There he is." Steve nodded toward a table against the far wall. His anger had cooled, and he spoke to her in a friendlier tone. "Your father has always met this customer in this establishment. The Zi are fanatics for ritual and tradition."

"Zi!" Leith grabbed Steve's arm, stopping him in mid-stride. "Are you serious? The Galactic Alliance has sanctions against the Zi as well as the Crucians because of their continual state of war."

Steve shrugged. "Hey, their loss is our gain. Your father's been dealing with the Zi for years. You'll have to take it up with him. Me, I just follow orders."

Too late now, Leith thought and let his arm go. Oh, why hadn't she asked Steve *who* they were meeting this time? Steve told her the appointment was with a valued customer and on Arreis as usual. Leith didn't want to run the company and left nearly everything in Steve's capable hands. When her parents said to follow Steve Hancock's advice, that he knew McClure Shipping inside and out, Leith took them at their word.

So far, everything had gone smoothly. She followed Steve's lead and let him handle the details. She wasn't even curious enough to ask who the customer was or what cargo they carried. She never dreamed they would be trading illegally.

"That big yellow and brown fellow is the Rep. Oh, yes, the Paxian is here. The Paxian is always with him," Steve commented as they waded across the room and dodged a staggering Hybrid. "The Rep is a little stuffy, and I hear they dominate their females, so he may take exception to your presence. If he refuses to deal with you, don't antagonize him. I'll handle it."

Rep was a derogatory term for the Zi, who were humanoid in form but of saurian descent. Leith had never even seen a Zi. Not many people had because they were a closed and secretive culture and preferred not to mingle with off-worlders. Neither Zi nor Crux was a member of the Galactic Alliance, so very little was known about either of them and their cultures.

As Leith and Steve approached the table, the Zi and the Paxian stood.

The Zi was big, about 230 centimeters tall. High black boots with thick soles and heels added to his height. Dark gray trousers, war jacket and gloves, tucked into a broad belt around his waist, were made of a durable wool-like fabric. For extra warmth, Leith assumed, if he remained true to his cold-blooded ancestry. A hexagonal patch of glittery gold-on-black set high on each shoulder, their symbols indecipherable to her.

Yellow and brown were too bland to describe his coloring. Tawny, Leith decided, and umber. Both colors etched over his glabrous head and hands, the only visible parts of his anatomy, as if a master artist had painted him tawny, then shaded the subtle scaling of his skin with dark umber.

Leith's gaze lingered over his elongated face, taking in the chiseled contours of chin and jaw and the arched ridges protecting the tympanic membrane on each side of his head. His brow protruded slightly, and Leith suppressed the urge to reach up and run her fingers along the crest. In the sweeping hollows created by prominent cheekbones and crested brow, exotic saurian eyes of clear amber stared back at her unblinking. She had the feeling he had studied her as meticulously as she had him.

"Where isss Cameron?" he hissed.

"My father is ill." She took a deep breath and wished she were anywhere in the universe but here. "For now, I'm handling the business."

The Paxian's sleek black feathers ruffled. He wore a voluminous cloak to protect his wings.

"I am called Corru." Most Paxians chose names that were easy to pronounce because the Pax language consisted of birdlike twitterings that most non-Paxians could not mimic. "This is Commander J'Qhir, the Warrior of Zi."

"Leith McClure." Before she could decide if offering her hand would be a requirement or an insult, Steve propelled her into the seat closest to the wall. He took the chair next to her as Commander J'Qhir reclaimed his. The Paxian drew heavy curtains together, enclosing the table to ensure their privacy, then sat down.

The Commander's saurian eyes had not left her. She, too, found it impossible to look away from him.

"I have alwaysss dealt only with Cameron," he said stiffly.

Leith hid her disappointment. The way his eyes penetrated hers she had expected him to say something quite different. She shrugged, trying to show she didn't care one way or another. It would be a relief not to have to deal with the Zi at all, but she couldn't reveal even a hint of that feeling. "As I said, my father is ill. I'm in charge, and I have the cargo. Take it or leave it. I'm sure we can find another buyer."

She waited for him to call her bluff.

Beside her, Steve fidgeted nervously. "Now, wait a minute. We seem to have gotten off on the wrong foot here—or claw, as the case may be," he said and laughed hollowly.

The Commander blinked once and slid his eyes, void of amusement, to rest on Steve. Leith had the impression that the Commander would like nothing better than to take his "claws" and wrap them around Steve's neck for that remark.

Surreptitiously, she glanced at the Zi's hands resting tensely on the table. Remarkably human in shape and form, they couldn't really be referred to as claws. He had four fingers of varying lengths and an opposable thumb, but his nails were blunt talons and tinted pale gold.

Suddenly she was aware that he was looking at her again, and she met his gaze boldly. "Do you want to go through with the deal or not? If not, there's no point in wasting our time— yours or mine."

Leith was surprised how harsh she sounded, but refused to make amends. Perhaps the Commander would take offense and call off the arrangements himself. She started to rise.

The Paxian made a chittering noise, and the Commander looked at him, nodding solemnly.

"I have no time to argue with younglingsss. The cargo isss needed by my people." He brought out a black velvet pouch and cleverly undid the complicated knot in the silver cord. He turned the pouch upside down and poured the contents on the table.

A dozen polished gems danced across the surface. Brilliant fire, red sparks radiating outward, glowed within the center of each crystalline stone. The Zi jewels!

Leith fell back into her chair. Collectors slavered over the chance to obtain one of the gemstones. The rich and the famous, from vid stars to royalty across the galaxy, coveted the prestige of owning one. She was no connoisseur, but even she could see the innate beauty in the stones. She held one against the dim light. It blazed brighter than a laserlight beam. She could only dream what one would look like in full sun. Carefully, she returned it to the others.

Steve, mesmerized by the sight, cleared his throat. "I see you brought the required amount."

"Yesss," Commander J'Qhir hissed. "I brought the amount ssspecified when lassst we ssspoke."

His sibilant speech had intrigued her from the moment he first spoke, but the obvious resentment in this last comment made her take her eyes away from the brilliant gems to rest upon his face. Were the slits in his amber eyes narrower than before?

The uneasiness she felt from the beginning had grown to a strange undercurrent of disturbance. Something was wrong between the Commander and Steve, but she couldn't pinpoint it. They didn't like one another, but it was more than that. If she got out of this alive, she swore she would ask more questions next time. Her premonition was so strong, she was certain none of them would survive unscathed.

The Paxian sat with slender hands folded on the table, his humanoid fingers long and graceful. He had expressed no interest in the gems, had not even looked at them when the Commander spread them out. Resembling a human more than the Zi, his eyes were round, a beautiful shade of blue, and yet they didn't seem real, as if they were glass replicas.

His feathers ruffled. "Perhaps we should proceed."

A peacekeeper. She should have known, of course, since it was the reason his world came to be called Pax in Terran Standard. She sensed the Zi Warrior trusted him, but his primary function was to act as a mediator if the meeting threatened to explode. His calming influence ensured that each side came away satisfied. Leith relaxed a little, comprehending the unlikely pairing of Zi and Paxian. Paxians were often used as peacekeepers when opposite sides were more likely to let their passions overrule common sense.

"Our carrier is docked in Bay 3," Steve said, unable to take his eyes off the gems.

"My warsssship isss in Bay 24." The Commander gathered the jewels and returned them to the pouch. Deftly, he retied the cord into the intricate knot. "My crew isss ready to transsssfer the cargo."

"And our crew is standing by," Steve replied.

The four stood. One of the few moments when the Commander took his eyes off Leith, he looked at the pouch clutched hard in his fist. "For my people," he murmured and, bypassing Steve's outstretched hand, gave it to Leith.

She tried to say thank you, but the words would trivialize the sacrifice of the jewels. Instead, she bowed her head briefly. His only response was his unblinking gaze.

"Uh, let me have them, Leith. I have the security belt," Steve said eagerly.

Too eagerly, it seemed to Leith. Reluctantly, she handed them over. Next time, she vowed, she would wear the security belt. The jewels would be safe. An ear-piercing alarm would sound if the belt was stolen. If forced open without the code, incapacitating electrical charges would be the thief's reward.

Grinning smugly, Steve placed the pouch inside the cavity and keyed in the code. Ashamed of Steve's eagerness to obtain the gems, Leith couldn't meet Commander J'Qhir's eyes. Didn't Steve know how difficult it was for the Commander to relinquish them? Or was it that Steve just didn't care? Only the need for the cargo outweighed the value of the jewels to the Zi.

Disgusted with herself for not asking what the cargo was, Leith could only assume they carried weapons. What else would a technologically inferior society at war need? She had heard all the stories of how the Zi were out to conquer the Crucians and rape and plunder the lush world of Crux. Their own world was hot and dry, little more than sand and rock, and they were running out of resources. The Crucians tried to compromise by sharing their bounty, but the Zi wanted it all.

Why had her parents agreed to trade with them? Supplying weapons to the Zi was a serious offense. If caught, they would all go to prison for life, if not face execution. What could they have been thinking? *If* she returned to Earth, she would have a long talk with her mother...

Her sympathy dissipated. The Zi Warrior deserved whatever befell him, but she didn't. Oh, she knew pleading ignorance would not save her. She'd hang along with the rest of them. It wasn't fair she found herself in this predicament. However, it was her fault for not asking questions.

"It will take a few hours to transfer the cargo," Steve said as they prepared to leave. "Would you like a tour of the carrier? It's the latest design, Galaxian class, and the newest addition to the McClure fleet."

What had possessed Steve to make the offer and prolong contact with the Zi? Leith was anxious to conclude this unpleasant business and return to Earth.

The Commander's response was even more puzzling. "Yesss, I would like to compare it to my warssship."

"Corru, would you care to join us?" Steve extended the invitation.

The Paxian shook his head, feathers ruffling then settling. "Thank you, no. I have another appointment this evening."

Halfway across the room, Steve stopped suddenly and Leith almost bumped into him. He glanced toward the farthest corner where a group of four or five humans gathered around a large table.

"Are you looking for someone?" she asked, raising her voice to be heard above a Biian harp being played too loudly.

Startled, Steve whirled on her. "I, uh, thought I saw someone I knew, but I was wrong."

They waited while the Peridots crawled through the door, then stepped outside. After the smoky, smelly interior of the bar, Leith drew in several deep breaths of crisp, clean air. She felt as if she hadn't taken a breath for hours.

Corru took his leave of them, grasping arms with J'Qhir and shaking hands with Leith. He disappeared into a dark alley. Steve led the way to the spaceport, walking ahead a few steps. With his long legs, the Commander could have outdistanced them both, but he matched his stride to Leith's. He stayed so close beside her their jackets occasionally brushed.

The few humans who came into contact with a Zi reported experiencing an innate aversion to them. Because of their saurian eyes, she supposed. Vertical slits for pupils surrounded by amber were distinctly different from human eyes, but Leith felt no repulsion when she looked at the Commander. What should repulse her was his warrior status, the Zi trying to conquer the Crucians, and this particular Zi involving her parents in illegal trading. That should make her furious.

Yet, there was something about this quiet, dignified male that contradicted all of these thoughts. She couldn't feel repulsion or fury toward him no matter how hard she tried or what reason she could think of to justify such feelings.

She felt something else and refused to identify it.

Leith frowned into the dark night, illuminated only by a sky full of stars and the pale double moons hanging overhead. They had only a few more hours, and then Commander J'Qhir, Zi Warrior, would be out of her life for good. She wouldn't have to wrestle with her conscience any longer.

※ ※ ※

J'Qhir trod slowly beside the human female, the *sa`aloh*. He had expected to meet with Cameron as usual. He had often spoken with Hancock to make arrangements, but Cameron would be present when the time came to make the exchange.

Unprepared for the *sa`aloh* youngling, he had been rude. He had broken one of the major tenets of the Zi Warrior: Be prepared for anything and all things and do not allow the unexpected to overcome. He had allowed the unexpected presence of the *sa`aloh* to jeopardize his mission.

He should, of course, report himself to the Council of Elders, but he was too old and had been the Zi Warrior too long to put himself at the mercy of the Council over a minor transgression. The mission would be completed to everyone's

13

satisfaction, which was the important thing. He had recovered his senses enough to accept the *sa`aloh* and her price.

Of course, Cameron had nothing to do with the cost increase. J'Qhir could accept inexperience as an excuse, but not greed. Yet, he had seen no greed in her wide blue eyes as she held the jewel to the light. He saw reverence and the comprehension of how precious the jewels were to his people. Hancock was as avaricious as a Crucian, and J'Qhir expected no less from him. The *sa`aloh*, however, acting in Cameron's stead, had to know of the increase and approve.

He tried to summon disgust for her and the price she demanded, but he could not find it. He glanced at her. His eyes were made for the night, and he could see nearly as well then as during the day. Deep brown hair cascaded down her back, shimmering in the double moonlight. Ivory skin glowed starkly against the dark colors of her clothing. He caught a whiff of her scent. By the sands, it was familiar but he could not place it.

His *vha'seh* tightened. How long had it been since his body had responded to a *sa`aloh*? Too long. The war and the demands of his position weighed heavily upon him so that he had no time or inclination to seek another lifemate after the death of T`hirz.

Now, his inclination was increasing of its own volition.

"Commander, will you return to Zi tonight?" Her harmonious voice broke their comfortable yet unbearable silence.

"Yesss," he hissed curtly, not knowing why.

She said nothing more, obviously stung by his discourteous manner. He could not blame her. He raised his eyes to the stars. He did not know how to conduct himself with this human *sa`aloh*.

He had spoken to few *sa`aloh'az* in his life. His mother, long dead, had rarely spoken to him after he reached adulthood. Even before he reached maturity, she had little say in the upbringing of her male offspring. She was a perfect Zi *sa`aloh* in all ways. She knew her place and kept any opinions, if she had any, to herself.

So also had been T`hirz, his lifemate. His binding with T`hirz had been arranged by his father. The daughter of a Council Elder, he had never seen her before the arrangement had been made. She had never spoken in his presence until the ceremony and, afterwards, she had spoken only when spoken to. She had never expressed curiosity about what he did, whom he saw, or where he went. He had found no fault with T`hirz's response. Was it not the expected behavior of a lifemate?

They had been bound for less than a season, their physical matings brief and painful for T`hirz. Then, before he ever knew if the seed he planted would bear, she sickened and died.

Shortly thereafter, his father died as well. Enshrouded in sorrow, he had suddenly found himself appointed the Warrior in his father's place. A dutiful son, he could not refuse the honored position any more than he could have rejected his arranged lifemate.

The appointment came in the middle of the Second War with the Crucians. By the time it had come to an end, any thoughts of finding another lifemate were long forgotten. He had decided it was unfair to subject anyone else to the all-consuming life of the Warrior. Besides, those *sa`aloh'az* he had known, who would have made perfectly acceptable lifemates, were all bound to others. He would have had to settle for another arrangement and—with all due respect to his father—this he would not do. Thus, he resigned himself to a solitary existence.

A circle of bright lights indicated they neared the spaceport. Hancock led them inside the circle, across the landing pad to the first row of bays. In Bay 3, the triangular ship rose like a monolith against the night sky, its quicksilver hull gleaming in the light.

"This is the *Catherine McClure,* named for Leith's mother," Hancock told him. "It's the latest model of the Galaxian class and the newest addition to the McClure fleet. The landing struts are made of titanium-jettite alloy and guaranteed to withstand more than one thousand times the weight of the ship."

J'Qhir watched as Hancock keyed in a code on his remote control pad. A ladder descended from the side of the ship while a door rose. They ascended the ladder with Hancock leading the way. J'Qhir climbed behind the *sa`aloh* and found himself eye-level with an intriguing part of her anatomy. Loose-fitting trousers and the bulky jacket left most everything to the imagination, but with each step up, one hip bent and revealed a plump curve on either side. So different from the straight planes of a Zi *sa`aloh.* He tightened even more.

Ssss, he should not react at all to the physical attributes of any *sa`aloh,* Zi or otherwise, but these curves tantalized him. Why in the name of the rock did this human *sa`aloh* make him think of *rhi`ina`a* more in the past hour than he had in the past decade? It was a relief when he stepped through the doorway and his line of sight was now above her instead of upon her. Hancock led them to the command sector, and he spoke into the comm to let the crew know they should begin unloading the cargo.

"I need to alert my crew to prepare for the transsssfer," J'Qhir said. When Hancock nodded, J'Qhir keyed in the frequency and quietly spoke in his own language.

"Oh, uh, Leith, would you mind conducting the tour. We were having trouble with an anti-grav skid earlier. I need to check it out with the crew."

"Of course. I'd be happy to show the ship to the Commander."

"Thanks. I'll let you know what I find out."

Hancock disappeared down the corridor leading to the back of the ship. Alone with the *sa`aloh*, her familiar scent played havoc with his senses. He stood as still as a stone, trying to keep himself in check.

"Command Central, of course," she said, hand outspread, pointing to each console in turn. "Navigation, communication—I suppose you know all this. Our technology is a little different from yours, but basically it's all the same."

Ssss, the implications of that statement made him tighten more. She could have no idea of where his thoughts led, but her round eyes widened a bit and she quickly led him down the corridor.

"The galley. We have to carry freeze-dried food now, but the Artilians are doing marvelous things with the replication process. This is the Liquidator. Using waste products, any beverage can be replicated as long as the specifications are logged into the computer banks. Would you care for something, Commander?"

"Water, thank you," he said.

She punched in a code, and they waited while the processor completed the operation. The doors slid open, and she handed him the container of water. She punched in another code, and this time a cup of brown liquid appeared.

"Terran coffee. Have you ever tried it, Commander?"

He shook his head.

"Would you like to try a sip? I like mine sweet with extra cream." She held out the cup to him.

He took it, his fingers brushing hers. Steam rose from the liquid.

"Careful, it's hot."

He turned the cup up to his lips and took a small sip. The sweetness was sickening to him and he frowned, handing the cup back to her. She laughed. "Perhaps you should try it without the cream and sugar. It might be more to your liking."

He gulped the water to wash away the taste and followed her to another section.

"This is Med One. We are equipped with the latest in diagnostic equipment so we don't need a doctor on board. The computer banks are uploaded with every conceivable injury and illness that can befall a human being and its treatment or cure. A robot surgeon handles the more complicated procedures. Xeno-biology programs will be available soon."

He had finished the water, but didn't know what to do with the container. Smiling, she took it from him and tossed both into a waste chute. Then she led him farther down the corridor.

"The hold and engineering are at the end of the corridor. These doors along here lead to the crew's quarters."

He stopped beside her when she came to a halt in front of one of the doors.

"This is my cabin. Would you care to see it?"

He nodded. She placed her hand on the identipad, and the door slid open. Inside, the lights were dim.

"Lights nine," she said, and the illumination brightened considerably.

Soft silver-gray carpet covered the floor. Sofa and chairs were grouped in one corner, dining table and chairs in another.

He watched her walk across the carpet to one side of the spacious bed. A silver comforter, puffed and soft, covered the bed.

"This room is obscenely luxurious compared to the crew's quarters. My father designed it particularly for my mother. He's been trying to talk her into making trips with him again, the way they used to when all they owned was one clunker of a ship and started McClure Shipping." She pushed a button on a comm pad. In the wall above the bed, panels slid apart to reveal a huge oval window. She pushed another button, and the lights went out. The starscape dominated the darkened room.

"In space, the scene is breathtaking," she murmured.

"I know," he said quietly and walked to the other side of the bed.

She laughed. "Of course you do. I was born on Earth, and I've spent most of my life there. By choice. I've traveled in space more in the past two months than I have in my entire life. I'm afraid it's still new to me. I hope the magic never wears off."

"It doesss not."

"Good. I always want to feel this way when I look at the stars."

She smiled, square teeth shining iridescently against the softer sheen of pale skin, and he tightened yet again. Each time he thought he had himself under control, she would say or do something or the light would fall on her in a way that he found indescribably pleasing.

In the name of the rock, why couldn't he get his mind off of *rhi`ina`a* for one moment? He was no better than a youngling who had yet to experience it for the first time!

"Commander, would you like to see the hold now?"

"Yesss," he said, and his voice sounded huskier to his own hearing. "That would be a good idea."

He moved to the foot of the bed, watching her as she did the same. As she drew near, the light from the window brightened considerably. They both turned as the double moons came into view, the larger pursuing the smaller across the night sky. Time passed in breathless anticipation as the chase continued across the expanse of window. At last, the larger moon overtook the other, and the two blended into one.

Rhi`ina`a in the sky. Even the celestial bodies conspired to drive him mad.

"My God," she whispered hoarsely as she stared at the conjunction.

Her round eyes were as big as moons, her lips moist and slightly parted. He did not think she invoked her God as a prayer. He thought—and he admitted it might be wishful thinking—she looked ready for *rhi`ina`a*.

He cleared his throat. "Perhapsss we ssshould visssit the hold now."

She nodded vigorously and turned back to the remarkable sight in the window. "Yes, Commander, I think we should."

Both of them hesitated as if neither wanted to make the first move. He felt the vibration first then the starscape moved, the moons quickly disappearing from view. He thought he suffered some kind of seizure, a result of long abstinence and the sudden influx of stimuli, but then he recognized it for what it was. Liftoff.

She was falling. As he reached out to help her he felt the enormous weight of an increase in gravity. He hadn't felt that kind of pressure since he was a youngling, flying the ancient warships that had no gravity sensors.

He fought the pressure, but it was too great. If he didn't give in, muscles would stretch and bones might break. He let himself fall forward, to the bed, and found himself atop the sa`aloh. She made a small *oof* sound.

The pressure did not increase any further or he would have crushed her.

"What's...happening?" Her words slurred, and she had difficulty speaking.

"Do I hurt you?"

She shook her head, one quick jerk to the side. "If you could—move a little—so I can—breathe."

He couldn't lift himself at all, and only with tremendous effort could he shift his upper body a little to the side, off her chest.

"Better," she said. "This shouldn't be happening. We should have felt some vibration, but the gravity sensors should have kicked in."

"The quessstion isss, why did we lift off at all?"

"I don't know. Have we been—hijacked? The gravity increase—to incapacitate—us?"

"That isss a logical conclusssion," he agreed. "There isss alwaysss that danger on Arreisss."

The side of his head pressed into the puffed comforter beside hers, his mouth close to her ear. His arm lay across her chest, but its weight was not enough to harm her. Part of his upper body lay upon hers, her arm beneath him, her hand in a most inconvenient place. She tried to rise, to pull free of the pressure, a natural reaction to one unaccustomed to the weight of a higher gravity. Her hand's movement did nothing for his sanity, and if she did not stop, he would not be able to hold it in at all.

"Relax, *sa`aloh.* You cannot essscape the presssure. Fighting it will only harm you," he advised. Her movements ceased, and he exhaled his relief.

His lower body ran along the length of hers, their lower legs off the bed completely. He felt the tension at the back of his knees, as if the pressure tried to bend them in a way the joints never intended. The mounting strain could not overrule what her moving hand had wrought or what she had unwittingly done to him all evening.

He was in danger from an unknown source, and all he could think of was her, spread beneath him, her body radiating a heat to rival that of the Bh'rin'gha Desert on Zi. Cold-blooded by nature, he always found himself drawn to heat, and humans were the most warm-blooded creatures of all.

He heard the doors open with a whoosh, but no one entered. He turned his head, straining his neck muscles, to see who held them captive. Out of the corner of his eye, he glimpsed—

"Well, well, what have we here," Steve Hancock said and laughed dryly. "You'd better watch it, Rep. That woman is cold enough to freeze hell over."

Chapter 2

Pinned beneath the Commander, his long length molded to hers by the heavy gravity, Leith felt a warm rush in her ear with every breath he expelled. The sensation trailed along every nerve, intensifying what her body had fought all evening long. If he did not move soon, taking his breath with him, she would implode.

Now, Steve's remark made her blush, and she was grateful the Commander couldn't see. The insult stung. She wasn't immune to members of the opposite sex, as Steve implied. Quite the contrary. She had just never been attracted to Steve, and his ego couldn't withstand the rejection. It was easier for him to believe she was lacking.

"Hancock, releassse usss at once." The sibilant command sent another shiver through her. Under other circumstances, the order would have sounded effective, but their apparent compromising situation relegated it to an indignant plea. "You will not sssucceed."

"Steve—?" Everything refused to work properly, including her jaw muscles. "What are—you doing?"

"Now, Leith, you've never been a stupid woman. Uncooperative and frigid, but not stupid. I thought you would have figured it out by now. I believe the Rep has. Am I right, Rep? Or is it true your brain is the size of a pea?"

"Sssss..." The angry hiss sent his breath straight into her ear as he struggled against the gravity. His need for retaliation outweighed caution.

"Relax, Commander," she whispered, reminding him of his earlier advice to her. "Save your—strength. You'll need it—when he lets us go—"

"What's that, Leith? Speak up, I can't hear you. Don't you know it's impolite to whisper in mixed company?" Steve laughed, a hysterical edge to the sound as if he were on the brink of madness.

"Steve—Dad is going to be so—disappointed—in you." Her jaws ached with the effort, but she hoped his genuine admiration for her father would snap him to his senses.

"You had to bring Cameron into this, didn't you? Cameron has nothing to do with this. And *everything*. Don't you understand yet?"

"You will be hunted down, Hancock, and you will not be allowed to live," the Commander said evenly. She noticed that he didn't say that *he* would be the one to find and kill Steve. Maybe he felt the same pall of doom hanging over them that she had sensed earlier.

Steve ignored the threat. "Haven't you figured it out yet, Leith?"

Her mind raced. Her father. Nothing and everything. She remembered Steve's covetous eyes on the Zi jewels. His pride in a ship that wasn't his. Would the real Steve Hancock voluntarily help with malfunctioning skids when a junior mech could be found to do the dirty work?

"Answer me, Leith!"

"Can't—hurts—"

"All right!" he barked. She heard him tap the comm pad on the bulkhead beside the door. "Carter. Bring it down to norm in Cabin One. Easy now. We wouldn't want to hurt them."

Steadily, the weight decreased. For the second time that evening, she drew in deep gulps of air as if she hadn't breathed for hours. She felt feather-light, as if she might float off the bed. The Commander remained atop her, but he was tensed, ready to take advantage of any chance Steve might give him.

"Don't try anything, Rep," Steve warned, stepping into the room. "I have a Blaser aimed at you, set on high. One shot and you're so much space gas—total vaporization in less than a second. If I even think you're going to try anything, you're a part of Rep history. Wiley and Phillips are here and armed."

The Commander eased from her carefully, so Steve wouldn't misconstrue any movement. Leith sat up—too fast. Vertigo swept over her, the room spinning as if she were in freefall. She held her head and closed her eyes, giving herself time to adjust. When she opened them again, Steve hovered over her. She looked past him to the Commander, held at gunpoint by Wiley and Phillips.

"Look at *me*, Leith!" Steve grabbed her chin and forced her head up. She caught movement in the corner of her eye. The Commander had taken a step forward as if to stop Steve. Wiley punched a Pulser in his side, and he halted, hands clenched, eyeslits narrowed until they had almost disappeared. Steve tightened his grip, and she was forced to look up at him again.

The madness in his dark eyes chilled her.

"You're disgusting, Leith. In the beginning, this was for us, you and me. We would have had it all—McClure Shipping, the Rep jewels, and the crysium, an added bonus. But you kept saying no, Leith, no to *me*. Now, you have to pay."

His grip loosened, and he stroked her face. She shuddered, trying to elude his insistent fingers. With an ugly sneer, he pushed her face, her head snapping to one side.

"You'd rather have the Rep clawing you than the touch of a man. To find you sprawled on the bed with *him*—"

"It's not what you think," she said without belaboring the point. In his state, nothing she said would convince him otherwise. She shrugged. "But then it's never been what you think. You never do quite get it, do you, Steve? Always a mark shy of warp speed. The Commander is more of a man than you could ever hope to be."

"Dry wit, condescending manner. Your life is in my hands, and you're still cracking jokes at my expense," he sneered, his face reddening.

"Did you expect me to beg?"

He chewed his lip, and then a smile crept into place. Another chill swept over Leith.

Steve drew back the Blaser, and she flinched, waiting for the blow. Instead, he took two steps back and brought it down, the butt catching the Commander on the side of his face. His head jerked, and he went down on one knee, a muffled moan escaping his bloodied mouth.

"No!" Leith sprang to her feet, then froze when Steve rested the muzzle of the Blaser against the Commander's temple.

"Look at *me*, Leith, and come to me."

She locked her eyes on a point beyond Steve's head, unable to look into his mad eyes, and walked toward him, stopping a meter away.

"Come *here*."

She closed the gap between them and focused in on him. "What do you want, Steve?" she asked quietly, careful not to set him off again. "Please take the Blaser off the Commander. I-I'll do whatever you want."

"You would beg for his life, wouldn't you? And more. Would you do more to save the Rep?" he added suggestively.

"What do you want me to do, Steve?" she asked again, her voice soft and compliant. Anything to save them. Anything to keep Steve's mind off the Blaser and the Commander. Her stomach heaved, but she would do anything at all to save their lives.

"I should take you here, in front of the Rep. Let Wiley and Phillips have a turn, to be fair. But we don't have the time." He moved the Blaser away from the Commander. "Get him on his feet, boys."

How many human men would have wisely kept silent during the ordeal instead of allowing their male pride to antagonize Steve further? She had said entirely too much, endangering the Commander and herself, out of habit. She had to keep in mind that Steve had crossed over into some uncharted territory in his own mind and wasn't the same man she was used to dealing with.

She forced a smile on her trembling lips to encourage the Commander. He tilted his head to the side and blinked once.

"Let's move out. We're running behind schedule, and we all know that McClure Shipping prides itself on being on time. Let's get them down to the restraining cells." Steve let Wiley and Phillips lead the Commander out before taking Leith by the arm.

They walked down the corridor to the hold doors that parted when Wiley placed his hand on the identipad. Stairs to the left curved down into the cavernous hold, the restraining cells to the right.

Isolated in space, light years from the nearest planet or Galactic Police Station, all but the smallest ships included some kind of restraining area. The Galaxian boasted two small cells replete with waste facilities, mini-Liquidators, pull-down bunks, and comm pads. Used by space-drunk crewmembers more often than dangerous criminals, the cells weren't meant to be uncomfortable.

As they entered the anteroom, Leith blinked against the cold harsh lighting. Steve immediately went to the console and keyed in settings until he was satisfied.

"Throw the Rep in Cell One," he ordered.

Wiley and Phillips shoved the Commander into the small chamber to the left. His bulk kept him from falling to the floor. He stumbled a few steps then turned and looked at Steve, unblinking. "You will die."

Steve laughed and punched a key. The forcefield shimmered across the width of the cell. "Not today, Rep, and not by your hand."

Once again, Steve didn't get it. The Commander was a vitally important officer in the Zi Force. His kidnapping and death would create an interstellar incident. As a result, the Zi would hunt down Steve and exact their revenge. In the most gruesome manner possible, Leith hoped.

Steve stepped around the console, his Blaser on Leith. "Wiley, Phillips, get up front with Carter. I'll take care of her."

After they'd gone, Steve pushed her forward. She glanced one last time at the Commander before she walked into the cell.

"Too bad, Leith. We could have had it all, you and me. But now, I'll have it all." He walked back around the console and punched a button. The forcefield shimmered into place.

"You'll never get away with it," Leith said. "How are you going to explain our deaths to the Galactic Police, the Zi government, and my parents?"

"Your deaths? Oh, didn't I tell you? You're not going to die, Leith, either of you. Well, we all die eventually, of course, but you won't die soon. If I were going to kill you, you'd be orbiting Arreis now." He hummed an eerie mix of nonsensical notes as he concentrated on fine-tuning the controls.

"You see, my original plan was to jettison the Rep into deep space—without a suit of course. You were supposed to have fallen in love with me by now. I would have easily talked you into staying behind so that you wouldn't have known anything about this at all. Then, when you wouldn't cooperate, I thought I'd keep you around for fun." He shook his head sadly. "But after that nasty scene I found in your cabin, I don't think I could stand to touch you now. The thought makes my skin crawl, if you'll pardon the expression."

He checked the chronometer. "I wanted to jettison you both, but I decided that's too quick, too humane. I want you to suffer for disrupting my plans. I have something else in mind for you." He headed for the door. "Sorry, but I have to run. We're meeting the Crucians soon, and I have to prepare. Not to worry, Rep. I won't tell them you're here. They'd insist on taking you into custody, and that would spoil my plans for you."

"Steve! Wait—" Leith called after him, but he just laughed and left the room.

As soon as the door closed behind him, the anteroom lights went out. Huge squares of light from their cells fell across the anteroom floor, and their shadows created blurry shapes within. The Commander was standing in the center of his cell as she had seen him last.

"Are you all right?" she asked, remembering the blow he had taken from the butt of Steve's Blaser.

"The bleeding hasss ssstopped," he said, knowing exactly what she asked.

She shook her head and smiled. A human man would have taken exception to the question, paced the cell like a caged animal, and spouted expletives and useless threats. The Commander's quiet dignity was more comforting to her than a thousand assurances that they were going to get out of this.

"Why did you sssmile?"

Briefly, she thought he could see through their adjoining wall, but she had never heard of any special abilities of the Zi. He had to refer to something else.

"When?" she asked.

"In your cabin, before they led usss here."

"Oh." She recalled how she had smiled at him, and he had tilted his head and blinked once. "I don't know really. To let you know I was holding up. Or maybe because humans have the peculiar habit of smiling in the face of adversity."

"Sss't, I sssee. What isss thisss forcefield?"

She had to think quickly to keep up with him. "I'm no electrotech, but I think it's some sort of low-voltage impulse field. Not enough to kill, but enough to make you—"

His shadow moved, and she heard the crackle, sizzle, pop as he tried to breach the forcefield.

"No, Commander, don't!"

Her cry came too late, but he probably wouldn't have heeded her warning anyway. His shadow oscillated, his feet leaving the floor. The electric cacophony escalated, the high-pitched squeal piercing her eardrums. She threw her hands over her ears, but her eyes remained affixed to his blurred shadow. She smelled scorched leather and burnt wool.

"Commander! Let go!" She tried to yell loud enough to be heard over the sound. "Can you hear me? Let go!"

His shadow moved again. As it disappeared altogether, she heard him hit the wall. With a final sizzling pop, the noise ceased. Then she heard nothing from the next cell.

She stepped to the adjoining wall, placing the flat of her palms on it. Now, she wished she had special powers and could walk right through it. Was he hurt? Dead?

"Commander? Commander, can you hear me?" She held her breath and strained to hear the slightest indication that he was alive—the scrape of a boot, the rustle of clothing, an exhalation of breath, anything. "Please, Commander, answer me! I can't tell if you're dead or alive."

Then she heard movement. "I am alive."

She rested her forehead on the wall and breathed again. "Are you all right?"

"No, I...I think I am all left."

She laughed a little, collapsing against the wall when she realized his command of Terran Standard wasn't as perfect as she had thought. Right, left. It made sense in a way.

"Did I sssay sssomething amusssing?" he asked stiffly.

"No, no." Now was not the time for an English lesson. "I laughed in relief. I was afraid your physiology might not be able to withstand the charges from the forcefield."

"I am sssinged, but there isss no permanent damage."

"Good. Can you stand?" She had yet to see his shadow again.

"In a moment."

"That was dumb."

"Yesss, I agree."

She paced the width of the cell, giving him time to recover. After a few minutes, she saw his shadow stand upright slowly. He walked with a limp.

"I'm sorry," she whispered.

"It isss not your fault. I had to sssee if I could break through the barrier."

"No, I mean I'm sorry Steve turned into a crazy dorgian. I'm sorry my thoughtless remarks caused Steve to hit you. And I'm sorry for not seeing what was coming so I could stop it. I haven't been paying too much attention lately."

"Your father'sss illnesss."

"My father's illness has me worried, of course. But no, not to the point of being unable to think of other things." She bit her lip. Whatever Steve had planned for them would result in their untimely deaths. She could be no less than honest now. "I didn't want to take over McClure Shipping. I didn't want to leave the safe and secure niche I had made for myself back home on Earth."

"What isss your niche?"

"The university, working toward my master's. That was something I knew and could deal with. Then my father contracted Peridotian Snow Fever. For the Peridots, it's no more harmful than a common cold, but for humans it can be fatal. Fortunately, Dad's was caught in time. He's been bedridden for about three months with another six months to go. Then there will be more treatments, and he should be back to normal in another few months. My mother was given the antidote in time, and she refuses to leave his side. His condition is serious, but they're expecting a full recovery."

"That isss good to know. I have much ressspect for Cameron."

"Thank you." Suddenly tired, she sat on the floor, resting her back against the adjoining wall. "The strange thing is, no one knows how he caught the Fever. The doctors said that he had to have come into contact with a Peridot who was in the final stages, that's when it's contagious to humans. But Dad hadn't been off-Earth during the time he was supposed to have contracted it. And Customs is very careful to check anyone coming to Earth for certain diseases."

"Had Hancock been off-Earth before that?"

"I don't know. What makes you ask?" Then she understood what he meant. "You can't think—Steve wouldn't risk exposing Dad to Snow Fever. It could have killed him!"

"I think that wasss hisss plan."

Leith closed her eyes as her stomach tied into knots. Tears slipped from beneath her lashes. Steve couldn't intentionally hurt her father. Cameron McClure gave Steve his first job out of college. He trusted Steve with the business, giving him more and more responsibility over time. How could Steve betray that trust? Steve was the son Cameron didn't have, and the replacement for the daughter that wasn't interested.

"Then it is my fault. I should have taken more interest in McClure Shipping. I should have been there for him."

"I do not think Cameron would blame you."

"No, he wouldn't, but that doesn't make it any less my fault." She buried her head in her arms.

❀ ❀ ❀

J'Qhir heard the muffled sounds, but said nothing. The *sa`aloh* wept. After all she had been through he had expected uncontrolled histrionics before now. He had been told that human *sa'aloh'az* were incapable of remaining calm under stress, especially when their cycles peaked. Either this was blatantly untrue or this *sa'aloh* was an exception.

He believed she was exceptional in many ways.

He walked the perimeter of the cell, looking for anything that could be used to his advantage. Burning pain shot up his right thigh, as if a knife drove into it with each step. His leg had bent under him at an unnatural angle when thrown from the forcefield. No bones were broken, but ligaments were stretched or torn. His left arm had almost ceased throbbing from where he'd charged the barrier. The left side of his head and both hands stung from electrical burns, but the raw flesh had already scabbed over. The Zi had the ability to regenerate skin growth at a rapid rate. Unfortunately, this ability didn't extend to ligaments, muscle, or internal organs.

The attack was "dumb", to use the *sa'aloh*'s word, but he'd had to try. Another tenet of the Warrior: Always attempt the impossible. He had done his duty this time and had gained nothing but aches and pains and burns...and the contempt of the *sa'aloh*. Sometimes the impossible was improbable.

He surveyed the room—Liquidator, waste receptacle, comm panel. His hands were deadlier weapons than circuitry components! The bunks. He crossed the room in three painful strides and pulled the top one down. Wire mesh, surrounded by a soft aluminum frame, supported a thin mat.

If he broke off a piece of the frame, could he short-circuit the forcefield with it? He thought not... Always attempt the impossible. With a hiss of exasperation to duty and responsibility, he grabbed one of the shorter tubular ends and braced himself against the bunk with his left arm. He pulled with all his strength. The metal screeched as the wire mesh broke free. Waves of pain shot through his hand, and his left arm began to throb anew. He wanted to scream with the metal. Instead, he released the tube, now jutting out at an angle.

He collapsed to a sitting position, his back against the wall. He held his hand, palm up, in his lap and positioned his left arm so that the throbbing was minimal. He breathed heavily, waiting for the pain to subside.

"What are you doing?" the *sa`aloh* called to him.

He inhaled deeply. "The imposssible."

"Did it work?"

"No."

"I thought not."

Shame washed over him. As the Warrior he was bound to protect those in his care. At the moment, the *sa`aloh* was under his protection, even if she was human, and he failed again and again to save her as well as himself. He had been able to save his people many times over. Why couldn't he save one small *sa`aloh*?

"Have you hurt yourself again?"

"Not again." He looked down at the torn scabs on his hand. In a few hours he would be able to try again. Perhaps by the time his skin regenerated, the rest of him would be well enough to make the attempt.

"Commander?"

"Yesss..." he said, trying to keep the discouragement from his voice.

"I'm going to try to sleep now." He heard her lower the bunk. "I suggest you do the same. Get some rest. We don't know what Steve will do next. We may have only a few hours. Lights zero."

He listened as she sat on the bunk, the metal creaking. Then she stretched out, her clothing brushing the mattress cover as she found a position so she could rest. He imagined her lying as she had on the bed in her cabin, her pink lips moist and slightly parted, her round eyes changing from blue to green.

He thrust himself up in one motion. The sudden movement set his leg on fire, and the throbs doubled in his shoulder. He welcomed the pain as it overcame another, more inappropriate bodily reaction. By the sands, why did the human *sa'aloh* do this to him?

Breathing heavily, he let down the lower bunk. Careful of sore muscles, he stretched out, his feet dangling over the end. In the name of the rock, sleep sounded like a luxury he needed to help his body heal.

"Lightsss zero," he murmured and closed his eyes.

❋ ❋ ❋

When Leith settled down on her bunk, she didn't think she would be able to sleep. Her mind wouldn't shut down, racing over the events of the past few hours and trying to make sense of Steve's betrayal. She had listened as the bunk groaned beneath the Commander's weight and he turned off the light. Some time later, she had finally fallen asleep.

Now, as she woke, her heart thudded wildly. A sound lingered in the air, a faint echo reverberating at the edge of her consciousness. Had the Commander called out?

She sat up, swinging her legs over the side. Strategically placed nightlights, creating a muted glow in the anteroom and cells, dispelled the darkness. She heard it again, the sound that woke her—a distant thump somewhere in the hold.

"Commander?"

"Yesss, I hear it. It ssseemsss Hancock completed hisss deal with the Cruciansss."

She dropped back onto the bunk and closed her eyes. The waiting was worse than Steve holding a Blaser on her. This time it was easy to fall back asleep. Too easy.

The next time she woke, Phillips brought foodpacks. She shaded her eyes against the anteroom light while he keyed in a code to release the forcefield a few centimeters from the floor. By her watch it had been three hours since Steve locked them up. Phillips shoved several packs in each cell, then quickly reset the forcefield.

"That'll take care of you for a while," he growled.

"You know my father will never rest until he finds out the truth," Leith began, but Phillips scurried out without acknowledging her, and the anteroom light went out.

She closed her eyes again and heard the crinkle of a foodpack wrapper and then the crunch of freeze-dried food as the Commander ate. Her appetite gone, the thought of food made her sick.

"Eat, *sa`aloh*. You need to keep up your ssstrength for the tasssksss ahead."

"I don't see the point, Commander. Steve said he wasn't going to kill us outright, but we can be sure that whatever he has planned, we won't survive long."

"Where there isss life, there isss hope. A belief of humansss, I think."

"Yes, it's one of our sayings. You can count on a human to have a saying for every occasion. Sometimes they contradict one another. For instance, 'Absence makes the heart grow fonder'. Yet, we have, 'Out of sight, out of mind'." She rested her arm across her eyes. "Sayings are just clever words strung together. They have no meaning."

"'Out of sssight, out of mind'," he repeated thoughtfully. "It doesss not mention the heart. Sssomeone can be out of the mind for a time, but never out of the heart. Sssss, the two do not contradict at all."

She couldn't find fault in his reasoning.

"If you do not eat, *sa`aloh,* they may not give you any more food. Now you are not hungry, but if many daysss passs, you will wisssh you had the food."

Steve might find it amusing to toy with them by withholding food. She set the lights on three and retrieved the packs. She punched in the code for boiling water then tore off the wrapper.

"It's better if you pour hot water over it and let it set a few minutes."

"Isss it? Our foodpacksss are meant to be eaten dry." She heard him punch in the code. "In a warssship, ssspace isss at a premium; in a war, time isss at a premium."

She poured the boiling water over the piles of freeze-dried crumbs in the plastic tray, turning them into a mush-like consistency. Each section had its own flavor, and although the granules didn't resemble what they represented, they satisfied the palate and provided essential protein, vitamins, and minerals a body needed to survive. A human body.

"These are made for human consumption. Can you survive eating nothing but this?"

"Yesss. My needsss are not much different than yoursss."

She smiled at the double entendre. She had to remember his English left something to be desired, so he had no idea what he said or how many ways it could be taken. Nevertheless, the statement brought images to her mind that were best forgotten.

She ate and tossed the empty tray in the waste chute. She heard his waste receptacle flush.

It was time to sleep, time to empty her mind of *everything* and find refuge in a dreamless void. She crept onto the bunk and put out the lights.

This time she woke with the Commander calling to her.

"Are you awake, *sa'aloh*?"

"I am now," she mumbled, rubbing the sleep from her eyes. She glanced at her watch. Another four hours had passed. Not long enough. She rolled over and closed her eyes again.

"Wake up, *sa'aloh*. Too much sssleep isss asss detrimental asss not enough."

"What does it matter?" she muttered.

"You are compensssating for lack of physsssical ssstimuli." There was a pause. "Sss't!"

Her eyes sprang open. She desperately tried to free her mind of what his "physsssical ssstimuli" suggested.

"Boredom," she said through a yawn.

"What, *sa'aloh*?"

"You mean that I'm bored."

"Yes, *sa'aloh*. You need to keep your sssensesss sssharpened, to be prepared for what isss to come."

She sat up on the side of the bunk. She loved the sound of the word he called her, *sa'aloh*, but she was afraid to ask what it meant. It might mean "bitch" or some other disparaging term. If so, she didn't want to know. She preferred to think it meant "dear" or "darling", something mildly affectionate.

"How do you propose I do that, Commander?"

"Talk to me. Pace your cell for the exercissse. Look at sssomething you have never ssseen before."

I want to look at you, she thought. *I want to rest my eyes on another living being.* His disembodied voice, especially now that it resounded with disapproval, had begun to get on her nerves.

She stood, pain gripping her abdomen. A full bladder screamed for relief. She had to do it, as embarrassing as it was. She dropped her pants and prayed that Steve or one of the others didn't pick this moment to run a bed check. There was no way to escape. If they managed to break free of the cells, there was nowhere to go. The ship scanner would locate them in a heartbeat—by the sound of their heartbeats.

The waste receptacle automatically flushed when she stood. She closed her eyes for those few seconds, then buckled her belt.

J'Qhir waited a few minutes.

"I am going to try again, *sa`aloh*," he called to her.

"Try what?"

"What I tried before."

"Which is?"

"The imposssible."

"Oh. Is it more possible now?"

"Marginally. The burnsss on my handsss have healed."

"Already?"

"Yesss. Zi ssskin regeneratesss quickly. My ssshoulder doesss not throb now."

"What, exactly, were you trying to do?"

"I attempted to pull one of the bunksss apart. The metal frame—"

"To use as a weapon?"

"No. I will try to ssshort out the forcefield."

"It won't work."

"Perhapsss not. But at leassst I am doing sssomething."

"A waste of energy."

He clenched his teeth. "At leassst I am not sssleeping away the few remaining hoursss of my life."

"To each his own."

A pause.

"Another human saying. One for every occasion, remember?"

Another pause.

"Do you think it will work, Commander?"

"I do not know."

※ ※ ※

J'Qhir braced his left arm against the bunk and yanked as hard as he could. The metal whined and his arm began to throb again. He twisted the tube, and with one last shriek it broke off in his hand.

He rubbed his shoulder. Now, how to do this without electrifying himself again. He couldn't hold the metal with his bare hands. He needed—

He looked down. Warmth crept into his face. Gloves. Tucked into his waistband. War gloves, two layers of wool for warmth with a layer of rubber in between. In a war, in the heat of battle, one did not have to worry about electrocution when making emergency repairs. He hissed in exasperation. Why hadn't he thought of the gloves when he charged the forcefield? His only answer was that his mind was clouded. His thinking had become impaired by—

"When are you going to do it?"

"Now." He jerked on the gloves and shoved the tube into the forcefield. Sparks showered him and sizzles, crackles, pops filled his ears. He held it until the tube started to bend and twist, but the electronic whine did not lessen.

He pulled the tube free, and silence settled over them. He tossed the piece of scrap, and it landed in a corner with a clank.

"Didn't work, did it?"

"No."

"I'm sorry. I hoped it would."

"I, alssso."

"Any more ideas?"

"Not at the moment."

They ate again, pouring hot water over the granules. Most of the flavors he couldn't identify.

"Mmmm, banana pudding. My favorite. What did you get?"

"I do not know. I am not familiar with the tassste of human food."

"The little section in the center is dessert. What does it taste like?"

He took a bite. It was difficult to describe unknown flavors. "Sssweet. Rich. Sssatisssfying."

"Must be chocolate cake. I had that last time."

The door to the anteroom opened, and Hancock, Phillips, and a third man walked in.

"Sorry to interrupt lunch, but it's time to go."

J'Qhir tossed the tray in the waste chute and stood, prepared. If there were an instant when he thought Hancock was off-guard, he was ready to take full advantage of it as long as it wouldn't endanger the *sa`aloh* or himself.

"What are you going to do with us, Steve?" Her voice trembled. Before she had sounded relaxed, but now J'Qhir could hear her fear.

"If I tell you now, it won't be a surprise." Hancock punched keys, and J'Qhir's forcefield shimmered out. "Come on out, Rep. Easy now. Carter, tie him up."

Hancock and Phillips held their weapons on him while Carter locked his hands in plasticuffs behind his back. Then Carter fastened his ankles with only enough slack for a half step. Hancock released the forcefield on the other cell, and Carter secured Leith's hands behind her back also. He knelt to lock her ankles.

"Never mind. She won't run with the Rep hobbled. Besides, where would she go?" He laughed.

All chances were gone, J'Qhir mused. He should have kicked Carter in the teeth while he knelt, but either Hancock or Phillips could have blasted him. That would have left the *sa`aloh* to face Hancock alone, and that was unacceptable.

If he could not save them both then he would do nothing. As long as he lived he could keep Hancock away from her somehow.

Hancock led them out of the restraining area into the hold. Their steps echoed throughout the empty cavern. The cargo was gone, sold to the Crucians. He had sacrificed the precious jewels for nothing.

The *sa`aloh* recognized the path they took.

"The lifecraft? Steve, where are you taking us?"

Hancock smiled and kept a tight hold on her arm. He turned them toward another door and laid his palm on the identipad. He pushed them through first.

The small lifecraft took up most of the bay. At a nod from Hancock, Phillips lifted the door. Hancock motioned with his Blaser. "After you."

"Not until you tell us where you're taking us!" the *sa`aloh* exploded. "I'm tired of all this, Steve. Tell us where we're going."

"I was saving it as a surprise, but since you're so impatient...I'm taking you to Paradise."

Chapter 3

Paradise, Arreisan Neutral Zone

J'Qhir spent the greater part of the ride to the surface of the planet straining against the cuffs and fighting the pain that shot through his shoulder with every move. By the time they entered the planet's atmosphere, he had given up. The cuffs were no looser and his shoulder throbbed mercilessly.

Hancock landed the lifecraft in a grassy meadow near the foothills of a mountain range. A herd of horned, quadruped creatures scattered in graceful leaps and bounds.

The whine of the engine wound down as the doors rose.

"Welcome to Paradise!" Hancock said and got out. The front seat swiveled aside leaving room for the occupant in the back to emerge—an occupant of smaller stature than J'Qhir. They'd had to remove the cuffs from his ankles for him to fold his large body into the seat. Now, he twisted himself out, fiery pain stabbing his thigh repeatedly.

When he straightened, the *sa`aloh* was by his side, the delicate arches of hair over her eyes wrinkled. "Are you all right?"

Lanette Curington

He wanted to smile at her—for encouragement?—but he
thought he might scare her. "I am...sssomewhere in the
middle."

Her brow smoothed as she smiled her understanding. Her
smile did not scare him at all.

"Paradise is in the center of the Arreisan Neutral Zone,"
Hancock explained. "It's one of the few known Terran-class
planets not colonized or plundered."

Hancock hauled out a flightpack. He led them several
meters away from the lifecraft and tossed the bag to the ground.

"You're leaving us here?" the *sa'aloh* asked, a hint of panic
in her voice.

Hancock nodded. "You and the Rep will be the only two
sentient lifeforms on the planet. No one ever comes here, Leith.
It's under Arreisan protection. Every pirate, every rogue, every
starman and starwoman knows better than to piss off the
Arreisans. They'd restrict access to Trader World in a
nanosecond and no one wants that. So everyone leaves Paradise
alone."

J'Qhir felt her disappointment and anxiety. If no one dared
to defy the Arreisans and visit this planet, then they were as
good as dead. It must be true or Hancock would not chance
leaving them here at all.

"How do you intend to explain our disappearance? The
Commander will have an entire government looking for him.
Dad knows enough people on the Galactic Alliance Board to get
them involved."

Hancock smiled chillingly. "After the Rep notified his ship
the cargo was ready for transfer, another ship was stolen out of
the port, and a message was sent to the Zi warship that the
transfer had been delayed indefinitely. You see, Rep, I've been
recording our meetings for a long time, preparing for this day.

46

When you and Cameron spoke your primitive language, *excluding me* from the conversation, you made it so much easier for me. I had to ask Cameron to teach me so I could understand what you were saying and carefully cull the message from all those hours of recordings. At that time, my plans included your immediate demise, but things change."

J'Qhir clenched his jaw. The Zi communications system was not state-of-the-art. They simply could not afford the latest equipment in all areas and communications was not deemed an immediate need. The crackling static of the old and worn out system would hide any signs that the message was cut-and-spliced from other recordings.

"When we return to Arreis, the ship will release a statement, in the Rep's own words, that he has renounced the Zi government and taken a human, Leith McClure, as hostage. Demands to be given later. Of course, another statement will never be released. The stolen ship will fly straight into a sun, to vaporize without a trace." He glanced back to make sure that Phillips was still out of earshot, then lowered his voice. "We're supposed to rendezvous with the lifecraft in a few hours, but I think we'll find the ship malfunctioned and poor Wiley crashed and burned with it. With Wiley gone there'll be larger shares for the rest of us and fewer witnesses."

"No one will believe any of that!" the *sa`aloh* snapped angrily. "You really have lost your mind, haven't you, Steve? The Zi government will never believe their top gun has gone rogue. Dad certainly won't believe it. He knows the Commander."

"It doesn't matter, Leith. The situation will cause so much confusion and accusation that by the time both sides, the Zi government and the Galactic Alliance, come to some kind of agreement, the trail will be cold. There will be no follow-up statement, no trace of either of you, and everyone concerned will assume you died in an unfortunate accident." Hancock shook his head sadly, but the smug smile remained on his lips. "I'll be by Cameron and Catherine's side the whole time, grieving with them, consoling them. I'll even express guilt because I was right there and should have seen it coming. I should have sensed what the Rep was up to."

Hancock broke into laughter as he called to Phillips and waited for him to key the lock open on the *sa`aloh's* cuffs. She rubbed her wrists vigorously. "It won't work. How can you explain the fourteen-hour delay in reporting my disappearance?"

Steve sighed in exasperation. "You really don't have the mental capacity for intrigue, do you? I'll tell the GPs you and the Rep were gone when I came back from repairing a malfunctioning skid. You left a message—which, by the way, I thoughtlessly erased—saying you and the Commander were going out for a while. Of course, I'll tell the GPs how well you two were getting along and wink suggestively when I say it. So I went to bed, and when you were still gone after I woke up hours later, I went looking for you. But Arreis is a huge place and filled with so many people, I couldn't find anyone who had seen you."

J'Qhir nodded thoughtfully. "How will you explain the ssship'sss disssappearance for fourteen hoursss?"

Steve frowned. "I won't. According to the spaceport log, the ship never left Bay 3."

"It *can't* work," she protested with less conviction.

"Well, let's find out, shall we?" Steve nodded again and trained his Blaser on J'Qhir. Phillips keyed the lock open while both held their weapons at the ready. "By the way, I tossed a few things in the flightpack. There are enough protein packs for a few days plus a few other things that might or might not be useful."

"Steve, this is insane," she called out as they watched the two men step backward toward the lifecraft. "What is the point?"

"Wealth, power, revenge. I have a dozen Zi jewels which will be a fortune on the market, as well as the crysium, another fortune. With you out of the way and Cameron's illness, McClure Shipping is as good as mine. I've been trying to convince Cameron to expand, but he won't listen. He insists on staying strictly Earth-based. And revenge? I told you you'd be sorry for turning me down, didn't I?"

"And the Commander? You could have easily sold him the cargo at an inflated price and kept the difference. Dad never would have found out."

Hancock shrugged. "I just don't like Reps. Good-bye, Leith. Who knows? You two might manage to survive, after all."

J'Qhir watched as the two men jumped into the lifecraft then shifted his gaze to the *sa`aloh*. Her round eyes were incredibly large as the doors lowered and sealed.

"Steve! *Steve!*" Before J'Qhir could stop her, she took flight, darting across the clearing toward the lifecraft. J'Qhir ran after her, giving in to the searing pain with each limping stride. The foolish *sa`aloh* would get herself killed on the spot if the craft took off with her so near. She reached it and beat her hands against the gray metal. "You can't leave us here! You can't! Steve, there has to be another way!"

He scooped her off the lifecraft and threw her over his good shoulder, turned, and ran as if the sandpits of the Bh'rin'gha sucked at his heels.

The *sa`aloh*'s legs churned in front of him, and her fists battered his back. The lifecraft lifted, creating a gale that reminded him of the windy season except void of grit. The force of it drove him to his knees.

The *sa`aloh* dropped away from his shoulder, but he could do nothing to soften her fall. He screamed as most of his weight landed on his bad knee, twisting it. He rolled to his side and doubled up, clutching the joint with both hands. Liquid filled his eyes as flames burned a path from knee to hip.

❄ ❄ ❄

Leith landed hard, her head snapping back against the unyielding ground. White dots sprang before her eyes. She thought she lost consciousness for a moment and dreamed the primal scream of a wild animal in the distance. When she opened her eyes, a flowing black mass obliterated the sky. She blinked and focused. Birds. A flock of birds moved across the sky in a rough V-formation. When they passed over, she rolled to her side and groaned. Her hips ached and her head pounded incessantly. She felt along her scalp and found the bump, as big and smooth as a Zi jewel.

Bruised and battered from the jarring ride on the Commander's shoulder and their fall, she dragged herself to her feet, every muscle in her body aching. She shaded her eyes against the glare of the afternoon sun. The lifecraft was gone. Steve really had left them stranded on this empty planet. She heard the Commander take a heavy, limping step behind her and whirled to face him.

"*You!* Why didn't you say something, anything?" she screamed at him. "Why didn't you threaten him? Or promise to shower him with a thousand Zi jewels? Anything, *anything* to buy us some time until we could find a way out."

She didn't care how awful he looked, standing on one leg, the other bent at an odd angle. She refused to allow the expression of pain on his face to move her.

"Why don't you answer me? I'll tell you why!" She flew at him and beat on his chest as she had the side of the lifecraft, emphasizing each word. "Because—you—have—no—excuse—"

His hands moved in tandem with hers until he caught her wrists and raised her arms in the air. Her eyes flooded with tears, making her angrier.

"You just stood there, all big and inscrutable, and didn't say a damn word!" Tears blinding her, she butted up against him, struggling to pull her hands free from his unbreakable grip. "Not a damn word!"

She slammed into him one more time, and they toppled over, crashing to the ground. She landed on top of him, and his face twisted in agony. His crested brow furrowed, his eyes squeezed shut, and his mouth drew tight, but his grip never lessened. She couldn't pull free, so she threw her body to one side. He rolled with her, and once again she found herself pinned beneath his long, heavy body, his hands holding hers above her head.

Her chest heaved with each breath, from the exertion, from his weight, from the tears that dampened her cheeks. With each breath she drew she smelled him, that unfamiliar alien scent that made her body react in a most peculiar way.

"Let me go!" she demanded hoarsely.

"Will you—ssstop fighting me?"

"Yes. No! I don't know. Let me go and we'll find out."

His head sank to her chest, his crest resting on her shoulder. His breath came in sharp gasps, intermittent moans escaping his throat. His hands trembled against hers. Her panic had overridden everything else, but now she realized what had happened.

"You're hurt!"

"Sssss, *sa`aloh*—"

"I mean, you're *really* hurt."

"If you do not ssstop fighting me, I will not have the ssstrength to fend you off."

"Well, why didn't you say something? How am I supposed to know when you just stand there and don't say anything?"

"I...sssscreamed when we fell—"

"Oh. I hit my head. I thought I'd passed out and dreamed the sound."

"I think I have torn a mussscle in my knee."

"You can let me go now, Commander. I promise I won't fight you any more."

He released her hands and slid away. Slowly, he raised his head, his crest deeply furrowed. Shifting away from her, he fell back and held the knee at an angle. He gasped for air and closed his eyes.

Leith sat up and waited for the pounding in her head to subside. She noticed the slant of the sunlight, a thinner light than Earth's Sol emitted. It was early evening as near as she could reckon. The air stirred around her, a breeze from the mountains. It was cool, almost chilly. The Commander shivered.

"I'm going to see if I can find the flightpack Steve left us. Maybe there's a medkit in it."

Ignoring the headache, she stood and scanned the area for the flightpack. She prayed Steve had been in a generous mood when he packed it and left them something useful. The tall grass swayed in the quickening breeze, and her eyes moved back and forth. She didn't see any matte black against the straw-colored grass.

She made her way to the patch of flattened grass where the lifecraft had landed and turned toward the Commander. She replayed the scene in her mind and saw Steve throw it down. Slowly, she walked the general area, pushing the tall grass aside with each step.

She found the bag by tripping over it. She slung it over her shoulder and as she hurried back to the Commander, she noticed the shadows were longer and the air had definitely grown chillier.

"I found it," she announced and let it slide to the ground. She sank to her knees and ripped it open. "Here are the protein packs—only six. They won't last long."

"They will keep usss alive until we find food."

"*If* we find food. What we find may not be edible."

"But we will eat—even if it killsss usss."

Leith nodded and dug deeper in the bag. She pulled out a flat plastic case, as square and thick as her palm. "Steve has a rotten sense of humor. MDVs. Micro disc vids. There won't be intelligent life on this planet for a million years, let alone electricity."

She drew her arm back to throw it as far as she could in the sea of grass.

"No!" the Commander said sharply. "We will dessstroy it later. We mussst leave asss little trace asss posssible of oursssselvesss and our technology on thisss planet."

They were on the verge of death, and it could come in any shape, form, or fashion at any moment, and he was worried about what local archaeologists might find a few million years from now. But he was serious. Too serious. His slitted amber eyes stared at her unblinking, and his mouth was a thin, straight slash. She lowered her arm and dropped the vid case in the bag.

"And I'll be sure to die someplace where my bones won't fossilize and change the course of history," she muttered under her breath. She rummaged some more. "Great. A mess kit for two. I'm sure Steve meant to tease us, but it'll be so much tastier boiling those toxic roots and sautéing those poisonous mushrooms and washing it down with water so full of deadly bacteria we can watch 'em swim."

The Commander tilted his head to one side. "You are being sssarcassstic."

"How can you tell?" Then she regretted the quip because he looked so—so naively somber. "I'm sorry, but I've honed my skills on Steve. He was always so easy to get, it was embarrassing at times. But I can stop if it's annoying you. Actually, I'm annoying myself!"

"No, I find human sssarcasssm fassscinating."

"Don't the Zi do sarcasm?"

"To insssult, not to amusssse. Then, of courssse, the one insssulted mussst retaliate, to protect the honor of hisss *uh'mir*—hisss clan."

"And how would he do that?"

"A duel in the desssert."

"Oh. Do you get to slap his face with your glove?"

"What, *sa`aloh*?"

"Nothing. An ancient Earth custom. The nineteenth century was famous for its duels at dawn."

"Ss'h. It takesss place at—what do you call it? Yesss, high noon. The hottessst time of the day. It isss a tessst of endurance."

"Is it to the death?"

"Of courssse, *sa`aloh*. Ssso you can sssee, sssarcasssm isss not a frequent occurrence."

"Remind me not to insult you sarcastically."

She pulled out a small carton next, saw what it was, and shoved it to the bottom. Steve really did have a rotten sense of humor. Tampons.

"What isss that?"

"Nothing." They were useful for now, but what would she do next month? With any luck, she wouldn't survive that long. "Oh, a laserlight!"

The cylindrical tube fit snugly in her hand. She aimed it at a tuft of grass and pushed the button. Nothing. She popped off the end but it was empty.

"Isss it not crysssium powered?" he asked stiffly.

"It *was*, but Steve thoughtfully removed the battery."

The laserlight was the most controversial use of crysium of all. A nifty little gadget, it could start a fire, dry out clothing, cut through most anything, and lead you through the darkness. A DNA detection field around the laser beam prevented one from cutting off one's finger or foot or accidentally decapitating a loved one. The field would recognize human and numerous other species, but she didn't know about Zi. She explained to the Commander that he had to be exceptionally careful around it.

The crysium battery would last indefinitely with daily use. As advertised, the housing would wear out before the battery. Crysium was found only on Crux, but with the sanctions against the non-allied planet, its import had been halted indefinitely. Pre-sanctioned crysium was legal, and the manufacturer of the laserlight claimed their product only used legal crysium batteries. Laserlights were relatively cheap, considering how long the speck of crysium would last. Leith had one, but conscious of the controversy, refused to use it. It was—

"Stupid, stupid, stupid!" She jumped to her feet and snatched off her jacket. "How could I be so stupid? Do you realize what this *is*? A *survival* jacket. I've had it for three years, but never actually had to use it to survive."

She spread the jacket, lining up. Without its protection, she shivered in the chilly breeze. She glanced at the Commander who, as usual, remained stoically silent. He watched her, but his eyes blinked slowly, sleepily. He was reptilian, after all. Didn't reptiles slow down when the weather cooled? Didn't they go into hibernation if it got cold enough? They'd have to find shelter and build a fire soon or she'd lose the Commander to his natural instincts.

"We'll look at all this fun stuff later." She pulled at several magnostrips, opening secret pockets, and examined the contents before she found what she wanted. "Here it is. The medkit. And here's a laserlight that works. I apologize, Commander, but this little baby will probably save our lives. Oh, good, a solar film!"

She opened the medkit and found the elastic bandage. "This will help your knee."

The Commander nodded and blinked slowly. His eyeslits were dilated and glassy. She shook out the solar film. Folded, it was no larger than the palm of her hand, but when undone it was large enough to wrap around two people. She doubled the silky silver material and draped it over his head and shoulders. His fingers shook as he grasped the edges together.

She pulled on her jacket and fastened the magnostrips.

The sun was sinking rapidly in the west. The west? She'd try a compass later to find out if that phrase had any meaning here. Now, she approached the Commander's leg.

"Does it hurt now?"

"Only...when...I...move."

"I'm going to pull up your trouser leg and wrap this bandage around it. The support should help."

He nodded again. Slowly.

She pulled the cuff of the woolen material out of his boot and carefully pushed it up above his knee. His leg was the same tawny-umber blend, but otherwise was no different from a human leg. The calf muscles were taut and well defined.

Occasionally, her fingers brushed his scaled skin. She was surprised to find it soft like rich, expensive leather. She shivered but not from the chilling breeze.

His knee was puffy, swollen.

"Tell me if it's too tight. I don't want to cut off the circulation, but I need to get it tight enough to support it."

The bandage was, supposedly, flesh-colored—light beige. As she wound it around his knee, she wondered if Zi bandages were tawny-umber. If Zi females wore face powder, what color would it be? If their children—no, younglings—had crayons, what color was Flesh in a box of one-twenty-eight?

"Is it too tight?"

"No...*sa`aloh.*"

She rolled the trouser leg down again, accidentally-on-purpose touching his smooth leather skin. It was all she could do to keep from running her hands along the length of his leg. She stuffed the cuff back in the top of the boot and sighed.

The sun neared the tops of the mountains in the distance. She'd taken entirely too much time bandaging his knee, rolling and unrolling his trouser leg. Another gust of wind stirred her hair and gave her goose bumps.

"We have to get you out of this wind. Is the solar film helping?"

"Yesss..."

The grassy meadow seemed to stretch forever to the "east", but to the "west", toward the mountains, she saw a dark stand of trees. About two kilometers, she guessed. Beneath the trees, they would be sheltered from the wind. There would be deadfall to build a fire.

The Commander turned slowly, following her gaze.

"I can...make it."

She tucked the laserlight in a jacket pocket, threw the medkit into the flightpack, and slung it over her shoulder. She squatted beside him and adjusted the magnostrips on the film so it wouldn't come loose. He laid his arm across her shoulders and leaned heavily on her.

For a second, before he found his balance and a comfortable position for his knee, she thought they were going to fall over again. His hands gripped her painfully, one on her shoulder, the other on her arm, and she bit her lip to keep from crying out. That strength, unleashed, could very easily crush every bone in her body.

This close to him, Leith caught a whiff of his scent. His smell, his power, his vulnerability, his color, his texture—all of it played havoc with her senses, teasing her body into a reaction that was *alien* to her and most inappropriate at that moment. Perhaps the fact that their lives were at stake was the active ingredient. Now or never, and her body was all too aware of it.

They found a rhythm, a steady gait that ate up the meters more quickly than she thought possible. Even so, the sun dipped behind the mountain peak, and she brought out the laserlight, setting it on array, to light their way.

In the distance, somewhere in the trees, an animal roared.

They both halted at the preternatural sound and waited while its echo died. Then they continued on their way. They had no choice. The stand of trees was their only hope.

The Commander was breathing heavily by the time they reached the trees. Leith's shoulders ached from his weight, and the headache, which had diminished earlier, returned with the strain.

The night sky overhead, full of stars but as yet no moon, disappeared as they moved beneath the trees. The leaves rustled in the breeze, and the animal roared again. An answering bellow sounded, farther away.

Leith played the light left and right. Night creatures, disturbed by their movement, scent, and light, scurried through the underbrush. A night raptor swooped low over their heads and dove to the ground. Its prey squeaked once then the predator took to the air again and disappeared in the night.

The Commander stopped and leaned against a tree. By the pale array, its crooked trunk with low gnarled branches looked as if it were trying to swallow him.

"I will...ssstay here. You continue...to look for a...sssuitable sssite."

"No. I think we should stay together. That animal, the one that roared, sounded too close."

He shook his head and drew the film closer against the cool night air. "I will ssslow you down. I need to ressst my leg."

"No—"

"Do it, *sa`aloh*." He sank onto one of the lower branches and carefully repositioned his leg.

"What if I get lost? How will I find my way back?"

"Call to me, *sa`aloh.* I will anssswer."

Not if a roaring beast has found you and made you his supper, she thought but didn't say aloud. "What if I find my way back to you then can't find the site again? We still might wander around all night long."

"I have faith in you. Go. Or we will ssstand here...all night long."

He sounded exasperated with her, and she didn't blame him. She didn't relish the idea of wandering through the woods in the dark alone with who knew what kind of night creatures out there waiting to pounce. She liked even less that she would have to leave him alone with nothing to protect himself. If only the other laserlight worked. Damn Steve anyway!

"All right. I'm going." She turned on her heel and headed in a direction at random.

Leith tried to remember landmarks, but in the pale light all of the gnarled, twisted trees looked the same. She heard a rustling to her left and moved the light, hoping to scare it— whatever *it* was—away. Two red eyes glowed from the brush, then quickly darted off.

She shuddered and called out, "Commander?"

He answered, and he was nearer than she thought he'd be. She hadn't gone very far at all. She had to get a grip. She was safe for now. They were more afraid of her than she was of them. She had to find a campsite *now.* The Commander was depending on her. She couldn't let him down.

She walked farther into the darkness, pushing aside limbs, stumbling over roots. She tripped over a dead limb and fell through a thick patch of brush and thought she'd landed in a dream.

The site was picture-perfect—a small clearing with a soft carpet of moss and grass and a fallen tree to one side. She blinked and pinched herself to make sure she hadn't hallucinated the scene out of panic-stricken hysteria.

She scrambled to her feet and pushed through the brush, the way she'd come. "Commander! I found it."

"Very good, *sa`aloh*."

She jumped. He was only ten meters or so away, using a crooked tree limb for a crutch.

"God, you scared me. What the hell are you doing here?"

"I followed you."

"How did you find your way? I don't think I would have found my way back to you, and I have the light."

"I can sssee well enough to follow *your* trail, *sa`aloh*," he said with a touch of disapproval. "And I would have to be deaf not to hear your crassshing through the undergrowth."

"Well, excuse me, but I wasn't a boy scout when I was a—a youngling."

He tilted his head to one side, the way he always did when he was perplexed.

"I would not think you would be a *boy* anything. Unlesss, I have confusssed your language again."

"Not at all," she said, puzzling him further.

She led the way to the clearing, parting the brush for him to pass through. If he hadn't been injured, she would have released it to slap him in his supercilious face. His disapproving comment on her skills hurt more than it should have. She hadn't been trained as a warrior so how could she be expected to act like one.

He expected it of her.

She thought she'd done a damn fine job of locating the perfect campsite—even if she'd had to trip over it to find it. Her feelings bruised, she didn't offer to help him to the fallen tree, but she watched him until he was safely seated, his leg positioned to cause the least amount of pain.

She tossed the flightpack to the ground at his feet. "I'll gather some wood for a fire."

It didn't take long to find an armload because deadfall covered the ground. She dumped it and went for another load. She placed a handful of dried leaves and grass in the center of the clearing, then a double handful of twigs, and larger pieces of wood on top of that.

With the laserlight set on medium intensity, she aimed it at the leaves and grass. Smoke curled upward and flames licked at the twigs. She changed the setting to array and balanced the tube on the log. As larger pieces caught fire, she put on more until it was hot and bright and they didn't need the laserlight array anymore.

Leith didn't realize how cold she was until the heat warmed her skin, even through the material of her trousers. The Commander, his injured leg held at an angle, eased himself to the ground beside her and rested his back against the log.

"All we need now are marshmallows," she commented as her stomach growled.

"Marssshmallowsss?"

"White puffs of pure sugar. You put one on the end of a stick and hold it over the fire until it's toasted brown and the inside is melted. Scrumptious."

"Ssscrumptiousss," he repeated slowly.

She was close enough to him that she could feel him shiver.

"Are you warm enough? I think the temperature's dropping by the minute."

He didn't answer. Was he going into hibernation even with the fire and the solar film? Leith, too, felt the cold on her back, the part of her away from the fire. The only way either of them was going to get warm was to double up in that solar film.

"Here. Maybe this will help." She pulled the magnostrips free and shook the film to its full size. He shivered violently from the exposure. She draped it over them and sat beside him, fastening it securely again. He was drawn to her body heat, leaning into her, and she didn't think he was completely aware of it. She drew the filament tie at the edge and the material crinkled as it gathered. She left a hole large enough for them both to watch the fire.

He drew even closer to her. Tentatively, she put her arms around him and held him. His breathing grew stronger, and his shivering stopped completely. She rested her head on his shoulder, the wool-like fabric of his war jacket soft against her cheek. She had expected it to be scratchy, but it was as fine-textured as cashmere.

Trapped beneath the film, all she could smell was *him*. She yawned, her jaws popping. Still, warm, quiet. Sleep lured her by making her eyelids heavy. She forced them open. She had to stay awake to keep the fire going or the Commander would phase-out again.

"Sssleep, *sa`aloh*," he said, and the tips of his fingers caressed her cheek briefly. "I will watch the fire."

❋ ❋ ❋

It was a hindrance, J'Qhir decided, that could sometimes be beneficial—his kind's weakness to the cold. Otherwise, he would not have had the chance to be this close to the *sa`aloh*. Her body heat radiated to him, permeated his skin, awakened him. He had been in a sleepy haze ever since the chilling winds began. The film helped but it only radiated his own body heat back to him. Her added warmth was more than enough to bring him fully alert.

His nostrils filled with warm air, saturated with her scent, and he finally recognized it—the *jhuhn'gha* flower. She smelled of flowers in the heat of the sun. He drew in her scent again, and his *vha'seh* tightened pleasantly.

He enjoyed the sensations he had not felt in a long time, but there would be no alleviation, no matter how alluring he found her. She was *qa`anh'al*, forbidden. Anyone non-Zi would be *qa`anh'al*. Yet, at this moment, with her asleep on his shoulder, her warm arms holding him, he allowed himself the luxury of thoughts of the forbidden.

Once again, he had found himself atop her. If he had not been injured and in pain, he would have enjoyed the experience so much more. Both times had been brought about by extenuating circumstances, but both times he had felt her softly rounded curves giving in to the hard planes of his own body. Once, he would like to lie along her length just to feel her softness and smell her flower scent. But he could think of no way to do it without frightening her—or perhaps raising her expectations? He shook his head.

His *jha'i* hardened at the thought of her lying pliantly beneath him, but he did not think she considered him in that way. He was probably *qa`anh'al* to her as well. She depended upon him for protection and survival and companionship. Nothing more, he thought sadly. They were too different, culturally as well as physically. Yet, they would spend a lifetime here together, whether that be days, weeks, or decades. In time, would he not give up his beliefs and traditions when the nights were too long? Would *she*?

Together, they had experienced more in the past twenty-four Standard hours than he would have experienced with his lifemate in a lifetime had she lived. Certainly, their conversation had more substance and meaning. Very few, if any, lifemated couples struggled with life-and-death decisions every minute of their lives together, even at the height of the Crucian wars. And how many Zi *sa`aloh'az* would manage it as well as she? None, he feared, not even T`hirz. *Sa`aloh'az* never voiced opinions, never took control of a situation, never did anything to attract attention to themselves except in the meticulous order of their lairs and the excellent care of their younglings. Was it because they could not, would not, or were not allowed to? Somewhere along the way, the reason had blurred and faded from the memory of his people. It was the way it was because it was that way. The Zi answer to all questions that had no answers.

She murmured in her sleep, and her arm dropped to his lap. Her hand always had a way of being in the right place at the wrong time. The light pressure was enough to cause him further discomfort. He thought he was at the point that the weight of a grain of sand would have the same effect. Yet that grain of sand would not have her warmth or her softness or her scent of the *jhuhn'gha*.

Carefully, he moved her hand away from that area. If she awoke, she would be embarrassed and so would he. He shifted his body in another position, easing the constriction of his *jha'i*. He should think of other things now, such as survival. Their first priority, in the morning, would be to find a source of water.

But the image of her, as she flew at him, hurling her passionate accusations as well as her fists, exploded into his mind. She was correct, of course. He had warned Hancock that he would not succeed, that he would be found and justice would be served. That should have been enough. Why did humans insist on ignoring the truth? Why did they demand those truths to be repeated until all meaning was lost? However, if Hancock's plan succeeded then the Zi would have no reason to hunt him down and kill him. Sss't, perhaps his threats were empty after all.

After they landed on this planet, he had said nothing more because he had said all he had to say to Hancock. Besides, the *sa`aloh* expressed her concerns and her fears—all of which he shared—quite eloquently. She had asked every question, made every point, so that he had no need to say anything.

What her human mind could not grasp was that the Zi mind did not easily use subterfuge, even as a last resort. Simply, he had not thought to bribe Hancock with the promise of more jewels. Truth, logic, reason—these were the weapons with which he fought. And, in the end, lost to Hancock's obsessive madness.

He had failed.

There was no other way to describe the outcome. He had tried his best, constrained by the Zi code of honor, and failed. Ideally, he should present himself to the Council of Elders, and perform the ritual every Zi youngling memorized but hoped never to engage. For the average Zi, the ritual would be carried out before the clan council. For him, as the Warrior, it should be performed before the Council of Elders—an impossibility right now.

He would not tell her because she would insist he not do it, give a multitude of reasons why he should not, and he would be tempted to listen to her. If carried out quickly, he would manage it before she could stop him.

The thought of the ritual was enough to drive everything else from his mind. He would pay his penance as soon as they found a permanent camp.

Chapter 4

Leith awakened with *something* tickling her nose and crawling down her face. Instinctively, she slapped it away, swallowed a scream, and sat up. A withered leaf fluttered to the ground. She picked it up. The porous surface looked and felt like a piece of dried sponge. It crumbled to dust when she squeezed it.

She was alone—but she wasn't supposed to be. She was outside, beneath a canopy of twisted trees... Suddenly, everything flooded her mind. The meeting on Arreis, Steve, how he'd kidnapped them and abandoned them on Paradise. *Them.* The Commander—

Leith flung aside the solar film and scrambled to her feet. "Com-man-der," she tried to call out, but her voice broke. Her mouth felt as if all the moisture had been wicked away, leaving her tongue as fuzzy as a wad of cotton. She chewed her tongue to make the saliva flow and swallowed hard. "Commander! Where are you?"

"Here, *sa'aloh*," he called from amid the trees.

She followed the sound of his voice, making her way through the twisted trees that looked as eerie in the daylight as they had at night.

"Over here," he called again, guiding her.

When she found him, she watched him from a distance for a few moments. She was again impressed by how big and imposing he was. Propped up by the crooked tree limb he used for a crutch, squeezing something into a little tin cup from the mess kit, and his face drawn in concentration, he still wore his dignity like an aura, an innate part of himself. She stepped closer to see what he was doing.

"Do humansss alwaysss sssleep ssso much? It hasss been daylight for over an hour."

She shrugged, unsettled by his censuring remark. "Stress," she said and swallowed again. "And interruptions."

He had awakened her twice to feed the fire, and it was for *his* benefit, after all. She could have made do with the solar film. He had done it gently, apologetically, but it had interrupted her rest, and both times she'd had trouble falling back asleep. Either he didn't understand her jibe or chose to ignore it.

"The leavesss of the twisssted treesss sssoaked up the morning dew." He plucked another leaf and squeezed. A few drops fell into the cup, and he handed it to her. "Drink, *sa`aloh*. Thisss will quench our thirsssst until we can find another sssource of water."

She peered into the cup and gave only a passing thought to what bacteria it might contain. Her parched mouth needed the moisture. She closed her eyes and gulped it down greedily.

It tasted like pure sweet water, and she told herself the spongy leaves had filtered out any impurities.

"Thank you."

"Now, we fill the canteen."

They spent an hour squeezing the precious drops into the cup and finished filling the canteen. She had grown bored with the process in five minutes, but he seemed to have an unending supply of patience. By the time they filled the canteen and the cups again, Leith's hand was cramped and her fingers stiff, the skin wrinkled like a prune.

When they returned to the campsite, Leith removed her jacket. The morning had grown warmer by the minute, even beneath the deep shade of the trees, and dappled sunlight played over everything. They feasted on a protein pack. Leith broke the grainy bar in two and gave him the larger piece. His body mass was bigger, and he was injured. It seemed only fair. They washed it down with their cups of water.

As Leith chewed the tasteless foodstuff, she thought of bacon and eggs and pancakes dripping with butter and syrup and hot aromatic coffee. To take her mind off *real* food, Leith spread her jacket and investigated its secret pockets.

"A mini omnilyzer! I had no idea it was here." The wafer thin, rectangular computer was about as big as her hand. Most analyzers were specialized, but the omnilyzer could do a little bit of everything, such as analyze the chemical content of potential food, chart their course, diagnose simple ailments and injuries, and suggest treatment. It didn't go into depth on any one thing, but was a survival tool like the rest of the gear in her jacket. She glanced at her cup then the Commander. "Should I? We've already drunk the water. Do we want to know what's in there? Of course, it might be nice to know that we're going to die, writhing in agony, as the bacteria turn our intestines to pulp."

He stared at her, unblinking.

She clicked it on and aimed the laser eye at the residue in the bottom of her cup, reading the results. "It's water, H-2-O. According to this, nothing toxic to humans. It doesn't analyze for xeno-physiology."

He nodded.

"How is your knee?"

"There isss ssstill sssome pain and ssstiffnesss, but the bandage and ssstaff have helped."

"Good."

She found a few more items in the jacket including a compass, which she tucked into her trouser pocket, and a knife. The Commander took the knife from her and pulled it from its sheath. Its keen edge gleamed in the shadowed sunlight. "I will keep thisss," he said and clipped it to his belt.

She put everything else into the flightpack as the Commander, using his crutch, thoroughly scattered the remains of the fire. Leith sat back on her heels and watched him.

"I suppose we do have to leave." She glanced around the perfect campsite and sighed regretfully.

"We mussst find water."

"I know, but this place is safe and familiar." She nodded in a general direction. "We don't know what's out there."

"We will find out."

Leith stood and tied her jacket around her hips. She converted the flightpack to a backpack and pulled it over her shoulders. She retrieved the compass and rested it in the flattened palm of her hand. The needle spun jerkily, one way then the other. The Commander limped closer and peered at it.

"Thisss planet doesss not have a magnetic pole."

"Or there is a strong magnetic field in this area."

"Or large deposssitsss of iron."

"Whatever the cause, it's useless." She put it back in her pocket and looked at him. "We should head for the equator, but—"

"But I am unable to travel fassst enough," he finished quickly, as if admitting his own weakness somehow minimized its impact on the situation.

"No. I was going to say that we don't know which way to go. We don't know which hemisphere we're in or the rotational direction of this planet. On Earth, the sun rises in the east so we would know in which direction to move toward the equator, but Paradise's sun could very well rise in the west."

She thought his face darkened a shade, but he turned away before she could be certain.

"Besides," she added, "if you were at your peak physical capacity, I would be the one slowing us down. With your injury, I would say we're about even. So, which way do we go?"

Leith spoke the truth, but she also hoped her words soothed his wounded pride. Human or Zi, a male was a male.

"The mountainsss."

"Any particular reason?"

"We ssshould have a better chance of finding water—a ssstream or ssspring." He looked up at the trees. "Have you noticed how many of the leavesss are dying?"

Her eyes followed his. She estimated about a third of the leaves on the twisted trees were brown and withered. A high breeze rustled the tops of the trees and some of the dead leaves broke free and fluttered down.

"Autumn," Leith murmured. "That means—"

"Winter isss near. The nightsss have already begun to turn cold." He struck the side of his leg in exasperation. "I will build a lair for usss."

His amber eyes grew wide and his mouth became a tight, straight slash across his face. He looked, Leith concluded, surprised.

"No, Commander," she said gently, not understanding but reluctant to ask. "There isn't time to build anything, just as there isn't time to travel toward the equator even if we knew which way to go."

He nodded, blinking rapidly. "Of courssse. We have to find ssshelter now and prepare for winter. The mountainsss ssshould have cavesss."

A lair, Leith thought, as she fell into step beside the Commander. Under other circumstances, the word would sound—well, romantic. Back home, there was a lodge called Shade's Lair, a sprawling building of cedar logs. Students from the university used it as a getaway—to relax, to party, or to enjoy intimate liaisons. Leith had been there once.

She had dated another student for a while. Khris—what was his last name? She found a certain satisfaction in not remembering. Khris heard about a big party planned at the Lair, and she agreed to go although it didn't really interest her. She did, however, fall in love with the lodge itself. She spent her time studying the rustic decor while Khris indulged in every recreational drug available. By the time she was ready to leave, Khris was ready to lead her upstairs. She declined as gracefully as possible. Khris insisted and became incensed at her refusal.

Up until that night, he had seemed to understand. He had broached the subject of sex during their short relationship, and each time she had explained her reasons for saying no. Each time he said he understood, but he really didn't. That night, high on drugs and alcohol, he called her many things, loud enough for the world to hear, including *frigid*. The same word Steve had used.

Embarrassed, Leith had fled the lodge. She was comfortable with her decision not to give in to the meaningless temptation of casual sex. She wanted to fall in love first, and she certainly hadn't loved Khris.

She had never been in love, never even thought she was in love. There were men she found physically appealing and some of them she had dated, but she'd never met a man who had taken her breath away, made her heart race with a glance, consumed her thoughts day and night. She'd never met a man—

She glanced at the Commander, who concentrated on placing his makeshift crutch securely before taking a step. Her one regret should have been never having experienced intimacy with a man, but it wasn't. She regretted that the life she'd chosen and enjoyed had been snatched away from her. And she regretted that she hadn't taken more interest in McClure Shipping. If she had, things would be different now.

If she had, she would have been by her parents' side, instead of Steve, learning the business. She would have made the trips with her father to Arreis. She would have met the Commander anyway. *If*, in this case, would not have changed the fact that they would have met, as they were destined to meet. They would have met sooner, been able to develop a normal relationship. Whatever a "normal relationship" with a Zi meant. They would have grown to know one another before—

Before what? she chided herself. Before he swept you off your feet and carried you away to his vine-covered lair and made a woman of you? She wanted to laugh at this flight of fancy, but then he would want to know what she found "amusssing". Would he be embarrassed, insulted, or appalled to know she thought of him this way?

She sighed. Besides, he wasn't the type. Too prim and proper, too dignified to let his libido overrule propriety. Too stuffy, Steve had said, and for once he'd been right. The

Commander would have met with them, concluded his business, went on his mirthless way, and never given her another thought. She would have dreamed of him and created elaborate fantasies as she usually did with men she found attractive. Dreams and fantasies were much safer than reality.

Ultimately, she would have been crushed by his reality. *A wife and sssix younglingsss back at the lair,* she could hear him explain. *Besssidesss, I find humansss repulsssive, all that hair...*and he would shudder.

"*Sa`aloh!*" the Commander called out at the same moment the ground moved beneath her foot.

Leith looked down. A brown snake, as thick as her arm and nearly as long, coiled up around her ankle. She screamed and jerked her foot, trying to shake it free. She lost her balance and grabbed the Commander's arm to keep from falling backward. He held them both upright as Leith shook her foot a few more times. The creature fell, landing on the ground with a plop.

It remained curled up. The Commander poked it with his crutch, and it wriggled into an even tighter knot. She could now see it had a segmented body. She got down on her knees and, using a stick, prodded it again and again until she saw the head was a darker brown spot. No eyes, no mouth, no fangs.

"My God, it's a worm! I thought it was a snake. I've never seen a worm that big."

"Ussse your analyzer."

"It didn't bite me."

"Find out if it isss toxic."

"Commander, I said it didn't bite me."

"That isss not why we need to know if it isss toxic. We need to know if it isss edible."

"*What?*" Leith leaped to her feet, away from the giant worm. She shook her head, and it turned into a full body shudder. "I am not eating a giant slimy worm. I don't eat Chinese noodles because they look like worms. I'll starve first!"

The Commander sniffed disapprovingly. "You may do jusssst that, *sa'aloh.*"

She shook her head again, refusing to retract her statement. There were cultures on Earth that survived on diets of grubworms, tarantulas, and insects of all kinds. They boiled them, steamed them, and battered and deep-fried them. Knowing that didn't make the worm any more appetizing to her. She flatly refused to eat anything that remotely resembled a worm. Or spider. Or insect.

"A *p'ha'al* of that sssize would make a tasssty pie," he said and sighed regretfully. Using the crutch, he gently rolled it out of their path.

Now, *she* stared at *him,* unblinking. "You eat worms?"

"Yesss, *sa'aloh.* We call them *p'ha'al,* but they are much sssmaller than thisss. The mountain wormsss have a better tassste and texture, but are more difficult to find. The desssert wormsss are easssier to locate, but do not tassste asss good."

"You eat worms," she repeated. "Well, maybe you had better bring this one along. We might not come across anything else—uh, edible soon."

"I have sssseen quite a few. They are plentiful."

She hadn't been paying attention. She had let her mind wander to other things. What else had she missed? Something she would consider edible but the Commander wouldn't? Lost in thought, she could have passed by a taco stand and not noticed. And the Commander wouldn't have said anything because the menu didn't include worms.

The thought of a taco made her mouth water and stomach rumble. A taco supreme and a milkshake, her favorite fast-food meal. She never should have thought of a milkshake.

"I would kill for a chocolate milkshake right now."

The Commander eyed her with disdain.

"It's a figure of speech! It shows how much I want a milkshake." She glanced at the worm again. "Tell you what, I'll kill the *felafel*—"

"*P`ha`al.*"

"Whatever—to get my milkshake and you can have the *pahapel.*"

"*P`ha`al.*"

"Worm."

The Commander stalked off, and Leith had to run to catch up to him.

The forest gradually changed from the twisted trees to trees with smooth trunks and feathery fern-like leaves. Some of the fern leaves had turned brown, and the limbs were heavy with seeded cones. Leith plucked a few and analyzed them as they walked. Non-toxic. She broke away the seed covering. The seed itself was almond-shaped but smaller and smooth, pale yellow in color. She popped it in her mouth and chewed. It was almost tasteless, but should be filling. She finished deseeding one cone and handed them to the Commander.

"This is much better than worms," she said and began cracking the seed coverings on the other cone. "And they're high in protein and fat."

The Commander shook a few into his mouth. "Not asss good asss *p`ha`al,* but it will do."

When she finished her cone nuts she picked as many as she could stuff in the flightpack. Then she plucked another from a tree and deseeded as they walked. She stored the nuts in a pocket of her jacket. The task kept her hands busy and her mind occupied. She had no time to think of the life she was forced to leave behind. No time to think of what could have been or even what might be. She broke off another cone and proceeded to deseed it. Time to think of food that did not curl up around her ankle when she stepped on it.

By then she had seen several of the giant brown worms, but had not pointed them out to the Commander. She desperately hoped they would not be forced to rely on them for nourishment, although the Commander would undoubtedly consider them a delicacy. She supposed she would eat them if nothing else was available, but all around them the forest teemed with life. She could hear the chittering of what she thought might be squirrel-like creatures, but she had yet to see one. Birds flew here and there amid the branches—brown, dull blue, vibrant yellow. They weren't much different from Terran birds. Now, if only she could find the Paradisian version of a chicken, there would be eggs for breakfast!

The slope of the ground increased, but the Commander compensated easily. She was almost glad he was injured. With his long legs and tireless stride, he would have left her behind long ago. She had difficulty keeping up with him now, and he limped and used a crutch.

The forest thinned somewhat, and the Commander suggested they stop to rest and drink. She was thirsty, especially after the cone nuts, and she was tired. She brought out the canteen and cups and poured each half full. They drank in silence.

Leith stretched out full length beneath the shade of a fern tree. The Commander chose a sunny spot and eased himself down, his back against a large rock. She watched him as he rubbed his knee.

"If it's bothering you too much, maybe we should wait a few days. I have a feeling a few days won't make any difference."

"No, sa`aloh. It doesss not hurt—much. The ssswelling hasss gone down, but the bandage hasss come loossse. We need to keep moving to find water and ssshelter."

She watched as he rolled up his trouser leg, easing it over the bandaged knee. His fingers fumbled with the length of elasticized cloth. He tried to tighten it without first completely unwrapping it. Leith shook her head. For someone so efficient, so competent, he could be impossibly clumsy at times. Then a picture came to mind—his taloned fingers deftly untying the intricate knot on the bag of Zi jewels. She would be just as clumsy trying that.

Afraid she might fall if she tried to stand, she crawled to him. "Let me do that."

"You need to ressst. I can manage, sa`aloh."

"I'm sure you can. But I—I want to."

His amber eyes glittered in the sunlight. Then he nodded and withdrew his hands. He leaned back against the warm rock, but his eyes remained on her hands as she finished unwrapping the bandage.

His knee appeared less puffy than the day before, but she really had no idea what an uninjured Zi knee looked like. She thought of asking him if she could uncover his other knee so she could compare the two. Why stop there? She might as well ask him to completely undress so she could compare him to the human male physique. The Commander would be shocked, of course, especially if his culture was at a point where the nude body was taboo.

On Earth, nudity was natural in many environs, such as swimming pools and the beach, and the norm in vids and advertising. The male body was not unknown to her.

Cleanliness, weather, and abrasive surfaces necessitated clothes, but many fashions revealed more than concealed. Leith had worn her share on numerous occasions, but she had no desire to bare certain parts of her anatomy while merely shopping or attending class or visiting another world such as Arreis.

"It isss an odd thing."

"*What?*" she asked since his remark seemed to coincide with her thoughts.

"Thisss bandage."

"Oh. Don't you have bandages on Zi?"

"Yesss, but not like thisss. Our medical technology lagsss far behind our martial technology sssince the Cruciansss began their warsss with usss."

She let all of her fingers and the palms of her hands slide over the soft scaling of his skin. His leg jerked.

"I'm sorry. I didn't mean to hurt you."

"You did not, *sa`aloh*," he replied. His voice was huskier than usual, like dry leaves rustling in the wind.

She began to wrap the bandage firmly. "The Crucians claim you started the war."

"Do they? Yesss, they would."

"Your government ought to reconsider joining the Galactic Alliance."

"Sss't, we have no time for politicsss! Every day isss a challenge to our very sssurvival. Each day we sssurvive isss a day of victory."

"If what you say is true, then your side needs to be told. The Crucians—"

"*If?* If what *I* sssay isss true? What reassson would I have to ssspeak falsssely now, *sa`aloh*?" He spat out a string of Zi as he brushed her hands aside and rolled down his trouser leg. "We are ssstranded on thisss planet, void of sssentient life sssave our own, with no hope of ressscue. Why ssshould I lie to you? Why ssshould I ever lie to you?"

"You shouldn't— You wouldn't— It's just a figure of speech." Flustered by his reaction, she didn't know how to make amends. "I'm sorry, Commander. I didn't mean—"

He lurched to his feet, and she rolled out of his way so he would have room to maneuver. He towered over her, his slitted amber eyes boring into hers, delving into what lay beyond, seeking something in her that she was afraid he wouldn't find.

"I command no one. I am *J'Qhir Zha'an Gha'na`ameht`h Rhilh meh Bh'rin'gha T`hagh'qohp'nij vuh Dhi`if'qha`al.*"

She was tempted to make a flippant remark questioning how he could remember it all, but the slits in his eyes had narrowed to almost nothing. His flat nostrils flared, and his mouth was set in a hard line. She had the uneasy feeling—and it was so uneasy she wanted to squirm beneath his relentless stare—they had crossed a boundary, moved past some point they could never return to. They had entered another realm of the Zi zone of their relationship, and she had no earthly idea what it was. If she had to ask, she would disappoint him. Asking what he meant would wound him beyond repair. She could do neither to him at this moment when he looked so solemn and, yes, lost.

"My name is Catherine Leith McClure," she said. It seemed lacking in depth and history compared to his, and she added, "I was given my mother's maiden name and my father's surname and I am called Leith."

"Leith," he repeated softly.

He held out his hand to her, bracing himself with the crutch. She remembered how the Paxian had grasped his arm, not his hand, as a gesture of friendship and trust. She raised her hand high enough to grip his arm, but he moved his hand into hers instead.

At some point, he had removed his gloves.

His cool fingers lay matched to hers briefly, then entwined with them even more briefly before slipping around her thumb and grasping the heel of her hand. Her smooth, pale skin against his tawny-umber texture constituted a study in contrast.

She didn't have to pull herself to her feet. He brought her up without a change in expression or a sound. Among humans, she wasn't considered a small woman. At 180 centimeters, she was tall, inheriting the McClure statuesque frame. She was impressed with the way he hadn't shifted a millimeter, had lifted her with one hand as easily as he would lift a rag doll. She'd never met a human male who could do that.

"Thank you," Leith said and smiled at him. She wondered if he would ever smile back. Maybe the Zi never smiled, but that didn't mean he couldn't. Finding a way to make him smile might easily turn into a life-long project. What else did she have to do for the next five or six decades? If they survived that long.

Their hands held for a moment longer than necessary, then he let go and looked up at the sky. "We ssshould move on," he said, and he sounded like rustling dry leaves again. "We have lossst enough daylight already."

"Are you sure you—" Leith began, but his eyes cut to her sharply. She bit off the rest of what she intended to say. Instead of asking if he was sure he shouldn't rest longer, she began again. "Are you sure we're headed in the right direction?"

"I am sssure of nothing except that if we do not find water and ssshelter we will die." He jerked on his gloves. "If Hancock had left usss on a desssert world, I could find water by the lay of the land or the texture of the sssand. But here...everything isss covered by treesss, grasss, and green plantsss. Here— sss't!"

Viciously, he stabbed his crutch into the ground and started up the slope in the direction they'd been heading all morning. After pulling on the flightpack, Leith followed behind, trying to make sense of what had happened between them.

❈ ❈ ❈

J'Qhir glanced back once to make sure she followed, then turned his eyes to the ground. He had to watch where he placed the staff or he would stumble and fall and disgrace himself further. His free hand bumped the hilt of the knife at his waist, a reminder of his debt.

He held out his hand and would not have been surprised to see tendrils of smoke curling from the tips of the glove. His fingers and palm stung from the contact with hers. His knee burned, but not only from the injury. He could still feel the imprint of her hands, each spot where a finger connected with his skin a concentrated pinpoint of heat. Like an uncontrolled youngling, his leg had twitched as his *vha'seh* tightened in response to her accidental touch. She thought she had hurt him. He was relieved she did not know what she actually did to him.

Her actions had prompted him to give her his *na`ajh*—his soul or spirit. No exact equivalent existed in her language. By the slight wrinkling of the delicate arches of hair on her brow and the puzzlement in her round eyes, she did not comprehend *why* he had given her his veiled name. She had not questioned him aloud so she understood the importance of the gift. It was enough for now.

They walked throughout the afternoon in silence. The shuffling of their feet, the tap of his staff, and the relentless crackle of cones being broken open the only sounds. She had filled her pockets and began filling his.

She kept several paces behind like a *sa`aloh* should... She would take offense, and he allowed himself a small smile since she was behind him and could not see. Then she had stepped closer and placed her closed fist into his jacket pocket.

By every grain of sand on Zi, he could feel her heat through the thick material. She filled that pocket, then started on another, lower one. Why in the name of the rock did war jackets have so many pockets? He stabbed the ground with his staff every time her hand entered one.

Late in the afternoon, they came across a little bush covered in bright yellow berries. Her round eyes grew rounder as she shot past him and scooped up a handful. She had almost put them to her lips before she remembered to analyze them.

"Well?" His mouth watered at the thought of something besides dry protein bars and nutmeats.

"We wouldn't die," she said as she threw the berries to the ground and stomped them, "but we'd be puking our guts out."

J'Qhir sighed. "Not a pleasssant consssequence."

"Looks like it's nuts for supper," she said with a false smile.

Wearily, he nodded.

Long before time to set up camp, as they passed an expansive thicket of thorn bushes, Leith halted in her tracks and tossed the flightpack to the ground.

"I'm too tired to take one more step!" She looked at him as if she dared him to argue, then settled in the shade of the largest tree.

He said nothing. His knee throbbed dully and needed rest also. He found a sunny spot, remembering to shift the knife to a more comfortable place before easing his cumbersome bulk to the ground.

The knife.

He would wait until they found or built a permanent shelter before performing the ritual. The actual ceremony lasted two exhausting Zi days and included fasting. He did not have the strength to follow these strictures now. Perhaps later, if he could do so without Leith discovering his intentions.

His eyes slipped over her still form, stretched out in the dying grass. Once again, he wished for the opportunity to lie atop her, merely for the pleasure of the experience. How would she react? Twice they had been pressed body-to-body, and he had seen no distaste in her round eyes. Would she be offended if he—

Sss't. Speculation was fruitless. She was *qa`anh'al*, and he was too old to waste his time on such things.

He forced his attention to the knife. His fingers ran along the smooth, unornamented handle. On Zi, he would have use of his clan blade. The ancient hilt had been ornately carved from wood gathered on the mountain nearest the Bh'rin'gha by an ancestor several millennia ago. Here, on Paradise, this plain knife would be just as effective.

He would try to perform the entire ritual, but if Leith proved too curious, he would execute the last part, use the knife, and accept the result. Leith would know nothing about it until he was finished, and then it would be too late. Certainly, she would look at him in disgust, but he would have to accept her disfavor. He felt a deep need to pay for his incompetence.

The sun sank lower and shade moved over him. When the first of the chill winds began, Leith awoke and rubbed her eyes.

"You shouldn't have let me sleep so long."

"You needed the ressst."

"But you're getting cold." She brought out the solar film and helped him secure it. Once more she had to gather wood while he sat idle, mindful of his injuries. He had whiled away the time he could have helped, his thoughts consumed with a rite that held no meaning on this planet. Or in her eyes. Survival should be his main concern at all times, at all costs. Could he be any more useless?

Thus, he had failed again.

He struggled to his feet and gathered what material he could find to start a fire. He had watched Leith and knew what was needed—dry leaves and grass, twigs, and small branches. He gathered them in a pile as she had done. When she returned with an armload of deadfall, he looked at her expectantly.

"Isss thisss the correct way?"

She tilted her head to one side, unconsciously mimicking his kind's way of displaying perplexity. He took no offense. He found the mannerism agreeable. It made her seem more familiar, more Zi... Is that what he wanted? Did he wish for her to be more like his own kind so that she would be more acceptable?

"You don't know how to build a fire?" The arches of hair over her eyes furrowed as she sank to her knees and laid the wood beside the small pyre he had prepared.

"On Zi, flammable matter sssuch asss wood is ssscarce. When heat or light isss needed, we ussse the glowing ssstonesss."

"Glowing stones?" Leith brought out the laserlight and set the leaves and twigs aflame.

"Yesss." He picked up a piece of wood as big around as his fist and twice as long. "The ssstonesss are plentiful on Zi and found buried deep within the mountainsss. They are made of a clear ssstone that trapped a natural chemical when it formed. When the ssstone isss ssshaken, a reaction between the liquid and ssstone generatesss heat and light."

She fed larger pieces of the wood to the growing fire then stopped suddenly. She grabbed his hand and held it between hers. Her warmth seeped through the thick gloves, and he wished desperately that he had removed them.

"Don't you realize what you have? Instead of your jewels, you should have been trading the glowing stones! They would be worth a small fortune on the market." Then, quite suddenly, she withdrew her hands from his and began placing more wood on the fire. The radiance left her face, and her smooth brow creased in a frown. "You could have exchanged them for the cargo."

He didn't understand her change in attitude unless she thought she had overstepped some boundary by touching him in a familiar way. He wanted her hands to hold his again, to have this small connection to her, but she moved away to the far side of the fire, cold and distant, in dimension as well as disposition.

J'Qhir wrapped himself tightly in the solar film. This night was not as cold as the previous one. When Leith curled up close to the fire without another word, he knew he would not have to share the solar film tonight.

Something had happened, and this time it was he who did not know the meaning of it at all.

Chapter 5

The shallow stream bubbled over smooth pebbles embedded in the sandy bottom. Leith leaned over the muddy bank and saw her reflection for the first time in days—tangled hair framing a dirt-smudged face. She wanted nothing more than to plunge into its refreshing coolness. She looked at it longingly and withdrew the omnilyzer. Offering a silent prayer, she aimed the laser eye into the stream.

A few bacteria, but nothing a human body couldn't adjust to. Zi? She didn't know and neither would the Commander. They took it on faith that his physiology was similar enough to human to be safe.

Leith put the gadget away and dipped her hands in, washing away two days' worth of dirt and grime. She splashed her face and scrubbed it clean. At last, she enjoyed the luxury of fresh water spilling through her mouth and down her throat. The dew they had collected the first morning had the musty taste of leaves and a sharp metallic tang from the canteen. It had saved them from dehydration but wasn't very palatable.

When Leith had drunk all she could, she dunked her head completely into the stream and washed her hair. Her scalp had itched for two days. She wished Steve had thrown in a bottle of shampoo among all the other useless things. She squeezed out as much water as she could, then finger-combed the tangles out.

She dumped the last of the dew, rinsed the canteen, and refilled it.

Now to find the Commander.

J'Qhir.

He had stopped calling her *sa`aloh* and now used Leith. After he told her his long, unwieldy name, she assumed he wanted her to call him J'Qhir, the only word she'd recognized. She had yet to say it out loud. It was difficult for her to think of him other than the Commander.

If she used his given name, wouldn't they become more...intimate? Would he consider it an insult if she didn't? More importantly, should she even care?

Last night, when he explained about the glowstones, she thought she'd found a way to save his precious jewels and perhaps bolster the Zi economy. Then reality had hit her in the mid-section like a laserblast. Whether it was jewels or glowstones, they traded illegally for weapons of war. And this Zi Warrior had somehow convinced her father to be a part of it.

How could she have forgotten?

She had lost sight of that important fact while they were at Steve's mercy and as they struggled to survive on this unknown planet. How could she maintain her integrity and fight her overwhelming attraction to the Commander while facing possibly decades with him as her sole companion?

Leith didn't think she could.

Flights of fancy were one thing. Leith could do whatever she wished in the fantasies in her own mind without compromising her principles. This was reality. She and the

Commander...J'Qhir were the only two people on this planet, and they probably were going to be here the rest of their lives.

Leith took one last, long drink of water. Now was not the time for introspection. She needed to find the Commander and lead him back to the stream. She hated to leave, afraid she wouldn't be able to find it again. For whatever reason, the mapping function in the omnilyzer didn't work. She could return the way she had come and use the k-counter to track how far she traveled in kilometers. If she could remember landmarks as well, she might succeed in bringing the Commander to the water.

Not the Commander, J'Qhir.

She practiced his name aloud, "J'Qhir." She liked the way the sounds moved in her mouth—the soft j, the hard k sound followed by an extra breathy rush of air, the roll of "eer" over her tongue. She repeated it. Maybe by the time she found him, she could use it as easily as he used hers.

On the other side of the stream stood a tall tree, long shaggy limbs hugging close to the trunk as they reached for the sky. Leith would keep that tree in sight as she headed in the direction she thought she had come.

Splitting up had been the Commander—J'Qhir's idea. She had awakened stiff and sore from sleeping on the ground. A night's sleep hadn't eased her resentment. She remained aloof while they ate from their meager supplies in silence. She remained unmoved by his dismay. She knew he had no idea what had disturbed her the night before, but she was in no mood to broach the subject of illegal cargo.

When J'Qhir had proposed they search in different directions, she had voiced her objections. She had no experience at that sort of thing. Just as she'd been afraid of losing him in the twisted tree forest the first night, she now feared losing him and never finding him again.

"You are more capable than you think, Leith," he reassured her. "But if you think you are lossst, ssstay in one place and I will come for you."

Patiently, he had explained they could cover twice the area in the same amount of time. He sounded as if he had confidence in her and her ability. She couldn't bring herself to object again. His amber eyes might register disappointment. He might make that sound of exasperation, "Sss't!"

Now, Leith grinned. She couldn't wait for the opportunity to explain how closely that sounded to a Terran expletive.

Leith had wanted to use his injured knee as an excuse, but she knew he already felt inadequate because of it. In the end, she conceded against her better judgment.

Looking back over her shoulder, Leith could still see the tall, slim tree in the distance. The k-counter read two-thirds of a kilometer. What would that be in miles? Converting metric to the obsolete system was an old game of hers. On Earth, the United States had been the last country to go metric in the latter half of the twenty-first century, mainly because space travel became feasible and metric was more exact.

Two hundred years ago, distance was measured in inches, feet, and miles. Weight in ounces and pounds. Volume in cups, pints, and quarts. There were yards, tons, and bushels. Those confused her sometimes. Now, what was the formula to convert kilometers to miles?

She glanced over her shoulder again and— The tree was nowhere in sight! She stopped and her heart fluttered. If she lost the tree, she lost the water and their only hope of survival. How could she be so stupid as to preoccupy her mind with nonsense *again*? J'Qhir had no business thinking her capable of anything or entrusting her with the simplest of tasks.

She keyed off the counter and backtracked, paying attention this time. Now, she saw how the land swelled into a gentle rise then receded behind her. She had walked over it without noticing, and as she descended the slope, the crest had come between her and the tree.

Had she come from this direction in the first place? She couldn't remember crossing the rise before finding the stream. Nothing looked familiar, none of the short scrubby trees or the sprawling bushes. Oh, why had she agreed to the separation?

She should sit down and wait for J'Qhir to find her. She didn't doubt he could do it, but it might take hours. It might be nightfall before he came upon her, when the wild beasts roamed and howled. No. She couldn't wait for J'Qhir to rescue her. She had to find a way back to the clearing.

By carefully examining the area close to the stream, Leith was able to pick up her original trail. She set the k-counter again. She recognized this way. The ground did not swell and surge. Yes, she remembered the two bushes that twisted together peculiarly. And the broken branch where she'd caught her jacket.

Feeling more confident, she glanced back often to make sure the tall tree was still in sight. She purposely broke many branches along the way and replaced the tall thin tree with a taller dead tree in her line of sight. Luck was with her because three hours later, the same amount of time it had taken her to find the stream, she found the clearing beside the thorn bush patch where she and J'Qhir had parted.

Commander J'Qhir had not yet returned.

Leith threw down her jacket and flightpack, then rested in the shade. She munched on cone nuts and sipped the fresh water. She was tired but growing accustomed to physical exertion. Anxious to tell the Commander about the stream, she wished he would hurry.

How long should she wait for him? An hour? Two? What if he never came, attacked by one of the beasts that roared in the night? What if she searched and found the tawny-umber remains—

A huge black mass started to move across the sky, and Leith scooted further under the tree. She leaned against the trunk and watched as the birds made their way to warmer climes. It was the second flock she'd seen since their arrival. Warmer climes...south for the winter... If birds on Paradise acted the same as birds on Earth, she now knew which way was south! She could tell J'Qhir in which direction they should travel when it turned spring.

When the birds had passed over, Leith stretched out again. Just as she settled, a distant drone slowly crept into her consciousness. The buzzing sound, not unlike Terran bees amplified many times over, grew louder with each passing second. Whatever made the noise moved at high speed in her direction.

Leith climbed to her feet and watched. Over the treetops a dark cloud swelled into mammoth proportions. The writhing mass filled most of the southwestern sky, partially blocking the sun, and in no way resembled the flock of birds that had just moved overhead. She stood frozen in indecision.

At that moment, J'Qhir broke through the trees at a dead run. He yielded to his injured knee, but his long legs covered ground faster than she ever could. Gasping for air, he shouted one word, "*Run!*"

Leith turned and ran.

She headed for the dense forest beyond the clearing and the thorn bushes. She ran as fast as her legs could carry her, but J'Qhir caught up with her quickly. So did the advance guard of the horde of flying creatures.

As J'Qhir took hold of her arm, several of the flyers shot past them. One turned in mid-flight and hovered in the air a few seconds. Although as large as a Terran hawk, it resembled a dragonfly. Several sets of wings buzzed noisily on a long, narrow body that tapered to a stinger point and curled underneath. Just as the insect dove toward her, J'Qhir propelled her to the left. It sailed harmlessly past, so close that its wing tips brushed her cheek.

He shouted, but she couldn't hear him over the drone of the horde. He led them toward the thorn bushes. She tried to stop, but J'Qhir's vise-like grip wouldn't let her. She yelled at him that the forest was close, but he couldn't hear her either. She glanced back and saw the main body of flyers nearly upon them.

Leith folded her free arm over her face and allowed J'Qhir to catapult them into the tangled thicket. Needle-sharp thorns tore at her skin as she landed face down, the jolt knocking the breath from her chest. She wanted to remain very still so the flyers wouldn't see her, but J'Qhir hauled her forward. They crawled until the growth that had been beneath them sprang upward to close off the aperture they had created with their desperate leap.

Dozens of the flyers tried to maneuver through the bushes. Some impaled their slender bodies on the sharp thorns. Others shredded their wings and dangled helplessly in the lacework of branches. A few made it through and aimed directly for their tender flesh.

The Commander batted at the fragile bodies, crushing them with his gloved hands. Leith could only watch. Bare hands were no match for those stinger tails. One buzzed near her head and she screeched, instinctively moving closer to the Commander for protection. She drew her arms in under her and buried her face in the space between his side and the ground, trying to make as small a target as possible.

She felt his body jerk to and fro as he fought the flyer. Its wings caught in her hair, and she waited for the sting. There was one last tug at her hair as the Commander grabbed it. Then she heard a sickening squelch. The horde had moved on, and she could hear once more. The Commander's gasps for breath were synchronous with her own.

Tentatively, she raised her head and shuddered at the sight of hundreds of flyers dying in the thicket around them. She rose to her knees, aware of stinging cuts on her arms and a scratch on her cheek. The Commander balanced on one knee and arm, his injured leg held out at an odd angle. She was about to ask if he was all right when she heard the angry buzz of a lone flyer behind her, drawing near. Before she could dodge it, the creature slammed into her back.

She felt no more than a pinprick just before the Commander reached around her to snatch it away and smash it to the ground.

"Leith!"

"I think we overreacted," she said just before white-hot pain seared her shoulder blade and spasmed through her muscles. Her whole body stiffened, and she couldn't move her right arm at all. With difficulty, she lifted her left arm and slapped her hand on his chest, her fingers closing over the soft material of his jacket. She clung to him to keep from toppling over.

"J-J'Qhir—I found—water," she whispered before the pain increased to an intensity she could no longer bear. She fell into his arms as she allowed her mind to shut down, then knew nothing more.

※ ※ ※

Wrapped in the solar film, J'Qhir fed the fire. How he had managed to do all that needed to be done before nightfall chilled him into immobility defied logic.

For one moment, one small portion of a heartbeat, he had almost succumbed to his despair. He considered plunging the stinger from one of the dying creatures into his own flesh and ending it all. Because in that one everlasting moment, he thought Leith had died in his arms.

She had lain as still as a stone, no breath passing through her pale lips. As he contemplated the thought of his own demise, her body convulsed, the shudder rippling through her like a wave. She breathed again. Shallowly, tortuously, but she breathed.

Carefully, he turned her over and tore her shirt away from the spot where the huge insect had stung her. The bump was as large as his fist. He unsheathed his knife. He couldn't take the time to fight his way through the brambles, hobble to the flightpack and jacket where she'd left them in the clearing, and fight his way back again. The poison would have time to work its way through her system, and she might be truly dead before he returned. He could only hope the blade was clean enough. He inhaled sharply, held her body on its side, and made the first incision.

Clear yellow fluid spurted from the cut. He sliced again, across the first. He squeezed, letting the poison drain to the ground, until only blood flowed freely, clean and red, and the lump had diminished to no more than irritated flesh.

He was loath to leave her, but he needed the medkit now. Awkwardly, he crawled to the nearest thorn bush. He couldn't leave the thicket the same way they had entered it. He grasped the thick stem close to the ground and yanked. The soil was dry and loose, threaded with spindly roots. The bush pulled free easier than he could have hoped for. It didn't take long to clear a path.

He retrieved the flightpack and jacket from beneath the tree where she'd left them and returned to her side. In the medkit, he found packets clearly marked. He spoke her language more fluently than he could read it, so he wasted precious minutes trying to decipher the lettering.

Gently, he wiped the area with a small pad soaked in an antibacterial solution. Then he dusted it with antiseptic powder. He applied a skinseal to compress the wound and stop the bleeding.

Her breath came in ragged gasps, and her chest shuddered with each inhalation. He laid his fingers along her wrist. The pulse was not as strong as he thought it should be. He knew next to nothing about humans. Compared to a Zi heartbeat, hers was much weaker. Perhaps it should be so.

Dried blood smeared her ivory skin from cuts on her cheek and arms, but none were serious. He too had suffered scratches from the thorns, but they would heal rapidly. Their minor wounds could wait until he had them encamped for the night.

Leith said she had found water. Now, he had to find it again.

He could leave her to hunt for the water by himself. He could follow her trail more quickly unburdened by her weight. Then he would return for her and carry her directly to the water source even more quickly. That meant two trips on an injured leg that could crumple beneath him at any moment. The alternative was to carry her with him now. He was unsure if he could even lift her.

The sun had moved closer to the mountaintops, and J'Qhir was aware of every second he spent in indecision. Leith would be appalled at his lack of command. *Think, stupid Rep!* he chastised himself using her language in his mind.

He couldn't leave her unprotected. What if the horde of flying creatures returned?

J'Qhir tried several ways to lift her to his good shoulder and rise with his good leg, but her weight overbalanced him. He couldn't find enough leverage...or enough strength to withstand the pain that clawed at his injured limbs when he tried to use them.

He had to build a litter.

By the time he found two suitable branches and entwined them with enough vine to hold her weight, the sun was much closer to the mountaintops. He mindfully rolled her onto the litter and placed the flightpack and jacket between her legs. He dug in the pack for the canteen and found it full.

He poured a little through her lips. Her throat automatically worked to swallow. After she had taken in a few sips, he turned the canteen up to his mouth. He gulped the fresh water, draining the container. He needed the liquid, and he didn't plan to stop again until he reached the water source.

Using the laserlight, he burned the path clear of branches and roots. He lifted the litter poles and started at a steady pace.

From the clearing he went "north", as she had called it, and easily found her trail. She had broken many branches along the way. He smiled briefly. Leith was capable of much more than she thought. Her broken trail would lead them directly to the water source. Spring or stream or ocean, he didn't know. Only water.

Pain was his constant companion. After a while he could no longer remember what it was like not to hurt. Each time he set down a foot, the jolt sent a laserblast throughout his lower body. Every bump of the litter jarred his aching shoulder. Soon the two blended into one unending wave that undulated along every nerve. Liquid filled his eyes, but he never lessened his pace.

As the chilling winds of evening stirred around him, incessant pain prevented the natural lethargy from overtaking his senses. He remained alert enough to continue placing one foot in front of the other. Each step taken was a step closer to survival.

He came upon the stream before he knew it. In his fugue state, he took too long to react to the realization that flowing water lay in his path. He plowed to a halt only after his boots sank ankle-deep in the muddy bank. He dropped the litter where he stood. He would make camp here, close to the water's edge.

He stumbled around in the twilight, dragging his leg, as he gathered wood. Somehow he had built a fire. Somehow he had found the film and wrapped it around his shoulders. Somehow he had located the small metal pot and filled it with water. All of these things he did, but now he had only a vague recollection of performing the tasks.

When he touched Leith an unnaturally high heat radiated from her flushed skin. He covered her with her jacket. He used several of the diaphanous cloths from the medkit to dip in water and wash her brow. The packets were marked *gauze*—a strong word for such flimsy material.

Now, after drinking his fill of fresh water and eating half a protein bar and a handful of nutmeats, he was warm and more clear-headed. He picked up each packet in turn from the medkit and squinted into the firelight. He hissed at his failing eyesight and wished he'd thought to bring his glasses. He'd left them aboard his warship on the desk in his cabin, which was no larger than the detention cell on the *Catherine McClure*. *If* his personal belongings hadn't been removed yet.

His disappearance—no, his apparent *defection*—would allow the Council to effectively eradicate his entire existence as well as bring dishonor to his clan. His distant relatives would be bewildered by this turn of events, but they would accept the Council's decision with grace. His clan would lose their land grants, mining rights, and their seat in the General Council. They would, in effect, be ostracized by society.

Elder M'bat'h would have no qualms about making the pronouncement. He followed the ancient Code to the letter. Elder P'hi'in would be smug. And poor Elder S'huhfh would be uncertain, but he would agree, cowed by the stronger personalities of the other two Council members.

With a hiss, J'Qhir turned his attention to the medicines. Many packets were labeled "to reduce fever". He tore open several. The small white pills fell into his palm. Leith would not be able to swallow them. He crushed four of them into a powder and mixed it in water. Holding the cup to her lips, he was able to get her to drink all of the mixture. He spent the next few hours bathing her smooth forehead with cool water.

Later, J'Qhir dozed and dreamed of the Bh'rin'gha. A part of him knew he dreamed for he often experienced this vision of an imaginary past when away from his home world. As the dream concluded, he cried out and jerked upright, sloshing water from the pot. The gauze cloths fell from his cramped fingers. He blinked at the firelight and looked to Leith.

He laid his hand on her forehead. Less heat emanated from her skin. He fumbled with the packets of fever reducers, crushed the tablets, and dissolved them in water as he'd done before.

"Leith," he murmured as he eased his arm under her head and put the cup to her lips. He had twisted his leg upon awakening and now his knee began its rhythmic throb. The tablets were also for eliminating pain, but their supply was limited. He had no idea how long Leith would suffer the fever. He could endure the pain. "Drink, Leith," he coaxed.

At the sound of his voice, the fringes of hair on her eyelids fluttered open revealing dilated eyes. Her hand wavered in the air then rested on his arm.

"Commander," she whispered. She blinked until her eyes focused and squeezed his arm. "J'Qhir..."

"Drink, Leith."

She swallowed the concoction, made a face and shuddered at the taste.

"Y-You found the stream?"

"Yesss. I followed your trail of broken branchesss quite easssily." He removed his arm from under her head. She wouldn't release his other arm. He set the cup aside with his free hand.

"What happened, J'Qhir? I don't remember—"

"A flying creature ssstung you." Tentatively, he covered her hand with his. "I drained the poissson immediately, but sssome sssseeped into your sssystem. You have a fever."

"Thank you for taking care of me."

A bit of warmth crept into his face. "Are you hungry? Do you want water?"

"Water."

He held the canteen, and both of her hands grasped his as she drank. When she had finished, she would not loosen her hold on one of his hands.

"Leith, I need to change the dresssing."

Only then did she reluctantly let him go.

He helped her to turn over, then pulled the skinseal away from the wound. She shuddered and her hand clenched the sleeve of her jacket, but she uttered no sound. The flesh was an angry red, yet he saw no sign of infection. He dusted antiseptic and used another seal.

As she settled, she found his hand again and held it. "Are you warm enough?"

"Yesss. Thisss night isss not very cold."

Her eyelids shut, and he thought she slept. He did not try to remove his hand and disturb her. She needed the healing rest. Besides, he found comfort in the simple contact.

"Tell me," Leith said suddenly, startling him.

"Tell you what?"

"Will you tell me about Zi?"

"Zi?" J'Qhir paused. "What do you wisssh to know?"

"Your home. What it's like."

"Zi isss a sssmall world. Mosssstly arid land. Sssand asss far asss the eye can sssee. Where there isss not sssand, there isss rock. Pilesss and heapsss and moundsss of rock. I am from the Bh'rin'gha, the largessst and driessst desssert on Zi. *Bh'rin'gha* meansss 'dry'."

"Bh'rin'gha," she repeated. "Tell me about the Bh'rin'gha."

"A vasssst area of white sssand from what we call the Burning Mountain to the Empty River."

"Empty River?"

"Sssome claim the riverbed once carried water from the mountainsss, but it wasss long before we began to record our hissstory. They sssay our world wasss once asss green and lusssh asss Paradissse, but a natural catassstrophe occurred—"

"Asteroid."

"What?"

"Scientists say a natural disaster occurred on Earth millions of years ago, too. The theory is an asteroid hit the planet and the dinosaurs, gigantic animals that roamed Earth at the time, were killed off by the impact and the winter conditions that followed."

"Sssscientistsss alwaysss have theoriesss. Sssome thingsss are not meant to be known."

"Once there was a theory that a certain plant the dinosaurs ate for a laxative became extinct." She paused. "They say the dinosaurs died of constipation."

He saw her smile and heard a strange gurgling sound, but he found nothing amusing in the extinction of any lifeform. Perhaps she was delirious from the fever.

"Sssleep, Leith. We both need the ressst."

"Only if you sleep with me. I'm cold."

"I need to watch the fire."

"Put all the wood you have on it. It'll last till morning."

"I might hurt you."

"You won't. Not much. It doesn't hurt too bad."

Sharing a blanket with a *sa`aloh* he was not bound to wasn't proper. Humans, he had been told, were not concerned with propriety. Humans did as they pleased without thought to tradition or custom and did not follow rules, even their own.

Leith did not know what she asked of him. Yet, their circumstances were unusual. They had to share the blanket because there was only one blanket on the whole planet.

J'Qhir tossed the rest of the wood on the fire. He unwrapped the solar film from his shoulders and laid it over Leith. The cool night air struck him immediately. He would not survive the remainder of the night without succumbing to the Long Sleep. He slipped in beside her, mindful of his knee. Her heat, intensified by the fever, enveloped him. Her body quivered then snuggled against his side.

"I will build a lair for usss," he whispered. The words eased his conscience superficially.

"What?"

"I sssaid I will build a lair for usss."

"No, J'Qhir," she murmured sleepily. "There isn't enough time. Winter..."

A sharp pain stabbed through his chest like a laserknife. He shouldn't be disappointed with her negative response. Leith had no idea of the meaning behind the words. She didn't understand exactly what she said no to.

J'Qhir closed his eyes, drifted into sleep, and once more dreamed of the Bh'rin'gha.

Chapter 6

Leith dreamed of chicken soup, and when she awoke, the lingering aroma still filled the air. She blinked and stared overhead. Firelight illuminated a cathedral ceiling of natural rock and created fluttering shadows in the darkened corners. She didn't know where she was, but she recalled the flying horde and experiencing indescribable pain. After that, her memories were vague—J'Qhir giving her medicated water, lesser pain as he changed the bandage on her back, giggling over some inane remark about dinosaurs...

"*Oh, God!*" She closed her eyes and covered her burning face in total and abject humiliation. Had she actually asked J'Qhir to sleep with her?

"Leith, you are awake!"

She jumped at the sound of his joyous voice. Her hands slid down her face, and she opened her eyes again to find J'Qhir hovering near, his amber eyes wide and expectant.

"The fever hasss returned." He reached for the medkit. "Your face isss red."

"No, I'm okay. I-I think I'm too close to the fire. That's all." Leith bit her lip. She wanted to bury her head under her jacket, which covered her upper body. Maybe she had suffered hallucinations with the fever. Or dreamed it along with the chicken soup. She could not have brazenly asked him to sleep with her...although she remembered she meant only sleep, nothing more. The worst part was she couldn't remember if he had complied or not.

To get her mind off that embarrassing subject, she glanced at their surroundings. "Where are we? What happened?"

J'Qhir recounted everything that had occurred after the flying creature stung her. She noted he mentioned nothing about their sleeping arrangements.

"Thisss morning, I walked upssstream until I found the cave. When I returned to the campsssite, you were awake and able to walk here."

After he told her, she recalled walking beside J'Qhir, holding onto him to remain upright. "I barely remember last night and this morning."

Pushing aside the jacket, she tried to sit up straight, but a bolt of pain shot across her right shoulder blade. She tried again slowly, at an angle, bracing her weight with her left arm.

"I dreamed about chicken soup, and I still smell it." Leith vigorously rubbed her nose. "Chicken soup would be wonderful, but I haven't seen anything remotely resembling a chicken on this planet."

"No chickensss." J'Qhir removed the cooking pot from the fire and poured some of its contents into a cup. "But there is sssoup."

"Where did you get soup?" She wrapped her hands around the warm cup and breathed in the heady fragrance of cooked food. Flecks of green and chunks of pale yellow floated in a creamy liquid. She put the cup to her lips, then stopped. "There's no *pahahel* in here, is there?"

"*P`ha`al.* No, Leith. No *p`ha`al.*" He filled the other cup. "I boiled sssome of the nutmeatsss until they were sssoft enough to masssh. I usssed your analyzing device to ssscan every green plant I could find. There aren't many left. Everything isss dying."

Leith held her breath and took a sip. She recognized the flavor of the cone nuts, but the rest was unfamiliar. She chewed a piece of boiled root and pretended it was potato. The soup was bland, but it was hot and nourishing.

"I-I have to go outside a few minutes."

J'Qhir nodded his understanding. "It isss night, and it isss raining."

He explained how tunnels in the back of the cave led to other caves. The tunnel to the far left led to a smaller cave he'd prepared.

"Can you rissse?" He moved to help her, but she waved him away.

"Yes, I'm fine." If she moved slowly and carefully, she felt only a little discomfort in the muscles of her right shoulder. Using the laserlight on array, she found the small tunnel entrance where J'Qhir indicated it would be. The tunnel was only a few meters in length and opened into a cave much smaller than the one they occupied.

Leith answered the call of nature and hurried back.

In their living quarters, she shone the laserlight around. The cave was like an upside down bowl, the convex walls curving to meet the floor. The floor space was roughly circular, approximately fifteen meters in diameter and the ceiling about the same at its highest point.

Here the floor was hard-packed dirt, unlike the loose crumbly soil in the latrine cave. A semi-circle of rocks and boulders, off-center and to the left, served as a reflector of heat and light for the fire J'Qhir had built in front of them. J'Qhir had nestled the bed where she had awakened up against some of the boulders. He had doubled the solar film and stuffed it with grass and leaves, she supposed. Another pallet of grass and vine lay on the far side.

Separate beds. Propriety, of course, but there was no one else for them to be proper for. They had one blanket. It seemed more practical to share it to conserve body heat. Perhaps J'Qhir thought she would be more comfortable with this arrangement. Or maybe he was.

Leith wished she could remember the past twelve hours more clearly. If she had asked him to sleep with her and he obliged, what was the point of separate beds now? She walked around the boulders, flashing the light in the shadowy areas to keep J'Qhir from wondering why she stood so long in one place. She didn't want to have to explain her thoughts.

A couple of armloads of damp wood lay scattered out to dry in an area off to the left. At the front of the cave, firelight flickered through a doorway. She discovered that this doorway did not lead directly outside. A short tunnel veered off to the left, and another doorway led outside. J'Qhir had built another fire just inside this entrance. From here she could hear the occasional drip of rain.

When she returned, she eased down beside J'Qhir and leaned back against a rock, careful to put most of her weight on her left shoulder blade. She picked up her soup and sipped it. "I think it's stopped raining. Why did you build the other fire?"

"Did you notice the floor of thisss cave? The dirt here isss compact, asss if it hasss been well usssed. I believe sssome animal hasss made itsss den here in previousss ssseasssonsss. The fire isss to warn it off if it comesss back."

"The animal that roars in the night?"

"Perhapsss," J'Qhir murmured, and it was then she noticed how tired he was. She was surprised to find that she could see the changes in his face. His mouth was drawn, and his eyes were bleary. He blinked sleepily.

"You must be exhausted. How is your knee?"

"It painsss me when I move."

"Well, when you finish your soup, you will move one more time to lie down on that pallet. It's very comfortable."

"No, Leith, it isss for you," he protested.

"Do as I say, J'Qhir. It's my turn to take care of you."

"Are you sssure you are well enough? Lassst night and thisss morning, I thought you were coherent, but you remember little."

"I'm sure. Finish your soup while I look at your knee."

Leith pulled his trouser leg out of the boot, taking her time pushing it upward. At one point, her palm lay fully against the side of his calf and the muscles spasmed.

"I'm sorry. I've hurt you again."

"No, Leith..."

Perhaps it was a sensitive area. This time it was difficult to raise the material over the swelling. She unwound the bandage to reveal the misshapen knee.

"You're not moving for the next few days," Leith ordered as she rifled the medkit for aspirin and antibiotics.

"There isss much that needsss to be done..."

"You won't be any good if you don't heal. It will only get worse."

She gave him the pills and water and hoped they wouldn't kill him. Maybe he was humanoid enough for the medication to help. She swallowed a couple of the antibiotics for her sting.

"I ssshould change your bandage."

Leith found another skinseal in the medkit and handed it to him. Then she turned her back to him and swept her hair out of the way. His talons pressed under the edges of the seal. The tips of his fingers lingered on her skin and a tiny ripple of awareness coursed through her.

She closed her eyes and enjoyed the sensations, wishing he would...or she had the courage to lean back into him, and find herself wrapped in his arms. It had been a long, long time since she had been held, had wanted to be held.

"Are-Are you having trouble with it?" she asked, her voice sounding husky and unnatural.

"No, Leith..." he murmured and peeled away the seal.

He dusted antiseptic, and then his fingers tenderly applied the fresh bandage. She had felt no pain and little discomfort. How could a large, bulky being accomplish such delicate procedures so gracefully?

"May I?" he asked politely and touched her hair.

She nodded, not trusting herself to speak. His fingers enclosed her hair and spread it over her back. He seemed to take extra care in putting it perfectly in place.

"Beg forgivenesss, but I had to rend your ssshirt to reach the wound."

"It's all right," she said and rummaged in the medkit. "There's a sewing kit in the jacket. I'm no seamstress, but I think I can mend a tear. Could you put some tape on it to hold it until I can get around to sewing it."

She heard the rip as he tore off a piece of medical tape. Once more his fingers brushed her skin as he grappled with the thin cotton material. At length, he held the torn edges together and pressed the tape over them.

Leith quickly moved away from him. She lifted her cup and found it shaking in her hands. She had to stop! He was bound to touch her occasionally, and she couldn't react like this every time he put a hand on her.

She drank her soup. When she turned back to him, he had finished rolling down his trouser leg and was removing his boots. She settled back against the boulder and watched as he drained the last of his soup as well.

"To bed," she said. He stared at her and blinked once. "I'll wash the dishes and tend the fire. You need to rest."

He shifted sideways until he was on the solar film bed. Leith rolled her jacket and tucked it beneath his head as he stretched out.

"No, you will need your coat for warmth."

"I'm fine. The fire is warm enough. Remember, I'm not as cold-natured as you."

He nodded, too tired to argue. He pulled his jacket closer, then reached out and laid his hand on her arm when she started to move away.

"I will build a lair for usss," he said sleepily, yet sincerely.

"Not tonight, you won't," she said with a smile as his eyes closed and his hand slid away.

Leith gathered the dishes and utensils and took them outside. The cold, damp air made her shiver and break out in goose bumps. It had stopped raining as she'd thought, and the dripping she'd heard earlier was water falling from the leaves of the nearby trees. By the glare of the laserlight she saw the stream was only a dozen meters away.

Leith flashed the light into the trees and beyond the rocks to scare away any unwanted night visitors. She hurried to the stream and scrubbed the dishes clean with white sand from the bank. Her fingers grew numb from the icy water. Just as she finished, a terrible crashing sounded amid the trees. Then that awful heart-stopping roar mingled with it. The sounds seemed to come from every direction at once. Leith grabbed up the dishes and ran back into the cave.

She careened to a halt inside their living area. J'Qhir slept soundly and had not heard the animal's scream of rage or her own wild rampage through the tunnel. Her heart pounding, she set the dishes near the fire to dry.

Leith gathered an armload of dry wood, some that J'Qhir had collected before it started to rain, and laid several pieces on the fire. She watched it a few moments to make sure it caught, part of her listening for the beast to crash through the doorway and reclaim its den.

Should she wake him? He had done so much in the past few days and needed to rest. She ought to be able to manage keeping an animal at bay the rest of the night. She would tell him in the morning, and then they could figure out what more to do.

As quietly as possible, she carried wood to the inner door and looked down the tunnel. It seemed so narrow and confining at only a meter wide and about three meters in height. The flames flickered as air currents shifted, but there was no other movement. Taking a deep breath, she walked down the tunnel.

She sat facing the opening, no larger than a regular doorway, although she was sure J'Qhir had to bend slightly to enter. She fed the fire until it blazed bright and hot enough to keep her warm even though she wore only the thin cotton shirt. She trembled, but not from the cold and not really from fright. Nocturnal animals feared bright lights and fire. Those on Earth did anyway. She had to assume animals reacted in the same way on Paradise. And she had the laserlight in her hand, set on high, just in case.

No, she still trembled from J'Qhir's touch. Wouldn't any male's touch have aroused her? Steve's hadn't. She had always been repulsed by his unwanted fondling and never could pinpoint why. He was handsome enough and, aside from his attempts at suggestive humor, he was pleasant enough. Her parents had trusted him implicitly with major responsibilities in the company. Leith knew now that her instincts toward him had been correct, but she didn't know *how* she had known.

Which brought her back to another problem... Every instinct told her that J'Qhir was as honorable and trustworthy as he appeared, but the facts told a different story. The facts were that he had somehow manipulated her parents into illegal trading and his warring people were bent on the devastation and destruction of their system's other world, Crux.

If her instincts had been at odds over the facts concerning Steve Hancock and were accurate, could the same be true of J'Qhir? Should she continue to believe in her feelings toward him until she could investigate further? Then Leith closed her eyes and laughed bitterly. How could she investigate anything? She was stuck here on Paradise for the rest of her life with no hope of rescue!

She didn't mean to go to sleep, but she kept her eyes closed as her thoughts tumbled and whirled. She tried to relax and clear her mind of everything, and she succeeded all too well. She had no idea how long she slept, but her neck was stiff when a noise awakened her. Her eyes flew open, and all she saw was a huge ursine form filling the doorway. Her mouth opened, but no sound could escape her tightening throat. She pushed back, trying to scramble away from the beast, but the solid rock wall behind her wouldn't give.

Bearlike, it reared on its hind legs and raised its forelegs over her, then its peculiar scream pierced her eardrums painfully. With one swipe of its powerful foreleg, it knocked the fire out through the doorway.

Light! She needed light or the beast would kill her here in the dark. She didn't want to die, not like this, and leave J'Qhir alone. The laserlight! Her hand still clutched the cylinder.

As blinded by the sudden darkness as she, the beast hadn't moved. She held her breath and tried to inch sideways down the tunnel. It heard her movements and grunted as it slashed a clawed paw toward her. She ducked to the side and felt the wind of the paw as it passed within centimeters.

There was no point in stealth since the beast could hear her every movement. Its eyes would recover faster than hers and would find her any second. Before she could even think through what she needed to do, she plunged down the tunnel, scrabbling on her back. The beast took a few precious seconds to consider what she was doing, and she gained a meter or so away from it. She brought up the laserlight, hit the switch, and cut a swath where she thought the beast's chest might be just as it turned and rushed her.

She must have missed. She crawled backward as fast as she could and cried out as she lost her grip on the laserlight. The beast moved forward, more slowly now. Something bumped the ground near her and rolled into the wall. The beast moved even closer, but much slower, and fell toward her.

With the last of her failing strength, she heaved herself backward one more time as the body of the beast crashed into the floor. Gritty dust filled her lungs as a thick spray of warm liquid covered her.

"*Leith!*" J'Qhir appeared in the inner door, using a burning piece of wood for a torch.

The light was enough for Leith to see the headless body of the beast at her feet. A few centimeters closer and it might have landed on her feet and broken her ankles. Then J'Qhir was by her side, staring in wonder at the carcass.

"Leith, are you all right?"

She couldn't speak, only nod. She swallowed, but her mouth was filled with grit and a sickening metallic taste. She worked up the saliva in her mouth and spat several times, getting rid of as much as she could.

J'Qhir helped her to her feet, but she was shaking so hard she couldn't stand on her own.

"I-I ki-killed it," she finally stammered. Bending over J'Qhir's arm, she vomited up every swallow of soup she'd had for supper.

※ ※ ※

Leith sat in the tunnel with the lifeless remains of the beast until she no longer trembled in shock. J'Qhir sat with her and listened as she related what happened.

"You dealt with the sssituation in a courageousss manner, Leith."

"Courageous?" J'Qhir had brought her the canteen. She used all the water to rinse out most of the grit and blood and half-digested soup, but her mouth still felt dry and tasted metallic. "I was scared stiff. I'm surprised I reacted at all. I just knew I couldn't die and leave you here all alone."

"Courage," J'Qhir explained patiently, "hasss nothing to do with lack of fear. Only one who isss unwissse would not feel fear. Courage isss doing what we musssst even when every inssstinct tellsss usss we have no hope of sssuccesss."

"Instinct..." Leith repeated.

"You reacted inssstinctively. You have good inssstinctsss, Leith. On Zi, you would be consssidered a great sssoldier...if you were male."

Leith ignored the insult. The Zi culture was different, and J'Qhir looked at things in a different way. She would just have to accept him the way he was.

Twice now, her instincts had been proven correct. She looked at J'Qhir as he stared at the head of the beast. Later, she would talk to him about her parents, about Crux. She would find the truth in him because here, as he had said a few days ago, he had no reason to ever speak falsely to her. She had a feeling she was going to hear a very different version of the reason for the Zi-Crux wars. And she hoped she would hear a reasonable explanation for the actions of her parents. Until then, she would go with her instincts and trust in J'Qhir.

After the shaking stopped, Leith asked J'Qhir to bring her jacket to her. She carried it out with her to the stream. She became chilled again instantly, and the water was icy cold, but there was no way she was going to let the splattered blood of the beast remain on her. She held her breath, dunked her head in the water, and nearly screamed from the cold. She scrubbed hair, face, neck and arms as quickly as she could, then squeezed out water from her hair. At this moment, not having hair like J'Qhir would have been preferable.

She removed her shirt and bra, donned her jacket, and rinsed her underclothing with numb fingers. She noticed that the fabric, treated with a stain-resistant compound, really did resist stains, even blood, as advertised.

Leith refused to remove her trousers. They too were stain-resistant and she grabbed up handfuls of grass, dipped them in the water, and washed down her trousers and boots. Clean enough for now.

When she turned back toward the cave, she saw movement. For a moment, her heart raced. What if the beast had a mate who had come searching for it? Then she flashed the laserlight. It was J'Qhir dragging the carcass closer to the cave entrance. He motioned for her to come to him.

"We have food and another blanket," he announced as he released the body and tossed the head to the side. "I usssed your analyzing device. The meat isss good."

"Can't this wait until morning," Leith protested. "You have to rest."

J'Qhir shook his head. "Leith, the sssmell of blood will draw other animalsss and the meat might go bad if we wait. I ssslept a while and feel much better. Build the fire again ssso that I can sssee and have warmth."

"But—"

"Do you know how to ssskin an animal? Do you know how to carve the meat?"

"Well, no, but—"

"Then do asss I sssay."

Leith did as he said. By the time her hair and clothing dried and, through trial and error, she erected a spit over the fire in their living quarters, J'Qhir had skinned the beast and cut the first slab of meat. She put the roast on, and soon the delicious aroma of cooking meat filled the cave.

Using deft, quick strokes, J'Qhir sliced the rest of it thin, and Leith used the laserlight to quick-jerk the meat. Soon a pile of jerky nearly covered the flat stone Leith had dragged from outside to work on.

"How are we going to store it? To keep it away from bugs and small critters?"

"Tomorrow we make basssketsss," J'Qhir said.

"I think you mean today." Leith nodded sleepily toward the opening where dawn had lightened the world.

"Good! You will be able to sssee to cut tall grasss and vine. Or young sssaplingsss sssince they are plentiful here."

Leith just stared at him. "How do you know how to do all this—this survival stuff?"

J'Qhir stabbed the knife into the remains of the beast carcass and leaned back against the rock wall, resting the backs of his bloodied hands on his thighs. "Thisss isss our way of life, Leith. Only three generationsss ago we had no idea anyone elsss in the universsse exisssted. When the Cruciansss came, our culture wasss very primitive. The Cruciansss claimed to come in peace. Sssince we knew no other way, we believed them."

"You didn't fight among yourselves?" Leith asked incredulously.

"Not for many centuriesss. There are talesss, of courssse, of battlesss fought between desssertsss, but we overcame our belligerent nature long ago. Until the Cruciansss came. They took our young and sssstrong, male and female. The Cruciansss promisssed them a visssit to a world of lusssh abundance and proposssed sssettlementsss if they found it agreeable. They would only be gone a sssshort while, the Cruciansss sssaid, but it wasss many yearsss before the Cruciansss returned without our people. Both of my grandfathersss had gone with them."

When J'Qhir seemed to be lost in thought, Leith asked quietly, "What happened to them?"

"The Cruciansss never intended for the Zi to sssettle on their planet. They ensssslaved usss, to work their crysssium minesss. They returned for more ssslavesss. We fought them and thousssandsss died, yet they captured thousssandsss more to carry back to Crux." J'Qhir shook his head and hesitated. "Perhapsss we have not evolved enough, Leith. The Cruciansss had never intended to return to Zi. Their plan wasss to breed thossse they captured the firssst time, but they found we do not breed in captivity. Our reproductive sssysssstemsss ssshut down when threatened."

"I am so sorry," Leith murmured, fighting back tears. He wouldn't appreciate what he might interpret as pity. "The Crucians tell a much different story. It was what I tried to make you understand before. Why haven't you ever told anyone what really happened?"

"It isss our fight," J'Qhir explained. "Our duty. No one elssse'sss. We are resssponsssible for our own."

"Sometimes it's all right to ask for help. It doesn't mean you relinquish the responsibility or sit back and let someone else take over."

J'Qhir nodded and sighed. "Of courssse, you are correct. Perhapsss it isss time to asssk for help. My people are very weary of fighting—and losssing. If we find sssome way to essscape thisss planet, I will approach the Council of Eldersss."

"Since the Crucians just came to capture your people, how did you attain space travel? I'm sure they didn't give you ships and teach you how to fly."

"It isss, in effect, exactly what they did," J'Qhir said with a trace of humor in his voice. "About the time my father reached maturity, the Cruciansss began to ussse Zi as a refussse dump. Mosssst of it wasss usssselesss trasssh, but they alssso left behind old warssshipsss and broken weaponsss. Leith, my people learn quickly when they musssst, and it helped that we had a few captivesss of our own to teach usss. We rebuilt warssshipsss and weaponsss from the ssscrapsss they dissscarded. Many died in the firssst attemptsss, but we finally moved out into ssspace and learned how to trade for what we need. By the time I wasss born, ssspace travel had become common and we were no longer at the mercy of the Cruciansss. We have not won, but we have not lossst either."

He straightened and, grabbing the knife, started slicing strips of meat. "Go, Leith. I have hunger enough to eat the ressst of this beassst raw. We cannot eat until our work isss done."

Leith left the cave and did as J'Qhir said. She mulled over what he had told her about the Crucians as she searched for the basket-making materials he wanted. Part of her problem was resolved for she knew he had told her the truth of the Zi-Crucian conflict. Now, all she needed to learn was the truth about her parents.

Chapter 7

Leith added to the twist of grass and secured it to the side of the misshapen basket with a narrow strip of bark. Surreptitiously, she watched J'Qhir seated on the other side of the fire. He had already finished one basket while teaching her the technique and had another half completed.

He made short work of the basket as he had the beast. His large hands worked quickly, efficiently, wasting no movement or effort. She wondered where his thoughts drifted. Did he think of Zi and wish to be home as much as she?

Leith sighed softly and looked down at her basket. After learning the basics she had quickly grown bored with the process. She had always needed to keep her mind busy, not her hands. She tried to concentrate on wrapping the bark around the grass, keeping it smooth and even, but her thoughts wandered again.

"I have been thinking," J'Qhir said suddenly.

Leith perked up. Neither of them was prone to small talk. He had sat close to her, showing her how to begin with a hank of grass as large as his thumb. He had patiently explained every step in his quiet, soothing tones. He told her how to create the circular bottom, weave the strips of bark around the grass, catching the previous round of grass to bind the two together, then how to begin making the sides when the bottom was as large as she wanted it to be. After he was sure she had grasped the concept and could continue without him, he had moved to the pallet on the other side of the fire, and they said little else.

She wished he had remained at her side. She had grown a little nervous with him so close, his hands on hers showing her how to hold the grass and bark. Her thoughts had then wandered into areas best left unexplored. His fingers, too, had trembled on hers. She thought that perhaps he wasn't comfortable in the role of instructor even though he was an excellent teacher. Or maybe he simply didn't like to be near her if he didn't have to be. She had shared her body heat with him under the solar film for several nights, but they now had the shelter of the cave and a warm fire. He didn't need her now, and obviously didn't want her near if he could avoid it.

J'Qhir halted his weaving and stared across the flames at her. "The mossst peculiar thing hasss happened. I have begun to *think* in Terran Ssstandard. But I digresss." He picked up his work again and continued. "Hancock sssaid Arreisss allowsss no one on thisss planet. Then how wasss he able to land the lifecraft without fear of retaliation from the Arreisssansss?"

"They must have no detection devices in place on or around the planet," Leith offered.

"Correct," J'Qhir agreed. "Yet, how do they maintain sssecurity? They would have to canvasss Paradissse on a regular basssisss."

Hope dared to rise within her. "That means they would have to physically come here and check the planet. Would they be able to detect the engine residue from the lifecraft?"

"Only if they ssscanned the area where it landed within a certain period of time." J'Qhir shrugged his broad shoulders. Silently, Leith appreciated the gesture. He had removed his war jacket earlier. His shirt, made of the same dark gray wool-like material, fit his body snugly and accentuated his breadth and musculature. "It ssseemsss Hancock would be taking a terrible risssk unlesss he had sssomehow learned their ssschedule."

"Anyone can be bought for the right price." Leith set aside her basket and stretched her cramped limbs. "Steve could have bought the information. Or he could have bribed the Arreisan in charge of monitoring the planet."

"What do you mean?"

"I mean that even if an Arreisan ship scanned this place tomorrow and found evidence of the lifecraft landing or us, it might never be reported or investigated because Steve had paid him off. Just as he bribed whomever was in charge of the spaceport log on Arreis. In the grand scheme of things, our presence here will not wreck the development of this planet. We won't live forever even if we do manage to survive to live long and healthy lives. The Arreisan has a nice retirement fund, and Steve has his revenge. Everyone is happy, and we are disposed of with a minimal amount of effort for anyone."

J'Qhir hissed thoughtfully. "I have moved among humansss for decadesss. I have read your literature and viewed your moving picturesss that tell ssstoriesss. I am, however, continually sssurprisssed at how treacherousss your people are among your own kind."

"Are you saying the Zi don't betray one another? What about that duel in the desert you told me about? Isn't that for vengeance?"

"To avenge persssonal insssult which isss alwaysss effected openly. We do not betray one another. Ssschemesss to dessstroy another Zi have been rare in our hissstory, and jussstice wasss ssswift and mercilesss." J'Qhir paused for a few moments then continued quietly. "Perhapsss becaussse we have had to battle a greater betrayal by the Cruciansss, we asss a people have been brought clossser together than mossst."

Leith shook her head. His self-righteous attitude irritated her. He seemed to think that his people were above such base actions and, therefore, superior. She picked up her deformed basket and threw it at him. Her aim was true, and it hit the side of his head before he could react.

"Leith!"

"You can't condemn an entire species because of the actions of a few. I'm the first to admit humans are capable of the most vile and despicable acts that can be conceived. But we are also the most loyal and dedicated you'll find anywhere in the galaxy."

J'Qhir frowned, his crest knotted tightly. "I did not mean—"

"Didn't you? No species is better or worse than another. Just different. 'The Zi don't fight amongst themselves. The Zi don't betray one another'. Human history is full of wars and betrayal, but on the whole we're just individuals trying to get through one day at a time."

J'Qhir merely stared at her unblinking.

Leith didn't know where the outburst had come from or why. Now that she'd had her say, the irrational anger dissipated as quickly as it flared up. Of course, he hadn't meant the comments the way she had chosen to interpret them. They were going to be here many long days and nights, and there would be innumerable legitimate arguments. There was no need to spin one out of thin air.

Annoyed at herself, she shot to her feet and snatched up her jacket. She suddenly felt cornered and closed in with no way to escape.

When she reached the inner door, J'Qhir called out to her, "Where are you going?"

"Where would I be going? Where else on this damned planet is there to go?" she snapped, then immediately regretted the words. She shook her head. It was best she leave for a while and cool off. "I'm going for a walk."

"Go with care," he said softly, and she was surprised he didn't try to stop her.

The cold night air chilled her instantly, and she put her hands in the pocket of her jacket. One hand found the laserlight and the other found the analyzer. She closed her eyes in relief that she wouldn't have to walk back into the cave right then.

She opened her eyes and stood for a while allowing her eyes to adjust to the night. The sky was a deep, dark blue and filled with a million stars. The Milky Way was a denser band running across the sky like a twisted ribbon. On Earth, she knew the stars and constellations, but here on Paradise she saw them from a different angle. Everything was different—no Big Dipper, no Orion's belt. She had no idea where Sol might be.

A brighter light from behind the trees caught her eye. She walked upstream a short distance and finally comprehended what she saw.

They had seen no moon since their arrival, but now a large crescent hung in the sky. She could see only the top third, the rest hidden by the woods. It was several times the size of Earth's Luna. When the moon became full, it would light up the night as bright as day.

Maybe in a few days when J'Qhir's knee was better, they could make their way up the side of the hill and find a place to view the entire moon.

She turned on the laserlight array and flashed it up through the sparse growth on the hillside. In the light of day, she could see the crest. Earlier when she'd gone out to gather the materials J'Qhir had asked for, she'd noticed a thick mist rising from one side in the crisp morning air. She hadn't the time or the energy to investigate then. She had found an open meadow beyond the woods and cut as much of the tall brown grass as she could carry. J'Qhir had sent her back twice more before she declared they had enough to make a thousand baskets.

Bleary-eyed and more tired than she had ever been in her life, she'd cut enough saplings to start a lumber mill and hauled them into the cave. On her last trip, she'd tossed the laserlight to J'Qhir as she passed him. He was wise enough not to say anything to her at all. She would have turned on him then if he dared criticize her quitting. She had paused long enough to turn the roast on the spit then collapsed on the nearest pallet and instantly fell sleep.

She slept for hours, hunger driving her to consciousness. For days, she had been living on protein bars, nuts, and water. She had heaved up the soup from the night before after killing the beast. She was ravenous. J'Qhir had waited until she awakened before eating the roast. She didn't think she would have been as considerate.

She had told J'Qhir about the mist. He, too, had seen it and said they would investigate it later when his knee had healed. But the mist intrigued her. If it had been evenly distributed along the side of the hill, she would have thought nothing more about it, but it had been concentrated in one place and as dense as a cloud.

Leith flashed the light over the ground. The slope was gentle and didn't look dangerous. She wouldn't take any unnecessary chances. A broken bone could be fatal with their limited medical supplies and knowledge. If the going became too rough, she would retreat.

As she worked her way around gnarled trees, patches of scrub brush, and boulders, she realized the slope was steeper than it had appeared. She decided to press on as long as she felt secure in her footing. Frequently, she broke branches to mark her way.

She stopped to rest and looked down. She could clearly see the silvery stream winding its way through clumps of trees and brush and piles of rock. Looking skyward, she saw the crescent had risen considerably and only its lower tip remained hidden. The view would be spectacular once the moon became full.

Leith shone the light higher up the hillside. She was close enough to the mist that the beam seemed to hit a blank gray wall only a dozen or so meters away.

She had been gone well over an hour. J'Qhir had probably started to worry. She glanced back the way she'd come, then looked ahead to the mist again. She really should wait for daylight, but she was so close. Curiosity overcame her better sense.

She had to cut wide to the left and circle back in toward the mist. It took much longer than she had expected. As soon as she had the thought of J'Qhir back in the cave growing edgy with concern, she was aware of every passing minute. Still, she couldn't give up. She was too close to turn back now. The misty swirls were only a few meters away.

Turning the laserlight to wide array she swept the ground in front of her and carefully stepped over scattered rocks and exposed roots. The wind shifted and curling tendrils of mist swept over her in a rush of warm, moist air. The scene would have been eerie had she not been so intent on finding out what lay beneath the mist.

She came to a solid rock wall that reached almost to her knees. The edge was smooth and rounded, and suddenly she heard the sound of rippling water. She picked up a stone and tossed it into the thick of the mist. A splash was her reward. Water. *Hot* water.

She almost plunged her cold hand into it when she remembered the analyzer. The water could be acidic or hot enough to peel the flesh from her bones or any of a dozen other things that wouldn't be good. She brought out the device and set the laser eye into the water. The readings were good—pure water with high mineral content and bathing temperature. Perfect.

This planet truly was Paradise.

Going downhill was much faster, especially after she found a shorter route. In no time, she was back beside the stream and headed for the cave entrance. She was surprised to find J'Qhir seated uncomfortably beside the fire at the outer door, still working on his basket.

"You are back," he said and sounded relieved.

"I went exploring. I know I shouldn't have in the dark, but I was very careful. I went up the side of the hill where I saw the mist this morning." She couldn't contain the excitement of her discovery. "You'll never guess what I found."

"Hot sssspringsss," he answered and set his basket aside. He twisted his bulk to one side, to rise without putting pressure on his bad knee.

Leith went to him and held out her arm. "How did you know?"

Gratefully, he accepted her help. "It wasss the only thing I could think of that would causssse the missst."

After he gained his feet, Leith took his arm and put it on her shoulder. "You are supposed to be resting your knee, not moving around so much."

"I wanted to be able to hear you in cassse anything happened."

"I'm sorry. I shouldn't have been gone so long." She bent under his weight as they walked down the tunnel. "And I shouldn't have snapped. I—I think I'm jealous. Your people have somehow overcome or avoided most of the pitfalls of human nature."

"I did not mean to sssuggessst our way is better than another'sss. We are not perfect, far from it. But our way isss different from yoursss." He lifted his arm away from her as they entered their living quarters. "Sssometimesss I think too different."

"Humans are better than they used to be." Leith walked near him as he limped to his pallet. "I think discovering and accepting that there are others besides ourselves have helped. We do have a bloody history, but hopefully we won't have a bloody future."

"Sss't! I left the basssket out there."

"I'll get it, but you have to promise you won't work on it anymore tonight. You need to rest. You look so very tired."

"Very well, Leith."

She retrieved the basket and when she returned, he was asleep. She sat on the solar film and began working on hers again, determined to finish the thing no matter how pitiful the result.

"I do have a quessstion," J'Qhir said, startling her.

"I thought you were asleep!"

"Almossst. Why did you damn thisss planet?"

She grinned sheepishly. "It's a way humans have of coping with frustration. I don't swear often, but when I do it's because I feel I'm helpless to change the situation I'm in. I shouldn't have damned the planet. I'm angry with Steve. I should have damned him...and I do. He'll get his in the end, I'm sure of it."

"Then you believe vengeance will take care of itssself?"

"I'm not sure, but it's a comfort to think so. I would like to believe in cosmic retribution, that the good we do, as well as the bad, will be rewarded, and that the universe keeps itself in balance. But most people can't wait. They want the instant gratification of seeing justice served. I think I have to agree. I would like to see Steve punished for what he's done."

"Then we are not asss disssimilar asss it ssseemed. The Zi alssso enjoy retaliation. Otherwissse, we would not fight the Cruciansss."

Leith waited, but he said no more. She quietly worked on her basket. Hours passed, and she finally did finish it. It wasn't as perfectly round as J'Qhir's, more egg-shaped really with one end larger than the other. If it didn't fall apart, it would hold the jerky as well as his. Her next one would be better, and the next one after that even better. Patience and time. She certainly had plenty of time. She'd have to work on her patience.

She stretched and yawned and looked at J'Qhir. He snored softly and she smiled. Would he be embarrassed to know? Or was snoring a sign of prestige among the Zi? There was so much about his culture she didn't know.

She crawled closer to him and when he didn't stir, crept closer still. She shouldn't...but she couldn't help herself. Lightly, she ran her fingertips over the protruding ridge of his browbone. Her touch disturbed him and he shifted in his sleep, mumbling words she couldn't understand. He might think in Terran Standard, but he obviously still dreamed in Zi.

She sat back on her heels and watched him. Her fingers itched to follow the sharply defined contours of his face, feel the soft leather of his skin. She shouldn't want him, but she did. How was it possible to desire someone so different?

Sitting here so close to him would not answer her question, but only exacerbate the problem. She crawled to her bed and closed her eyes. They were the only two people on the whole planet. It was inevitable, wasn't it? Patience and time, she thought again. They certainly had the time. She would definitely have to work on her patience.

❀ ❀ ❀

Leith waited until the warmest part of the day, the middle of the afternoon, before she climbed the hillside once again to the pool. The afternoon temperature had risen so high she was perspiring by the time she reached her destination. J'Qhir had suggested she wait until he could accompany her to make sure nothing unfavorable happened, but she couldn't imagine swimming nude while J'Qhir watched. Not that he would actually watch, but he would be near and she would be too aware of him.

Impatiently, she built a small fire in a natural alcove. She undressed and washed every piece of clothing she wore, except her jacket but including her blouse, which she had repaired several days ago. She spread them out over rocks near the fire to dry. Now, she was ready to bathe.

She was a strong swimmer and often swam alone. She wanted to dive right in, but she had no idea how deep the bottom was or what might be in the water. She had visions of a Nessie-type monster rearing out of the water and gulping her up in one bite. Shivering, she tossed a few rocks in and watched the water ripple. Nothing else disturbed the surface.

Now or never. She braced herself on the rock wall and lowered herself into the water. Her toes reached an outcropping of rock, and she found it was a natural ledge that ran along most of the side of the pool. Taking a breath, she pushed off and swam the perimeter.

The pool was roughly oval shaped and about the size of a small swimming pool. The warm water felt heavenly on her skin. She scrubbed at her hair and face and wished for soap. Somewhere out there in the vast greenery of this planet was a plant that had soap-like qualities, and she was determined to find it before she died!

Sometimes it was easy to laugh at their situation, but more often than not she wanted to cry in frustration. Now was not the time for tears because she enjoyed the hot water too much. She swam until her arms grew tired then sat on the underwater ledge. She had to give her clothes time to dry before she dressed again. She leaned her head back and closed her eyes.

She was glad she had talked J'Qhir out of coming. She found the idea of him seeing her unclothed...disturbing. Disturbing in the same way she felt the summer she turned thirteen and suddenly Marq Casijian wasn't just another one of the guys. He was someone she wanted to kiss. And more, she could now admit with a smile. At that age, for her, kissing seemed the ultimate goal. She never did get to kiss Marq, but a year later Drew Garrison thoroughly taught her how to kiss. Marq and Drew were still friends of hers. She saw Marq occasionally and Drew now worked for McClure Shipping, as one of their best pilots.

So many years later, she now couldn't imagine anything more serious than kissing Drew while her mind could conjure up all sorts of images of J'Qhir. Because of their situation, she told herself over and over. If Steve had never put them alone on this planet, they would have gone their separate ways and nothing would have ever happened. She knew that for fact, but it didn't change the explicit dreams she'd had the night before.

She shook her head and emerged from the water. The cooler air made her shiver. She rushed to the alcove, welcoming the heat of the fire. She allowed the water to evaporate from her body and dressed, then spread her hair close to the flames. When her hair was dry, she put out the fire and made her way back down the hillside.

Tomorrow would be J'Qhir's turn.

The next few days they entered into a set pattern. J'Qhir still needed to stay off his leg so it could heal, so Leith went out foraging for anything that resembled food. The beast jerky would have to be supplemented with whatever plants, nuts, and berries she could find until winter set in. Then they would have to make the foodstuff last for as long as winter did. They had no idea how long that might be.

Leith set out early in the morning carrying the empty flightpack and returned to the cave around noon. She left whatever she had been able to find with J'Qhir. He spent his time making baskets and drying what she brought in. In the warmth of the afternoon, they took their turns in the pool. The mineral-rich water helped his knee. He still limped and sometimes used a crutch, but he proclaimed it didn't hurt nearly as much as it had as long as he didn't overdo.

After lunch, Leith would head to the pool on her days or spend the afternoon gathering deadfall to stack near the cave. They were lucky that the weather held and although the mornings and evenings were cold, the afternoons were as warm as springtime. They had had no frost as yet.

In the evenings, after another meal of dried beast or soup, they worked on baskets. With practice and patience, Leith's efforts did improve, but they still weren't as good as J'Qhir's.

133

One day as Leith returned from her turn in the pool, she turned upstream instead of returning in the direction of the cave. After an hour's walk and finding nothing new, she had almost decided to go back when a bit of white past a clump of brush caught her eye. She circled the brush and found a bed of strange-looking plants.

The ground was marshy, soaked with water from either the stream or an underground spring, and the plants were thriving in spite of the cold nights. Each was as tall as her waist and bent under the weight of numerous white pods. Several had broken and leaked a white, creamy substance. She pulled out the analyzer and nearly jumped for joy. The substance was edible and high in sucrose. Sugar!

She plucked off one of the pods and broke it open, touching the thick liquid to her tongue. It would be an acquired taste, but one she was willing to work at. It was sweet and that's all that mattered. Now, if only she could find a chocolate tree.

She didn't have the flightpack along so she ate her fill then carried a handful back to the cave. J'Qhir hadn't liked the sweetened coffee she'd given him on the *Catherine McClure*, but he might like these sugarpods.

When she reached the outer door, she noticed the fire there had nearly gone out. Before she could frame any thoughts about why J'Qhir hadn't kept the fire up, a long keening wail echoed from within, then cut off abruptly and a low chanting began. The monotone sounds reassured her. He hadn't broken into song the other times he had been injured. Some Zi ritual that she probably shouldn't interrupt, but she was curious.

She crept toward the inner door, careful not to make a sound. Perhaps she could watch from there and not disturb him. As she neared the door, a blast of heat engulfed her. No wonder they had run low on fuel if he stoked the fire this hot every day while she was gone. He had never complained about being cold. In fact, when she came in for lunch, the fire was very small and he usually had his jacket off.

She stepped inside and felt as if she was entering a furnace. A sheen of sweat covered her almost instantly. The fire was a blazing inferno, flames reaching halfway to the ceiling. She waited while her eyes adjusted. Through the flickering flames, on the other side of the fire, she saw J'Qhir.

His eyes were closed and he knelt, thighs spread wide. He chanted in guttural, earthy tones. His hands clasped over the haft of the knife and raised it up over his head, the blade pointing down and glinting wickedly in the firelight. His voice grew louder as he slowly brought the knife toward himself.

Chapter 8

"*No!*" she shrieked and ran to him, dropping the sugarpods.

Startled, his eyes flew open and his hands fell. "Leith—"

She snatched the knife from his grasp, flinging it into a darkened corner. The clatter of metal on rock echoed hollowly. He struggled to his feet, lurching awkwardly because of his injured knee. She didn't offer to help. He had gone to his knees by himself, and he could get himself up again. Tears welled in her eyes. When he stood erect, she doubled up her fist and hit him square in the chest.

"What the hell do you think you're doing? Are you trying to kill yourself?"

"Noooo, Leith!"

She hit him again. "Some stupid arcane suicide ritual?"

"No—"

"Is it that bad, being stuck here with me?" She tried to blink back the tears, but they spilled over and flowed down her cheeks. "How could you leave me here alone?"

He shook his head. "Not sssuicide. It isss sssomething I mussst do..."

"Then, what were you doing?" She wanted to hit him again and again and again. And he would let her, she knew. He would stand there and take it, as he had done that first day. He would let her beat on his chest until she passed out from exhaustion and never lift a finger against her. Knowing that, she wrapped her arms around herself to resist the temptation to hit him one more time.

"The Admisssion of Failure."

"*Failure?*" she cried out incredulously.

He stiffened at the ridiculing tone in her voice. "I have failed many timesss. I failed to protect you. I failed to ssstop Hancock. I failed to—"

"Where did you get the idea it's your responsibility to protect me?" She clenched her hands into tighter fists. She desperately wanted to hit him again, to knock some sense into him if nothing else.

"It isss my duty, the duty of the Warrior." He looked down at her, his amber eyes glowing from the firelight. "Asss sssoon asss you were threatened in my presssence, you fell under my protection."

"I'm not Zi!"

"It doesss not matter. Anyone in danger in the presssence of the Warrior isss protected. Or ssshould be. I have done a very poor job of protecting you."

Leith shook violently. Honor and duty and responsibility were all well and good, but he carried it too far. "Wh-What is this ritual? If you weren't going to commit suicide, then what were you going to do?"

"The ritual isss to atone. Asss the Warrior, my failuresss affect all of my people. It isss required that I brand myssself ssso that all may know I have failed."

Leith didn't want to hit him anymore. She wanted to enfold him in her arms and hold him close. She wanted to take away his pain and ease the anguish from his face. His crest was knotted tightly, and his eyes burned. Not from the firelight as she first thought, but from the turmoil within his soul. She had to handle this delicately. She couldn't make light of what he perceived as his failures, and she couldn't scorn what he was driven to do.

Instead of embracing him, she reached out and took his hand. "I don't understand how you think you have failed. If you failed, then we both failed," she said quietly.

"It isss my duty—"

"There was nothing you could do to stop Steve. There was nothing either of us could do that wouldn't have gotten one of us killed on the spot." She squeezed his hand, and his fingers tightened around hers. "We're alive. We're surviving. How can that be a failure? As long as we stay alive, we're thwarting Steve's plans. I consider that a success."

"I ssshould have sssaved usss," he whispered hoarsely.

She didn't know what to tell him. She could say it a thousand times, and he wouldn't believe her. He would think he should have found a way to stop Steve. She reached for his other hand and held them firmly.

"Nothing I say will make a difference, but you have to promise me you won't ever do this again." She couldn't bear the thought of his tawny-umber skin carved by a blade with his own hand, and the scar it would leave. She couldn't stand by and allow him to brand himself for something he had no control over. "And you have to promise that you won't ever do this again over something you think you have failed to do."

He looked miserable. She could see the indecision in his eyes—the need to do as she asked, to please her, weighing against the compulsion to follow the rules he lived by.

"Promise me."

"I can-not." His voice broke over the words. His honor would not allow him to do it just because she asked.

She searched for a reason, something practical he couldn't refuse. Then it came to her.

"J'Qhir, you have to promise that you will never do this again. If you cut yourself, you could develop an infection. We don't know that the antibiotics work on you, and even if they do, our supply is limited. You could very well die from an infection. So you have to promise that you won't do this again, ever."

She waited while he considered her reasoning. His eyes lightened, and she thought he looked relieved. He tilted his head to one side and nodded once.

"I promissse, Leith."

"Good." She did not doubt his word. "I know that it's difficult for you to go against your beliefs, but some of them just won't work here."

His hands tightened around hers. "Yesss. I have dissscovered thisss already," he said, his voice barely audible. Then he spoke again the words he'd said to her before, "I will build a lair for usss."

Leith started to shake her head, but stopped. She didn't know why he insisted on constructing a shelter when the cave was perfect for their needs. Was there some hidden meaning to the words she couldn't decipher? She had answered in the negative each time. Perhaps he had to hear a positive answer to satisfy some Zi need she couldn't understand.

"All right, J'Qhir, you do that. When we travel south and find a place with a warmer climate, building a lair would be fine."

His hands tightened on hers and for a moment she thought he was going to smile. He didn't, but he seemed contented with her answer.

She pulled free and wiped the perspiration from her face. "It's so hot in here I can't breathe. I'm going to step outside while you lower the fire and—" Her gaze swept over him, head to toe and back again, and her eyes widened. "And you, um, can get dressed."

She turned and fled.

Outside, she headed for the stream. She splashed her face with cold water several times, washing away tears and sweat, and to cool her burning face. She needed lots of cold water. She sat back on her heels and rested her forehead on her knees.

She had learned two things about the Zi. One, nudity was not taboo to them. He had stood before her not wearing a stitch and didn't try to hide a thing. Two, he didn't have a *thing* to hide.

J'Qhir had spoken of younglings. Of course, the Zi had to procreate, but Leith had seen no evidence of how this could be accomplished. His chest was a paler solid shade of tawny, and his skin was ribbed toward his abdomen. Below, there was...*nothing.* She had noticed some sort of vertical decorative mark about ten centimeters in length but nothing else.

Leith sat a long time and pondered the implications of her discovery. His unique physique rendered any kind of intimacy an impossibility...and made her recent dreams pure fantasy. Just her luck, she sighed. She would get marooned on a deserted planet for the rest of her life with a being incapable of sexual intimacy as she knew it. Worse, she thought she was falling in love with him.

Leith didn't know if it was love or not and decided it was a waste of time trying to decide. It didn't matter what she felt, or thought she felt, they were stuck with one another.

❋ ❋ ❋

"We scratch a grid in the dirt, like this." Leith drew two vertical parallel lines, then crossed them with two horizontal parallel lines.

J'Qhir carefully did the same.

"Well, we only need one grid at a time, but—" Before she could finish saying they would use his later, he quickly smoothed the dirt over his. She sighed.

"We have to keep score." She wrote an L and drew a horizontal line after it. "Hmmm, I have no idea how to spell your name."

J'Qhir drew a few glyphs composed of graceful arcs and lines. Leith wrote a J beside them.

"That's how I would write the initial sound of your name."

J'Qhir nodded. "Like ssso."

He painstakingly printed J'QHIR in block letters. Leith smiled. She half expected to see his tongue sticking out of the corner of his mouth. The letters were perfectly formed, like a child would write when practicing his alphabet.

"Terran Ssstandard," J'Qhir proclaimed.

A fanciful name for English. Leave it to the English-speaking people of Earth to make their own language standard across the galaxy.

"Very good." Leith then drew a C with a horizontal line beside it. "That's for the Cat."

J'Qhir's mouth turned down and his crest furrowed. "Who isss the Cat?"

"It's very easy to play to a draw in this game, so when there's a tie, the Cat wins." He still looked puzzled. "That's the way I played it when I was a child. Youngling. It's not supposed to make sense now."

"Ssss..."

"Now, the first one to get three X's or three O's in a row wins."

J'Qhir quickly marked three X's diagonally across the grid. Leith clamped her lips together and tapped her stick against the bottom of her boot.

"Um, it's not a race. It's a game of strategy. We take turns." She smoothed out the dirt and re-drew the grid. "Since you're so eager, you go first. Do you want the X's or O's?"

Off to the side of the grid, J'Qhir precisely lettered one X and one O. He studied them a moment. "Thessse two figuresss are diametrically opposssite."

"They're what?"

"Diametrically opposssite. One isss a complete curve and the other isss composssed of ssstraight linesss."

Leith bit her lip. She didn't know if she did so to keep from laughing or crying. Or slapping him upside the head. Somehow she resisted that urge.

"So they are. Do you want to play or not?"

"Yesss, Leith." He rubbed out the two letters. "I will ussse the X."

He drew an X in the center of the grid. Leith drew an O in the upper right corner. J'Qhir put an X in the center right. Leith blocked him by placing an O in the center left. They continued until each had taken four turns, and there was only one square open.

"It's a tie," Leith pointed out and made a mark beside the C.

"But there isss no way to win," J'Qhir protested.

"Not if the first player always begins in the center square."

"Yesss... Then what is the purpossse of the exercissse?"

"It's for children, to make them think, I suppose." Leith rubbed out the grid and the scoreboard. She stood. "You're no fun. I'm going to bed. Good night."

"Good night, Leith."

❉ ❉ ❉

The next evening, after another long, exhausting day of hauling deadfall and scanning for potential foodstuff, Leith spent the better part of an hour creating a checkerboard in the dirt. J'Qhir watched her, completely absorbed in her actions, and didn't say a word.

His intense silence wore on her nerves, but she said nothing either. She had scratched out sixty-four squares. To differentiate between the colors, she pressed a flat piece of bark in every other square. Earlier in the day she had scoured the bank of the stream for two dozen uniform pebbles, twelve white and twelve brown. She had painted one side of each with sugarpod juice and laid them in the sun to dry to a glossy finish. They could turn one over to be "crowned" instead of trying to balance one rounded stone atop another.

Now, Leith set the pieces on the bark squares, glazed side down. When she had all twenty-four in place, she rested her hands in her lap.

"It's called Checkers. This is the checkerboard. It's supposed to be made with black and red squares, but we have to make do with what we have."

J'Qhir nodded, hanging onto her every word.

Leith pointed to the stones. "These are checkers."

"I thought you sssaid the game isss called Checkersss."

"Yes, but each playing piece is called a checker. The brown ones are yours and the white ones are mine. You move the pieces in a certain way, diagonally forward only. The object of the game is to move your pieces across to the other side while capturing as many of your opponent's as you can." Leith took one of her stones and placed it upside down on the far side to demonstrate. "When a piece gets to the last row, it's considered a king and can now be moved forward or backward, but still only diagonally."

She then prepared a simple jump position and demonstrated how to capture.

"I'll go first," she said as she replaced the stones in their original positions. "There is little action during the first few moves, but it gets better."

Leith thought they would be evenly matched because of her familiarity with the game and his quick grasp of strategy, but she was wrong. He obviously planned out moves far in advance, and she didn't stand a chance. As the game came to a close, she had never even reached the edge row on his side. He had kings all over the board and a pile of white pebbles beside him.

"I concede," she said rather than give up her lone piece.

"A very interesssting game," J'Qhir said as he gathered up all twenty-four stones.

"Well, yes, you would think so." Leith wiped out the board in one stroke and sifted out the bark chips. "Since you won."

"You are angry."

"No." She shrugged. "I never cared for the game anyway."

"You sssound angry that I have won your game."

"I'm tired, that's all. I'm going to bed. Good night, J'Qhir."

"Good night, Leith."

✽ ✽ ✽

"No games tonight," Leith announced when they'd finished tidying up after dinner the next evening. She sat cross-legged on her solar film pallet, and J'Qhir did likewise on his beast blanket. They had taken the skin to the pool and scrubbed it clean of vermin and matted mud and blood. It had finally dried out enough to use. J'Qhir wanted her to use it since it was her kill, but she explained that he would feel warmer next to the fur. In truth, she had no desire to have it as a trophy. "Tonight we sing."

J'Qhir seemed to brighten. Leith knew she had lost patience with him the past few nights. She had chosen elemental games to pass the time, but they were too simple for J'Qhir's analytical mind. He was too good at them. What she planned for this evening was a child's song, but she didn't know what else to do. She couldn't face many more evenings of having nothing to exercise her mind.

"I like musssic. My mother could play the *ohsiroh* exquisssitely."

"I don't play any musical instruments and I'm not much of a singer, but this is an easy song." Leith taught him the words to "Row, Row, Row Your Boat", then the melody. J'Qhir's voice was rich and deep, and he picked up the tune and carried it easily. Leith joined in and their voices blended well, her higher pitch a nice contrast to his baritone.

Leith urged him to sing alone one more time. In the classic rendition, Leith started in with "Row, row, row your boat" as J'Qhir began the "Merrily" line. J'Qhir stopped abruptly.

"You ssstarted too late."

"I was supposed to. It's the way the song is sung."

"You ssshould have told me."

"I wanted to sssurprissse you," Leith said then clamped her lips together. She hoped he hadn't noticed. It was too easy to mimic his long, drawn-out s's. She caught herself doing it from time to time. She was afraid he might think she mocked him and take offense. "Shall we try again?"

J'Qhir nodded and started the song. Leith joined in at the appropriate time. They went through the ditty several times and finally Leith flubbed it. Suddenly, she found herself singing along with J'Qhir, word for word. He cut off in mid-sentence, and his crest furrowed.

"But now you are sssinging the sssame wordsss with me."

"That's the point. To see how long we can keep it going before someone loses their concentration and makes a mistake." Leith sighed. "It's usually sung by a group around a campfire. Maybe we just don't have enough people to make it fun."

J'Qhir shook his head. "The wordsss do not make sssensssse to me. Perhapsss if the sssong had meaning it would be easssier to sssing."

Leith stood and straightened her blanket. "Some songs aren't meant to make sense. They're sung for the way the words flow together. Do all Zi songs make sense?"

"Yesss. They tell ssstoriesss and confirm truthsss about the nature of our people."

"We have those too. We have an entire industry devoted to music, its creation and performance. There are individuals and groups who make a very good living with their music." Leith lay down, curled on her side, an arm beneath her head. "Not from songs like 'Row, Row, Row Your Boat', but longer, more complicated pieces. We have more sophisticated games than the ones I've shown you. These things are mostly children's games, just to pass the time."

"I sssee. It isss ssso with usss alssso." He was quiet a few moments. "Life isss not a dream."

"Oh, I agree considering our lives have turned into a nightmare." Leith closed her eyes. "Tomorrow night is your turn. Good night, J'Qhir."

"Good night, Leith."

❋ ❋ ❋

J'Qhir used the checkers Leith had made and set the white stones in a pile in front of her, keeping the brown ones for himself. He had drawn three concentric semi-circles in the dirt, the ends connecting to the wall of the cave. With his forefinger, he marked a dot in the middle of the center space. At two meters he had drawn another semi-circle. At four meters, a straight line which they crouched behind.

"We take turnsss tosssing a ssstone againssst the wall." He demonstrated. The stone banked off the wall and landed in the second band, but very close to the innermost line. "Now, it isss your turn. The object isss to land your ssstone asss clossse to the center mark asss posssible."

Leith had never played pitching pennies, so she had no idea how hard to throw the stone. She tried to gauge the distance and the heft and let it go. The stone careened off the wall and sailed several centimeters past the outer band.

J'Qhir said nothing, but moved to the two-meter arc. Leith knelt beside him.

"Now, you choossse whether to try to move your ssstone clossser or an opponent'sss farther away by propelling another ssstone and trying to hit whichever you choossse."

He positioned his hand so that the bent knuckle of his index finger rested close to the line. The stone nestled in the crook of his finger, his thumb pressed hard against the underside of his finger ready to release and shoot the stone. Like playing marbles, Leith realized, although she had only played a few times during childhood. At first she was amazed that his people and hers had developed the same shooting technique, but then she realized it wasn't too remarkable. There were only so many ways to manipulate a humanoid hand.

J'Qhir let go and the stone shot toward his, pushing it closer to the center. He sat back on his heels.

"My turn?" Leith asked, picking up a stone, and J'Qhir nodded. Leith positioned herself, fixed the stone in her hand and shot. The stone arced up and over J'Qhir's and landed past the other side of the third ring.

She could have sworn she heard a snort from J'Qhir. He made some barely audible sound, but whether it was suppressed amusement or disapproval, she didn't know.

"This is very similar to a game called marbles. It's been ages since I've played," she defended herself. "More than fifteen years."

"The lassst time I played thisss game was the ssseasssson my mother died. That wasss...ninety-eight yearsss ago."

148

"In Zi years," Leith guessed. "Do we continue playing or do you get my stones now?"

"We clear the playing field now." J'Qhir reached for his stones. "I alwaysss ussse Terran Ssstandard. Othersss ssseem to have trouble making the converssssion."

As he spoke, Leith leaned over to pick up her widely distributed stones, but froze as his words sank in. *Ninety-eight* Terran Standard years—

"Leith, ssstop!" J'Qhir shouted.

She snatched her hand back and looked the floor over, expecting to see a snake or bug or something, but she didn't see anything. "What's wrong?"

"You losssst the ssstonesss, and they are not yoursss anymore."

"I wasn't going to keep them," she snapped.

"A Zi doesss not touch what isss not hisss—or hersss."

She was tired of playing games and tired of his rules. And she was stunned to find she was desperately attracted to and maybe falling in love with someone over a hundred years old. She dreamed of him when she slept and daydreamed of him when awake. If it was as simple as her body finally awakening to its sexual needs, why did she dream of J'Qhir? Wouldn't her subconscious conjure an image from the men she'd dated or found attractive or the latest vid stars? Why J'Qhir, unless it was he she truly desired?

Leith asked as calmly as she could, "How old are you?"

"One hundred, eight." The grammatical correctness of his response only served to emphasize the antiquity of the number.

"I'm twenty-one."

"A youngling," he said softly, and she could almost hear the amusement in his voice.

"I'm not a youngling. I'm an adult!" The pronouncement only made her sound more childish. "What I mean is, it may seem very young to you, but I've reached maturity."

That sounded worse! Leith's face grew hot and she crawled toward the fire. She piled on more wood to keep her hands busy. With luck, he would think her rosy tint was a reflection of the flames.

J'Qhir walked around and carefully lowered himself onto his beast blanket. He tucked one leg underneath him, but kept the injured one at a more comfortable angle. He pulled out his weaving and squinted into the light

"The average lifessspan of a Zi isss over two hundred, fifty Terran Ssstandard yearsss. A dissstant relative in my clan isss nearly three hundred. Yesss, twenty-one isss very young." He bent to his work.

❋ ❋ ❋

"Tonight we tell jokes," Leith announced the next evening.

J'Qhir shook his head. "No, not tonight, Leith. We have much work to do."

"We can make our baskets while we talk. Jokes are easy. Have you ever heard a knock-knock joke?"

He shook his head again, his mouth pressed into a grim line. She couldn't imagine what he had against jokes.

"Don't the Zi do jokes?" she asked.

He nodded reluctantly and shrugged. "But I have no way with telling them."

"Then I will tell you jokes."

"That would be unfair." He would not meet her eyes. "Can we not have one peaceful evening?"

"I suppose…"

150

Leith tried to concentrate on making her basket, but jokes kept running through her mind.

"Just a few jokes, please. Then I'll be quiet. I promise."

J'Qhir closed his eyes and said wearily, "Very well, if you mussst."

It had occurred to her earlier that she had yet to see him smile. It was still on her agenda, one of the things she meant to accomplish before she died. She thought she might as well start now, and it looked like it was a good thing. She was going to have her work cut out for her.

"Knock-knock jokes are based on puns. I say, 'Knock, knock'," and you say, 'Who's there?'"

"Why would I asssk, 'Who isss there?' when I know you are the one sssaying 'knock, knock'?"

He still would not meet her eyes, keeping his gaze on his work. She had the feeling he was being purposefully obtuse this evening. Something was wrong, but she couldn't pinpoint the cause.

"Because I will answer with a name or word or phrase. Then you will repeat my answer and add 'who'. For example, I say, 'Knock, knock' and you say, 'Who's there?' Then I say, 'Isabel' and you'll—"

"Who isss thisss Isssabel?"

Still, he had not raised his eyes.

"If you let me finish, you'll find out. Then you say, 'Isabel who?' and I finish with the punch line, 'Isabel ringing?'"

Leith smiled although the joke wasn't particularly funny, especially since there was no bell ringing. It worked better in school when the bell sounded for a change of classes. It actually worked best when one was about ten years old.

He didn't laugh, didn't smile, didn't raise his head.

151

"Knock, knock."

He waited a few moments, then said, "Who isss there?"

"Amos."

"Amosss who?"

"A mosquito bit me. Knock, knock."

She thought she heard him hiss under his breath, then, "Who isss there?"

"Andy."

"Andy who?"

"And he bit me again."

Leith smiled widely. Those two had been her favorite when she was very young.

He was silent a moment, then asked, "What isss a mosssquito?"

The smile dropped from her face. "A small flying insect, very annoying. They bite, suck blood, and leave an itchy bump behind."

"Ssss."

Leith slumped in dejection. She wracked her brain trying to remember at least one funny joke of the thousands she had heard in her life. As with games and songs, she couldn't recall any but the most basic. Rules wouldn't come, lyrics were only half-remembered... Then it came to her, a joke Steve had told her on the way to Arreis.

"Three starmen walk into a bar, a Danid, a Hykaisite, and a Peridot. Each orders a glass of Numerian brine. When the drinks are served, three flyworms buzz near and one lands in each glass. The Danid wrinkles his nose, pushes his drink aside and orders another. The Hykaisite tosses the flyworm away, and gulps down his drink. The Peridot picks up the flyworm and starts shaking it over his glass shouting, 'Spit it out, ya farking dorgian! Spit it out!'"

Leith held her breath. It was interstellar humor, something he should understand. If that one didn't make him at least smile, nothing would, and she might as well give up. She watched him closely. He blinked rapidly, more than once or twice, and his jaw muscles clenched tightly. Then...he smiled!

Chapter 9

J'Qhir's appreciation of the humor overcame his self-control. His mouth curved at the corners, edges parting to reveal the two rows of his sharp teeth. Leith's eyes widened— By the rock, what had he done! He had been told the baring of his teeth would frighten humans. They would perceive it as a threat and react defensively. He had been so careful for so long and now—

Leith jumped toward him. She threw her arms at him and pressed her face to his, her soft pink lips closing in on his mouth. Instinctively, his body tensed and his jaws snapped shut to cover his teeth.

"*Ow!*" she yelped as he backed away from her and staggered to his feet. She clamped a hand to her mouth. When she withdrew it, a drop of blood stained her fingers. "You-You-You *bit* me!"

"Leith, b-beg forgivenesss," he stammered. Then he shook his head. He straightened his rigid form and glowered down at her. "I did not *bite* you. Your flesssh ssscraped acrosss my teeth. What did you expect when you attack me in thisss ssstrange fassshion?"

"*Attack* you?" Leith stared at him incredulously. It hadn't taken decades after all to make him smile. It had only taken the right kind of joke. She was so elated she had reacted before she

154

could consider the implications or consequences. She had thrown her arms around his neck and pressed her mouth to his. Deep inside, she hoped he would respond as a *man*. She should have known it wouldn't be so easy. He wasn't a man, he was Zi...and he thought she had attacked him!

Leith tried to control the laughter but couldn't. She clamped both hands over her mouth to suppress it, but giggles escaped in short bursts. He stared at her, his crest knotted in confusion, his eyes unblinking, his mouth a grim slash. His serious expression sent her over the edge. She nearly doubled over, laughter wracking her body.

She has finally gone mad! J'Qhir thought in alarm as he watched liquid stream from her eyes and her arms wrap around her waist. She jerked spasmodically and strange deep-throated sounds emitted from her. He damned himself as she had explained he should do when one caused a terrible calamity to befall another. He had provoked her attack then driven her insane. All because he had smiled.

J'Qhir didn't know what to do to help her. He could only watch her collapse onto the beast blanket pallet, then fall to her back in a coughing fit. Between hacking coughs, her body shook and guttural noises continued to escape sporadically.

He eased down beside her, allowing his good knee and arm to support his weight. She glanced at him occasionally, but each time her body convulsed and she closed her eyes against the sight of him.

Every time she looked at him she would be reminded of the frightful appearance of him baring his teeth. J'Qhir decided he would have to leave her.

"Leith," he whispered so as not to scare her again. His fingers ran through the ends of her brown hair. How many times had he crept close to her in the middle of the night and touched the silken filaments as she lay sleeping? "I will go away, deeper into the cavesss. I will not frighten you again."

Her wet round eyes popped open. A gurgle caught in her throat, and she coughed once to clear it. "*What?*"

J'Qhir turned away from her. If she didn't look at him, she wouldn't become hysterical again.

"I will move deeper into the cavesss. You won't have to sssuffer my uglinesss any longer." There. He said it. Among his own kind, he was considered neither homely nor comely. All Zi looked remarkably similar. To humans, especially a female, he had to appear brutish even without the baring of his teeth. How had she withstood his countenance this long?

He felt her stir behind him, no doubt preparing to pack up his share of their supplies and send him on his way. Suddenly, she was upon him. Her hands latched onto his shoulders, pressing him back until he lay supine beneath her. Brown hair brushed his cheeks and neck. His *vha'seh* tightened and his *jha'i* threatened to release. He lay as still as a stone so that he would not disgrace himself beyond redemption.

"Are you crazy?" she snapped, her full lips parted, showing square teeth so unlike his own. He did not know if her people considered her beauteous. To him, humans were so different from Zi, there was no way to compare. He only knew his heart beat faster whenever she looked at him, and his blood pounded wildly through his veins whenever she was close to him. His *jha'i* felt as if it might explode at the slightest pressure.

He shook his head and turned away from her. "Leith—"

Warm fingers cupped his chin and brought him around to face her. "I didn't attack you, J'Qhir. I kissed you."

"Kisss?" The touching of lips, a custom of many species, including humans.

"Yesss..." she murmured, subconsciously mimicking his sibilant speech pattern. "I'm sorry I laughed. It's been so long since I've had something to laugh about, I couldn't stop once I started."

"You—You were *laughing?*" Blood rushed to his face and burned hotly. Only two circumstances caused a Zi to give off any extra heat—acute embarrassment and *rhi`ina`a,* the mating ritual. Blood vessels expanded and engorged. The dense accumulation of blood caused the extra warmth. Stimulation of certain nerve endings—sss't! Recitation of his ancient studies did not lessen the expansion and engorgement of either set of blood vessels at this moment. "Leith, I have ssseen you laugh, but thisss...thisss wasss not laughing."

"It was very funny that you thought I attacked you." She rubbed the back of her hand over his cheek. "There are different kinds of laughter, just as there are different kinds of kisses. Don't the Zi kiss?"

"No. Full frontal approach isss consssidered an act of aggresssion."

Leith nodded and sighed. "You're not ugly when you smile, you know. I bet all the Zi girls back home think you're quite a catch."

"A catch?"

"An expression. Remember, humans have one for every occasion."

"I remember," he said seriously.

Leith shifted until she lay beside him, her side pressed close to his, her chin propped in her hand. She frowned slightly. "Is there a Mrs. J'Qhir back on Zi?"

"There once wasss, but ssshe died many, many yearsss ago. Our binding wasss arranged by our fathersss." He did not know why he felt the need to explain. "Her father isss a member of the Council of Eldersss, and I think he hasss alwaysss blamed me for her dying while under my protection."

"I'm so sorry," she said very softly.

"But no, I have no lifemate now or I could not have—" He stopped short. He almost told her that he could not have asked the question of her. If he did, he would have to explain its significance. He was afraid she would draw away from him. "Or I could not have you thisss clossse."

"No younglings?"

"No. My lifemate died before there wasss isssue."

She made a strangled sound in the back of her throat. "Um, just because you have no lifemate doesn't mean there couldn't be younglings."

He felt his face grow warm again. She could not truly believe he would dishonor himself or a female in such a way. "No no. It isss *qa`anh'al*—forbidden."

"But accidents happen, no matter how careful one is—"

"No. It never happensss becaussse it isss not done."

"Never?"

"Never."

"Oh." Her lips remained pursed and her round eyes blinked languidly then widened. "Oh!" she said again and started to move away.

Quickly, J'Qhir rolled his bulk over until he had captured her. He lay along her length as he had envisioned so often. Not forced by unnatural gravity, not as a haphazard result of falling, but simply to experience the pleasure of her softly rounded body beneath his.

He blinked once when she did not resist.

He was careful to keep most of his weight off her as well as his injured knee. He slipped his arms underneath hers, which raised to accommodate him, and planted his elbows on either side of her torso. His hands entangled in her lustrous hair, cupping the back of her head.

He closed his eyes and breathed in her scent, the sweetness of the *jhuhn'gha* flower. His body absorbed her wonderful heat through the woven fabric of their clothing. He wondered what it would be like with nothing between them, to feel the prickle of her body hair, to touch the fleshy mounds that rose and fell with each breath.

He wondered how long she would allow the impropriety to last. If she were Zi, she would have cried out in outrage long before now. She was not Zi...and he was pleased she was not.

"Pleassse to explain what isss kisss?" He mangled the Terran Standard syntax, but he was too distracted to care. Her fingers lazily traced along his jaw, around the sweeping eye socket, over his crested brow. Her accidental touches had driven him mad, but her deliberate caresses plunged him into incoherent insanity.

"A kiss can mean different things at different times. It can express respect, affection, passion, or love." Her fingers found his tympanum and explored it thoroughly, delicately, sensuously. "I finally made you smile, and I was excited about the achievement. So a kiss can also express joy at accomplishing something one sets out to do. I'm sorry if I frightened you. Is kissing *qa`anh'al*?"

"No. We know nothing of kisssing." He opened his eyes and looked directly into Leith's. "Would you ssshow me how to kisss?"

A tingle had already worked its way through Leith's body, down to her toes. If she taught him how to kiss, including demonstrations, she would be on fire with unfulfilled longing. She suspected he would, too. *Becaussse it isss not done.* Didn't

159

he mean premarital relations were *qa`anh'al*? If they continued the kissing lesson, but could go no further because of his mores, they would be left physically frustrated. Was it wise to teach him how to kiss?

His amber eyes watched her expectantly, his mouth slightly parted, sharp teeth gleaming. The scratch on her lip was nothing more than a small sore spot. Kissing him would be a dangerous adventure.

Perhaps he was only curious. If the Zi hadn't discovered kissing, maybe the act wouldn't arouse him at all. Therefore, it wouldn't lead to anything more—for him.

Leith placed her free hand on the other side of his head and drew him closer to her. "One can kiss there." She lightly touched her lips to one high cheekbone. "Or there." His crested brow. "Or there." Tenderly, she brushed his mouth with hers.

The tingle turned into a burning flame and settled in the pit of her belly. She suppressed the instinctive surge of her hips toward his and the urge to spread her thighs for him. All natural reactions, but she didn't want to tempt him against his taboos.

He trembled beneath her fingertips, his breathing as harsh and ragged as her own.

"There isss more?" he whispered gutturally.

She nodded. "I have to be careful of your teeth. They're very sharp."

His crest, a thick fold of skin running across his browbone, rose up and out a few millimeters. He's *preening*, she thought in amazement.

"Is that considered a compliment?"

"Yesss..."

She ran one finger along the lower rim of his mouth then over several of his teeth. "J'Qhir, you have the sharpest teeth I have ever seen."

His crest inflated a little more.

She wanted to laugh, but didn't dare. He wouldn't understand at all, and she didn't want to hurt his feelings. Instead, she slanted her mouth across his, moving her lips. Carefully, she ran her tongue over his teeth then probed deeper. He caught on quickly and his tongue met hers, flicked against it teasingly.

The burning flame moved lower and became a throbbing ache. She couldn't stop the undulation of her hips this time. For the first time in her life she was completely and totally aroused. And the only time in her life, the only male she had ever truly desired could not take advantage of the situation.

Leith sighed deeply, a long shuddery breath. "W-We have to-to stop now or—"

"Or?" he prompted.

She looked into his amber eyes. "We have to stop or *not* stop."

"Not ssstop?" His crest had returned to normal. He cocked his head to the side and blinked once. "Do you want to not ssstop?"

"I want to not stop, but I don't want to expect more from you than you can give." Once again, she ran her fingers along the hard contours of his face. She frowned. "Honestly, I don't know if it's physically possible."

"Sss. *Rhi`ina`a*—the mating between male and female. Kisssing isss part of thisss ritual?"

"Most of the time. Not always, but usually." She noticed he offered no opinion whether he thought it possible or not. "The

161

day I walked in on you when you were doing that failure ceremony...you...I didn't see..."

She closed her eyes as heat infused her face. They were on the verge of mingling those body parts, why was it so difficult to talk about them?

"Leith, they are internal, protected from the high temperaturesss on Zi."

Biology hadn't been her best subject, nor one of her favorites, but she remembered the basics. Human male genitals were located outside the body because spermsemen, to remain viable, required temperatures slightly lower than normal body temperature. Since Zi was a hot world and the Zi body temperature was naturally lower, it made perfect sense that Zi male genitalia would be located inside the body, protected from the heat.

"Okay, but what you said before. You implied that—that *rhi`ina`a* is not acceptable unless the couple is married."

"Bound," he corrected. "It isss the way of my people."

"It was the way of my people up until a few centuries ago. Even when it was supposed to be forbidden—*qa`anh'al*, most did it anyway." Thoughtfully, she bit her lip. "But it's not that way with the Zi, is it? You don't ignore your rules and customs, do you."

"No. If we were on Zi and we were obssserved asss we are now, we would be ssshunned, cassst out from the clan. No Zi would ssspeak to usss or interact with usss. However, no Zi female would have allowed a male thisss clossse. And no Zi male would have presssumed—"

"Then we have to stop," Leith whispered. "I won't let you do anything that is forbidden to you."

She tried to extricate herself from him, but he held her fast.

"We are not on Zi, Leith. I will never sssee Zi again, nor you Terra. It isss difficult to go againssst what one isss taught from birth—but not imposssible."

"J'Qhir—"

"If you wisssh to ssstop, we will ssstop. But Leith, do not wisssh to ssstop becaussse of me."

"Are you sure? I don't want you to feel guilty afterward. I don't want our lovemaking to be something you regret."

"No regretsss." He took a deep breath. "Lovemaking. I do like the sssound of the word. Can we ssshed our clothing now, Leith?"

At her nod, he started to rise, but she stopped him. She fumbled with the antiquated loops and buttons on his jacket, undoing each one slowly. When she finished, he shrugged it off. His heavy shirt overlapped at the front with a tie at the side. She pulled the string loose and tugged the ends of the shirt from the waistband of his trousers. She pushed the shirt over his shoulders bulging with muscle.

"Your turn," she said mischievously.

J'Qhir had to sit up to keep from exerting pressure on his bad knee. Leith sat up also. His taloned fingers grappled with the thin cloth of her shirt, sliding it up and over her head. Her bra confused him. He ignored the front fastenings and pulled it over her head too. He stared at her breasts and her nipples hardened under his scrutiny.

"Touch them, J'Qhir."

Tentatively, he cupped them in his hands and held them almost reverently for a few moments. Then he carefully released them. Leith sighed and decided the finer points of foreplay could be covered later.

He was unlooping his trousers and Leith did the same. They wriggled free of pants and underclothes, socks and boots. Leith finished first and stretched out on the pallet. When J'Qhir was done, he lay on his side next to her. He placed his hand on her shoulder and eased her over onto her stomach. He clutched a handful of her hair as he latched onto the back of her neck.

"What are you doing?" she asked as he mounted her. He froze and released her instantaneously.

"Isss thisss wrong?"

Leith squirmed beneath him until she turned over and faced him. "Not wrong. It's one way to do it... J'Qhir, I've never done this before and I want this first time to be the—the most proper way."

"Never?"

"Never."

He fell to the side, leaning on an elbow. "I thought human femalesss—I have been told human femalesss are promissscuousss."

"Some. Not all. Not me. Who told you this?"

He blinked twice and shook his head. "Sss't, it doesss not matter."

"Oh, let me guess. Steve Hancock?" When he didn't answer, she laughed. "It's okay. The next time you recall something Steve told you, just remember the source. Steve is not exactly the most reliable source of information. He misled you simply for the joy of it."

He nodded solemnly and stared down at her unblinking. "But, Leith, I am not sssure how to proceed."

Leith raised up, propping herself up on her elbows. Her gaze traveled over his tawny ribbing, rippling ribcage, the softer area of his stomach, to his abdomen. As she had observed once before, he lacked the obvious, yet displayed a distinctive bulge in the area above where his legs joined his torso. Leith ran her hand over the bulge. Something moved within, and J'Qhir grunted deep within his throat.

Her exploring fingers discovered what she thought was a decorative mark was actually an opening. The vent spread beneath her hand and something damp and soft-yet-hard nudged her fingers.

"Leith...if you do not ssstop, I cannot hold it in."

"It's all right. I have a place for you to put it."

J'Qhir allowed her hand to guide his to her point of bifurcation. He felt a vent, not unlike a Zi sa`aloh's, hidden beneath the triangular pelt of dark curls. At her urging, his fingers sank into her liquid heat and she gasped. Inner muscles contracted around him, and her hips pushed upward to meet his hand.

Encouraged, J'Qhir delved deeper. Sounds escaped her throat, low and primal, and caused *his* breathing and heart rate to quicken. He did not understand why her action should cause a reaction in him, but he did not think he should ask her at this moment.

Since he'd never had the opportunity to explore the interior of a Zi sa`aloh, he had no idea how similar or different they might be to human. He could not imagine a Zi this *hot* or this *wet*. He probed deeper until the tender flesh seemed to resist his advancement.

"Don't—" Leith began and had to clear her throat. "Don't break it."

He yanked his fingers from her and his eyes widened. "Break you? I did not mean—"

"No, you didn't." Leith laughed. "There's a membrane, a barrier. Proof that no man—no *male* has been there before you.

Every human female has one. It has to be breached, but I would prefer that you do it with—" She broke off, unable to say the word again. They were nude, about to make love, and she couldn't say the word.

"*Jha'i.*"

"Yeah, that's it. Do it with your *jha'i.*" She only hoped *jha'i* meant what she thought it meant.

"You enunciate the Zi wordsss very well," he complimented her. "Except for *p`ha`al.*"

"I'll work on it," she said wishing he would get on with it. Her limbs quivered, and she ached terribly where his fingers had explored. "J'Qhir, can we please do this now or I think I'm going to implode."

J'Qhir couldn't resist running his hand through the small patch of hair again. "You will feel pleasssure?"

"Yes. Don't Zi females feel pleasure?"

He shook his head and entangled his fingers in the spirals. This hair was not as fine and silky as the hair atop her head. "It isss an endurance for them. It mussst be done quickly to caussse them asss little pain asss posssible."

"Have you ever done to them what you've done to me, the touching and caressing?"

"No! It isss not our way."

"That may be why. A human female body has to be stimulated to accept the male. Otherwise, it can be painful."

"Have you been ssstimulated enough?"

"More than enough. Please, J'Qhir..."

He lowered himself between her outspread thighs, pressing his vent against hers. She wrapped her legs around him and held out her arms.

"Hold me, J'Qhir."

He gathered her up and held her as close as he could. With a deep sigh, he at last allowed himself to let it go.

Uncertain what to expect, Leith cried out, mostly in surprise, but partly in delight. Immediately, J'Qhir withdrew.

"I'm all right," she assured him, whispering directly against his tympanum. "Can you do that again?"

"Yesss, Leith."

Once more his *jha'i* thrust into her, and she rose to meet it. There hadn't been pain as she had expected. A moment of discomfort, then only pleasure. Molten heat flowed from some center place throughout her limbs as her hips undulated against his. She had heard the expression "going nova" to describe climax, but she thought now it was an extremely inadequate description.

Through a white haze, she was aware that J'Qhir's body was very still.

"You should move with me, J'Qhir," she murmured against his tympanum.

After a few attempts, he matched her rhythm, his body naturally falling into its role. With the added friction of his thrusts, her back arched, casting her body against his. Waves of pleasure rippled through her, and she whimpered with each one. J'Qhir thrust into her a few more times until his entire body went rigid, then shuddered violently over her. Primeval noises sounded deep in his throat as he pulsed within her again and again.

When he had finished, he rested his crest against her brow, gently rubbing back and forth, and murmured words she couldn't understand.

Chapter 10

"Look! Isn't it beautiful," Leith whispered and snuggled closer to J'Qhir, pulling the solar film more securely around them. The full moon had just cleared the tops of the trees and filled a good portion of the sky.

"It isss a wondrousss sssight," J'Qhir agreed, his voice lowered as well.

J'Qhir leaned against the back wall of the well-protected niche they had found near the top of the hill. Leith sat between his thighs, her back pressed against his chest. J'Qhir had wrapped himself in the beast blanket and with the solar film and her body heat, he had assured her he was warm enough. She had wanted to build a fire, but he pointed out the firelight would interfere with their viewing of the moon.

"Our moon back on Earth is much smaller, but when it's full it can be very bright," Leith explained. "Do you have a moon on Zi?"

"We have three moonsss, but they are very sssmall. Much sssmaller than the moonsss we obssserved that night on Arreisss and their light isss harsssher than thisss sssilvery glow. When all three are in the sssky sssimultaneousssly, they barely illuminate the night. It isss a rare occurrence and it isss called *zar'az jha*. If we know sssomething doesss not have a chance of being accomplisssshed in a long time we sssay, not until the three moonsss."

Leith laughed. "I can't believe it! We have a similar saying—once in a blue moon. It means something that only happens every once in a great while. We usually have only one full moon in a month, but sometimes there's a second and it's called the blue moon."

"We do find more and more that we have in common," J'Qhir said and ran his fingers through her hair. She enjoyed his caresses. She tilted back her head and kissed him lightly on his cheek.

A few days had passed since they had become intimate. She had expected awkwardness or embarrassment, but felt neither. Leith was more comfortable with him than she had been with anyone in her life.

J'Qhir had been perplexed by the outcome. "Physssical pleasssure," he had explained, "isss not attained during Zi *rhi`ina`a*. Physsssical releassse, yesss, but not the intensssse joy I experience when our bodiesss join and peak."

She had fallen asleep, completely contented, in his arms. Later, when he had awakened her by kissing her cheek, her brow, and finally her lips, she was surprised but pleased and eagerly accepted him again. The third time, she had sleepily received his kisses and him, but her sated body refused to cooperate and would not peak.

The fourth time—in as many hours it seemed, but she hadn't checked her watch—she laid her hands against his chest and prevented him from settling atop her. "What are you doing?"

"*Rhi`ina`a*," he said as if the word actually answered her question.

"I mean, as much as I enjoy it, we don't have to do this all the time. I would like to get some sleep and so should you."

He looked down at her, blinked once, then fell back on his side, propping himself on his elbow. "Sss'h. *Rhi`ina`a* isss not sssimply the act of joining, Leith. When Zi male and female begin *rhi`ina`a*, their biological rhythmsss coincide. When the female'sss cycle isss at the fertile ssstage, ssso isss the male'sss. Once *rhi`ina`a* hasss begun, they sssequessster themssselvesss from otherss. It isss a continual processs until the female isss no longer fertile, thusss ensssuring there will be isssue."

Leith had stared at him wide-eyed. "Are you saying once you start, you don't stop until the female's not fertile anymore?"

"Yesss. In a Zi female, thisss could be asss long asss a Ssstandard month."

"And how long is a female's cycle?"

"It lassstsss one Zi year." He drew in a sharp breath. "It isss not thisss way with humansss?"

She shook her head. "No. With humans, lovemaking can occur at any time, whenever two people decide they want to do it. Physical need drives them, and most people try to avoid fertility, but it's not something they *have* to do. It's something they *want* to do."

"Then sssleep," he said and gathered her into his arms.

Leith had closed her eyes, but his restlessness kept her awake. He tried to lie still beside her, but she could feel the slight twitches in his limbs.

"J'Qhir, is this something you *have* to do?" He didn't answer immediately, and Leith sat up to look at him. "Is it?"

"Yesss, asss long asss you are in your fertile ssstage."

Leith smiled at him. "Human female cycles last about a Standard month. I should be fertile only a few days every month."

His eyeslits grew wider. "*Every* month?"

"Yes."

"Sss't."

She ignored the sound of dismay at the prospect of going through *rhi'ina'a* every month. She was as bewildered over the possibility of experiencing it only for a short time every year.

"Well, I don't think fertility is something we really have to worry about. We are much too different."

"I concur. But we are enough alike that I react to your cycle asss I would a Zi female." He paused. "No, I react more ssstrongly. I have wanted to lovemake with you sssince we were aboard the ssship."

She leaned over and kissed him as he had kissed her each time before making love to her—cheek, crest, and mouth. "And I wanted you from the moment I saw you."

J'Qhir pressed his crest to her forehead and rubbed slowly back and forth. The care with which he made the contact stirred her. She had never before considered the forehead to be an erogenous zone. She lay back pulling him with her.

"I thought you wissshed to ssssleep."

"Not if you need me."

"I do not want to presssume—"

"No, it's all right," she assured him and ran the tips of her fingers around his tympanum. "I do have a question before you have your way with me. Will you be able to do this at times other than my fertile stage?"

"Normally, no, but with you I believe ssso. Your fertile ssstage lassstsss only a few Ssstandard daysss, but I have had thisss want of you much longer." He settled himself on top of her, drew her close, and thrust inside her. "I think the way your cycle continuousssly ebbsss and flowsss will make it posssible."

"Mmmm," had been her only response.

Now, as they sat together watching the huge moon move across the sky, Leith decided J'Qhir was correct. The urgency of his need had waned. After two days of joining several times during the day and even more at night, J'Qhir hadn't awakened her at all the previous night and had approached her only once this day.

She also hoped he was correct in that he would be capable after her fertile period was over. It would be unsettling if they had to endure an intense flurry of lovemaking over a few days' time, then nothing until a month later. Human bodies weren't made for such a schedule—or perhaps it was a schedule she didn't want to become accustomed to. Surely, over time their cycles would adapt to one another.

"Ssshould we go back?" J'Qhir suggested. "I can no longer sssee the moon."

"I suppose." Leith leaned out and looked up. The moon had moved directly overhead, but only a quarter of it was visible, the remainder hidden by the unscalable jagged rocks at the very top of the hill. Gray clouds seemed to be building to what she had determined as north. If it snowed heavily and grew colder, they might be trapped in the cave for who knew how long.

Leith stood and held out her hand for J'Qhir. His knee still hadn't healed, and he needed help sometimes, especially in the confining space of the niche. He retrieved his staff, and they started down the hill at a slow and careful pace.

When Leith saw the mist rising from the pool, she stopped. "Let's go for a moonlight swim."

"The cloudsss, Leith." J'Qhir pointed toward the darkening sky with his stick. "It could sssnow at any time."

"And we might not be able to leave the cave for days." Leith turned toward the pool. "We'll have plenty of time to get there if it does begin to snow."

J'Qhir followed more slowly.

Leith started pulling off her clothing as soon as she reached the pool. She had found it was best to undress and get in the water as quickly as possible. The wind fluxed with the unstable air currents, sometimes enveloping her in steam from the pool and sometimes frigid air sweeping down the hill and sometimes a disconcerting mix of both.

She had doffed her jacket, shirt, boots, socks and was removing her trousers, standing on one leg, trying to pull them off the other. To keep her balance, she hopped around...and saw J'Qhir leaning against a boulder, watching her with widened eyes. She stopped and had to put her leg down to keep from falling over. She felt slightly foolish wearing only underclothes, her trousers wadded at her ankles.

"What are you doing?" She asked that question a lot lately.

He blinked. "Watching you."

"Yeah, I can see that." She held back a smile. "Why?"

"I enjoy the way your body movesss."

Leith had tried to prod him into embarrassment, but it was she who became flustered instead. She didn't understand how he could have enjoyed her clumsy one-legged dance. How could he enjoy her at all when she was so different from what he should want? But wasn't he just as different from what she should want?

"Why?" she asked again.

"I do not know. I have never wanted to watch a Zi *sa`aloh* the way I watch you."

Zi *sa`aloh*...Zi *female?*

"*Sa`aloh* means female?" She choked on the question.

"Yesss." His crest wrinkled. "Thisss upsssetsss you?"

"Yes. No." She frowned at him. "I'm not sure. All that time you were calling me 'female' as if I were nothing more than a—a generic gender. As if I were *nothing*."

"You called me Commander."

"That's your title."

"No. It isss a title Cameron usssed. He explained that Commander sssoundsss lesss antagonisssstic than Warrior, the title bessstowed upon me by my people. *Commander* meansss nothing to me."

"I'm sorry, I didn't know..."

"Beg forgivenesss, Leith, but we were ssstrangersss at the time. I would have been uncomfortable usssing your *na`ajh*."

Veiled name, he had defined the word one night when she asked him to tell her his complete name again. She repeated the syllables until she had them memorized. J'Qhir had explained a Zi rarely shared his *na`ajh* with anyone besides his lifemate. It was a sign of trust and something he had never given to another being, not even T`hirz. Leith felt truly honored by his confidence.

"What rank is Warrior?" Leith asked as she tried to tug her foot free.

He tilted his head and blinked slowly. "I do not undersssstand what you asssk?"

She rested her foot again. "If you're not a commander then what position do you hold in the Zi Force?"

He blinked once more then said suddenly, "No, no. Warrior isss not equivalent to sssoldier, although I do underssstand why the title isss misssleading. The Warrior doesss not participate in battle."

"There's only one Warrior?" Leith tried again to pull free of her trousers.

"One at a time. Our word *Ga`ar'ja* wasss taken from the old sssstoriesss of warsss fought between desssertsss. The Terran Ssstandard word 'warrior' isss an ancient word, isss it not? It isss why I chossse it."

"Yes, you're right." One final yank pulled her foot from the twisted trouser leg. "But if the Warrior doesn't war, what does he do?"

"The Warrior never wagesss war. He isss the people'sss greatessst hope..." J'Qhir's voice softened and trailed off. He lowered his eyelids and bowed his head. "Not that I am the bessst. My father accomplisssshed far greater deedsss during hisss ssshort tenure. Hisss untimely death came during the fiercessst of our battlesss with the Cruciansss. There wasss no time to carry out the rite of sssuccesssion to choossse another. At the time, I wasss indeed a sssoldier. I wasss called upon to ssserve in my father'sss ssstead."

"I'm sure it's an honor you deserve," Leith said quietly. "But you still haven't explained exactly what you do."

He nodded. "The Warrior ensssuresss the sssurvival of the people. The ssstrongessst malesss are called to battle and many die. Sssomeone musst provide for thossse left behind—the old, the ill, the younglingsss, and the femalesss—asss well asss the sssoldiersss themsssselvesss."

A chill crawled over Leith's body that had nothing to do with the cold. She wrapped her arms around herself. "Then the cargo—"

"The cargo wasss sssuppliesss—food and medicine and Terran wool—badly needed by my people."

"And-And Steve knew this?"

"Yesss, Hancock knew," he growled harshly.

"He sold it to the Cruciansss anyway."

"Sss't, yesss. He knowsss the Cruciansss have laid wassste to much of the mountainousss region. The *qhal'* is nearly extinct."

"The *qhal'*?"

"A quadruped with long hair. We ussse the animal for food and weave itsss hair for clothing. Three Ssstandard yearsss ago, Cameron helped usss move a sssmall herd to another planet ssso the *qhal'* can thrive and one day repopulate the mountainsss of Zi."

"I'm sorry!"

J'Qhir shook his head. "Do not apologize for the Cruciansss or Hancock."

"I don't. I-I made assumptions that were wrong. I didn't know—"

"I know what you thought, Leith. Jussst asss you asssumed I wasss a sssoldier, you asssumed I bought weaponsss from your father."

Ashamed, Leith nodded, unable to speak.

"But it did not matter to you," he said softly. "Had our posssitionsss been reversssed, I do not think I would have been asss forgiving."

Leith swallowed hard. "I hope you don't think too badly of me. I found it difficult to believe my parents would be involved in illegal trading. After I came to know you, it was equally difficult to believe you would ask it of them."

He gathered the blankets closer together. "Trade with the Zi isss illegal no matter the cargo."

"I know, but sometimes the humane purpose of an illegal act overrides the law. I should have guessed sooner, or at least asked you."

He blinked slowly. "The wind hasss ssshifted. Pleassse finisssh undresssing."

The cold draft reached her then and she shivered violently, but his suggestive request kindled a warmth in her that she didn't think possible after their numerous bouts of lovemaking over the last few days.

With chattering teeth, she undressed slowly and never took her eyes from his. She unfastened her bra, easing the magnostrip apart, and let the garment fall over her shoulders and down her arms. She ran her hands down the sides of her body, her fingers slipping into the waistband of her underpants. She had no idea if what she did aroused him until he made a brief, guttural sound. He said nothing more and never moved. His eyes devoured her, never blinking.

The wind changed again, blowing steamy air over her goose-bumped flesh. Slowly, she slid the underpants down her legs until they fell to her ankles. She pulled her feet free of them, took a few teasing steps toward J'Qhir, then turned and dove into the water.

Leith came up and slung her hair back, wiping water from her eyes. She found the underwater ledge and braced her knees against it. She crossed her arms on the rim of the pool and rested her chin on them.

"My turn to watch."

"Leith!"

"It's only fair."

He hissed, but dropped the blankets from his shoulders. He braced himself against the boulder to remove his boots, then quickly peeled off his jacket, shirt, trousers, and underclothes. At last he stood wearing nothing, but before she had a chance to comment, he sliced into the water and came up spluttering.

"I feel cheated. You undressed too fast," she teased.

"The wind ssshifted again," he murmured and turned, swimming away from her.

Her clean, strong strokes caught up to him quickly. After sitting in the chill night air, the warm water felt good flowing across her skin. They made several laps, then J'Qhir perched on the underwater ledge at the narrow end of the oval near where they'd dove into the pool. Leith also sat on the ledge further up the side from him.

"You come from a hot, arid world. Where did you learn how to swim?"

"Here, in thisss pool."

Shocked, Leith stared at him. "You didn't know how to swim until you came up here?"

He shook his head, unconcerned.

"You could have easily drowned. Why didn't you tell me? I would have taught you or at least made sure you didn't kill yourself."

"I have obssserved ssswimming." He shrugged. "It ssseemed a sssimple enough processs."

"You could have drowned," Leith repeated. She shuddered at the thought that he might have died.

"But I did not."

"Just because the worst didn't happen, doesn't mean it was the right thing to do." She pushed free of the ledge and floated closer to him. "You put yourself in jeopardy when you didn't need to."

"I honessstly did not think of the consssequencesss. I had no difficulty learning to move in water." He reached for her hand and pulled her to him. "But you are correct. I ssshould not have made the attempt without you."

"No, you should not have." In their own special ritual, she kissed his cheek and crest, then tilted her head and placed her lips on his mouth. The hard contours did not yield and mold to her as supple human flesh would, but his thin, flickering tongue more than made up for it. The warmth he had ignited earlier with his request fanned into a hotter flame in the pit of her belly. She pressed the hard tips of her aching breasts against his chest and let the natural fluctuating current rub them back and forth. He still hadn't decided what to do with them. The Zi did not have breasts.

"You invite me."

"Yesss..." she answered breathlessly.

Beneath the water, she slid her hands down the ribbing of his torso and massaged the hard bulge around his vent.

"I thought—"

She quickly kissed his mouth, stopping his words. "Don't think."

Leith trailed her tongue along his jaw, neck, and across his chest. Taking several breaths and holding the last, she went under the water. She eased her fingers inside his vent and probed until his *jha'i* released into her hand. This was the first time she had actually seen the thing that gave her such pleasure. J'Qhir never released until he was securely nestled against her.

She stroked it a few times, and it lengthened and stiffened under her gentle touch.

179

The clarity of the water and the brilliant moonlight allowed her to see he wasn't quite like a human male. Although she had never examined one this closely, she had seen enough of them in vids and ads to detect the differences. The head was not as large in proportion to the smoother shaft and there was no curvature. Its color was milky white and the texture was incredible softness over incredible hardness. His hands tangled in her hair and tugged, as if he meant for her to stop. Instead, she placed her mouth over the tip and suckled.

His hands tightened and he peaked almost immediately, a flood of warm semen filling her mouth. She choked a little at the suddenness, but she stayed with him until the rigidity left his body. Then she was all too aware of the ache in her lungs and the need to breathe. At the same moment, J'Qhir pulled her up by the strands of her hair. She spat water mixed with his seed and gulped steamy air as he held her above the water. When her breathing returned to normal, he crushed her to him.

"*Qa`anh'al!*" he whispered the one word feverishly. "What do you do to me? You make me crave the forbidden more than I have craved anything in my life...even the sssalvation of my people."

"I'm sorry!" she cried out and flung her arms around his neck. She hugged him fiercely as tears burned her eyes. "I beg forgiveness, J'Qhir. I didn't know. I swear I won't do it again if you don't want me to. Tell me, J'Qhir, teach me what is right and wrong for you so I'll know."

"No, Leith, do not beg my forgivenesss. I am not worthy. You are not at fault." He raised her head and looked into her eyes. "I do not blame you. You tempt me, but I am not forced to give in to the temptation."

"I'm not trying to tempt you."

"I know. There isss no guile in what you do."

She blinked back the tears. "I don't know your ways. I only know mine. On Earth, it is perfectly acceptable for two consenting adults to engage in sexual activity of any kind. There is no stigma attached. Nothing is forbidden."

"On Zi it isss much different. But here, there isss only you and I." He laid her head on his shoulder and pressed his cheek to hers while he fondled strands of wet hair. His voice lowered, and he seemed to be talking more to himself than her. "We may never leave thisss planet. How can I deny usss by adhering to the rulesss of a place I will never sssee again?"

"Have you given up hope?" She allowed tears to fall. If he had given up hope of rescue, what else did they have to look forward to? Years, perhaps decades if they were lucky, of trying to survive and nothing more.

"No, there isss alwaysss hope, but I mussst alssso be realissstic."

"Expect the worst and you won't be disappointed."

"Sss'h. Another of your human sssayingsss."

"One for every occasion."

A cascade of water droplets sprinkled over them. The gray clouds had moved over, covering most of the moon. Leith looked up to find snow falling all around them, thick and fast, but the steam turned the snowflakes to rain directly above the pool.

"We mussst return to the cave."

Leith emerged first and gathered their clothing. As they dressed J'Qhir grew lethargic from exposure to the cold. She helped him finish dressing and wrapped the blankets around him.

After a slow and careful descent down the slippery slope, they welcomed the warmth of the cave. Shivering, Leith piled wood on the fire until it was a raging inferno while J'Qhir huddled close to the flames. They had enough fuel to last a week or longer if used sparingly, but J'Qhir needed the heat now.

Leith undressed and laid out her clothes to dry. Then she sat across the fire from J'Qhir, running her hands through her wet hair to untangle it and allow it to dry faster. Through the flames, J'Qhir watched her.

Suddenly, he threw off the damp beast blanket and spread the solar film over the grass bed. He pulled off his clothes and came around the fire toward her. In one swift motion he picked her up and laid her down on the silky film. He rubbed his forehead gently against hers.

"I would never have watched a moon rissse with T`hirz. Or joined her in the bathing pool. Had ssshe lived, we would never have touched the way you and I do, even ssso many yearsss after our binding. There isss no reassson other than it isss not our way."

Bracing himself on one hand, he used the other to brush her hair aside and expose her ear. He leaned closer and traced the outer rim with his thin tongue. The warm, wet caress sent a chill across her skin and she shivered.

"It isss fassscinating that sssuch a sssmall touch pleasssuresss you."

His breath passed over the wet trail he'd left behind, and Leith moaned, closing her eyes. "Mmmm. It pleasures me very much."

His tongue traveled down her neck and chest, studiously avoiding her breasts, then across her quivering belly.

When he stopped, Leith opened her eyes and saw his eyeslits were very narrow.

"I want to tasssste you the sssame way you have tasssted me. Tell me what to do."

Leith told him and was exquisitely pleased with the results.

Lines of numbers marched across the cave wall where every afternoon Leith had marked another day's passing. She had begun the crude calendar three Standard weeks before, the night after the full moon. She had started with their first day and calculated Paradise's days as well as Earth's. It was now April 6 on Earth.

Leith laid aside the chunk of chalky rock and sighed. Someday all of this would be left behind. If they survived the winter, they would head south to warmer climes. She didn't know if leaving the area where Steve had dropped them was a good idea, but she knew life would be much easier for them if they could find a place with temperate weather.

Leith returned to the fire and her work. J'Qhir had showed her how to make twine by twisting fibers they found underneath tree bark. She had experimented with braiding the lengths of twine into a thicker rope. She was still impatient with the twine and rope making, but it seemed to go faster than making baskets.

After the short snowfall the night of the full moon where less than ten centimeters had fallen, they had experienced another warm spell. They had taken the opportunity to return to the cone tree forest. They had built a litter with sides and brought back as many cones as it could carry.

Leith had experimented with the sugarpod juice and found that the liquid, when spread thin on a flat rock and quick dried with the laserlight, formed a leather that could be rehydrated when boiled in water. It was an excellent way to preserve the last of the pod juice.

Now, J'Qhir entered the cave and unslung the flightpack from his broad shoulder. He had insisted his knee was well enough for him to take a turn at gathering when the weather was warm enough. Leith didn't believe him, but she dared not call him a liar. J'Qhir leaned on his makeshift crutch for a moment before he eased down on the other side of the fire. Leith said nothing. If she asked him, he would tell her he was all right. She knew different. His knee hadn't healed properly, and he would never be able to walk without a limp and pain. He said long soaks in the pool helped, and they probably did temporarily.

She asked him if he was hungry, but he said no. Leith hid a smile. The day she first thought of trying to dry the sugarpod juice, she was going to use the pan from the mess kit, but couldn't find it. After searching the cave, she went looking for J'Qhir to see if he knew where it was. She had found him in the woods with a small fire. He was cutting up one of the giant worms and cooking it in the pan. Quietly, she left him with his secret. On the days she found the pan missing, he wouldn't eat of their stored food. She didn't mind and thought of telling him she knew. But everyone needed a guilty pleasure. She had the sugarpods and he had worms.

With the beast jerky, cone nuts, sugarpod leather, and assorted nuts, dried berries and greens, they had a good chance of surviving the winter if it wasn't too harsh or too long.

Leith bent her head over the rope she was braiding and sighed softly. She still craved a chocolate milkshake!

Chapter 11

"Do you feel it?" J'Qhir whispered and halted the lovely rhythm their joined bodies had achieved.

"Not anymore..." Leith murmured and kissed his tympanum. She wriggled her hips against him impatiently.

"No, Leith. Lisssten!" he hissed and withdrew from her completely. His arms tensed around her. "I hear it now. Do you hear it?"

Leith groaned. *Now* was not the time for J'Qhir's acute senses to pick up the Paradisian version of an ant tunneling through dirt fifty meters away.

"Sss'h!" he warned sharply.

Leith forced her body to remain motionless although she desperately wanted to resume their course to its natural conclusion. How he could stop *at this moment* was incomprehensible to her, yet a part of her hazy mind recognized the urgency in his voice. She strained to hear any strange noises over the gentle lapping of the water and the wind soughing through the trees. The sooner she assured him she could hear nothing, the sooner they could return to what they were doing.

"I don't hear anything," she said and pressed her body against his again. Over the past few weeks, they had made love here in the pool as often as in the cave. She supposed by the time their lives were over, they would have made love over much of the surface of the planet. She nestled her head in the space between his shoulder and neck and dipped her hand beneath the waterline in an attempt to lure him back.

"Leith! A ssship!"

In one quick motion, he hauled her up and out of the water. She clung to his neck as he ran to the alcove. He slowed as colder air gusted around them, but he reached the fire. He set her down and picked up his clothes.

"We h-have to h-hurry," he said haltingly. "It might b-be an Arreisssan ssship."

Leith dressed quickly, her clothing still damp from laundering. The thought of rescue filled her with a different kind of excitement.

"What if it's a pirate ship?" she asked as she drew on her jacket and raised the hood over wet hair.

"Then we mussst convince them it isss in their bessst interessst to take usss with them."

She helped wrap the beast blanket around him and fasten it in place with the sturdy twine. Then she spread the solar film over him.

"Leith, you need thisss."

"You need it more. I'll get cold, but I won't shut down." She adjusted the film and secured the magnostrips.

They kicked dirt over the fire and descended the side of the hill. J'Qhir had pinpointed from which direction the sound came. She hoped he hadn't mistaken another horde of flyers or some other native fauna for the engine of a ship.

J'Qhir led them past their cave and through the woods. As they neared a clearing she remembered from her foraging, he motioned for her to be quiet.

Silently, they moved to the edge of the grassy glade. Passion, adrenaline, and steady movement had kept her warm. Now, standing still, the cold crept into the edge of her hood and sleeves. Her fingers were numb from exposure, and she shoved them into her pockets.

"It isss Terran," J'Qhir whispered.

Leith nodded. The Rover class ship was larger than the lifecraft, but much smaller than the *Catherine McClure*.

The door opened and a ladder ejected. A humanoid emerged dressed in a silver thermosuit, complete with hood. He scanned the immediate area then spoke to someone out of their line of vision before descending the ladder.

"Rohm'dh!" J'Qhir exclaimed at the same time Leith recognized him for a Zi. "What isss Rohm'dh doing on a Terran ssship?"

The second humanoid had exited and was halfway down the rungs. When he set his feet on the ground he was taller than the Zi. Long, unruly brown locks were pulled back and fastened at the nape.

"Drew!" Leith pointed. "Drew Garrison!"

Suddenly, Leith found herself running as fast as she could, running toward Drew and rescue. When Drew recognized her, he broke into a run also. When they met in the center of the glade, she threw her arms about him and he swung her up and around. Both were laughing and Leith was crying as he put her down. She held Drew's lovable face in her hands and kissed him soundly.

"Leith, Leith!" Drew grinned widely and hugged her again. "Everyone thinks you're dead."

"Not for lack of Steve trying. Steve Hancock marooned us here."

"We know, Leith. We pieced it together."

A third humanoid had emerged from the Rover. It was Corru, the Paxian who had attended their meeting on Arreis.

"How did you three get together?" Leith asked, but her voice trailed off as J'Qhir joined them. J'Qhir. She slipped from Drew's arms and studied J'Qhir. As usual, his face was expressionless. His eyes flickered once toward the other Zi before shifting back to her.

She understood completely. No open expression of their relationship. Nothing to give away their intimacy. She couldn't tease him or touch him or kiss him. Couldn't make love to him. If she remembered the layout of this class ship correctly, all areas on the upper deck except the facilities were open. No privacy. They wouldn't even have a place to talk. If she didn't find a way to have a few minutes alone with J'Qhir before they left, she had no idea when it would be possible.

Rohm'dh could not even suspect there was more to their relationship until J'Qhir was ready to bring it out into the open.

J'Qhir's saurian eyes, slits narrowed to almost nothing, pierced Drew coldly.

"Captain Drew Garrison, a pilot for McClure Shipping and an old friend," Leith introduced him.

"Hey, I'm not that old," Drew teased.

"This is Warrior J'Qhir."

Drew held out his hand, but J'Qhir ignored it. Drew shrugged and put his arm around her again.

"I want to thank you for taking care of Leith—"

"Msss. McClure isss quite capable of taking care of herssself," he said crisply, then turned and limped toward Rohm'dh. They spoke in the low, guttural tones of Zi.

"Not too friendly, is he?" Drew observed. "It must have been a rough six weeks, stuck with him."

Leith smiled at J'Qhir's retreating back. "He doesn't know you, that's all. He's quite...friendly once you break through his reserve." Leith tore her eyes away from J'Qhir. "How's Dad?"

"He's doing good. He still has a few months of recovery, but he's on schedule. No setbacks."

"Oh, I'm so glad. I've been worried about him. And Mom?"

"She's fine, too, but neither of them took your alleged death well. They didn't accept it at first, and they couldn't believe J'Qhir would do what Steve and the media said he'd done. Hell, I couldn't believe it either, but none of us suspected Steve."

"It came as a shock to me, too. And I don't completely understand why he didn't kill us outright instead of marooning us here. This planet is a paradise. He should have known we had a good chance of surviving."

"Basically, Steve is a coward. I've known that about him for years. If he got caught, you two would still be alive. He wouldn't be charged with murder."

"What about Wiley? Steve hinted he fixed the stolen ship so Wiley wouldn't survive."

Drew shrugged. "I don't know what to tell you. I don't know what was going through his farking mind."

Leith glanced at J'Qhir who was still deep in conversation with the smaller Zi. She looked back to Drew. "Do Mom and Dad know you came looking for me?"

Drew shook his head, dark brown hair coming loose from its fastening. "I couldn't tell them, Leith. Didn't want to get their hopes up. I took a vacation leave and borrowed the *Starfire*. Before all this came up, Cameron had been urging me to use one of the smaller ships and take some time off. He thought it strange that I chose to do it in the middle of this crisis, but he agreed."

"As soon as we get aboard, I'll put a call through to them on LinkNet," Leith said.

"If you can get through. A transmitter in this sector blew. Calls have to be re-routed, and it's taking a helluva lot longer than usual for them to go through." Suddenly, Drew threw his arms around her and hugged her until her feet left the ground. Over Drew's shoulder she saw J'Qhir watching them. "Are you ready to go home?"

Oh, yes, she wanted to go home...but she wanted to stay, too. She wanted more time with J'Qhir. She would never wish they hadn't been rescued, but why couldn't it have been later? They never had a chance to speak of a future off Paradise. Once they left the planet, everything between them would change.

"Leith? You are ready to go home, aren't you?"

"Of course," she answered quickly and slid from Drew's bear hug. "I'm sure Warrior J'Qhir will want to wipe out every trace of our presence on this planet before we leave. Come on. I'll show you where we've been living."

Leith took his hand and tugged. She had to get away from the sight of J'Qhir right then. At the thought of the cave, she suddenly remembered their sleeping arrangements. If Rohm'dh saw it before Leith could rearrange things, he would know they had shared a bed. For J'Qhir's sake, he couldn't see the lone pallet of grass and leaves.

When Leith and Drew reached the trees, she broke into a run, pulling him faster. When Drew hesitated and didn't move fast enough for her, she let go of his hand and sped faster through the woods.

"What's wrong, Leith?" he shouted after her.

"I'll explain later," Leith called over her shoulder.

Inside the cave, Leith started tearing the bed apart and tossing the leaves and grass on the fire. She did it methodically, mechanically. If she stopped to think about it, she might cry. She and J'Qhir had shared and discovered so much in this one place. She could hardly bear to destroy it.

Drew entered the cave and walked to her. "God, Leith, you look like you've lost your best friend."

Leith smiled up at him. "You're my best friend and you're not lost."

"No, but you were." Drew squatted beside her and helped burn the bedding. "We thought you were dead and, I tell you, Leith, something inside of me died too."

"Oh, Drew." She patted his hand. "Hey, now that you know I'm alive, maybe that part of you will resurrect itself."

"Already has," he said with the boyish grin she remembered from childhood. "I felt it come back to life when I saw you run across that clearing."

By the time J'Qhir and Rohm'dh arrived, Leith and Drew had cleared away every trace that she and J'Qhir had shared one bed. J'Qhir stopped short just inside the doorway, and his gaze swept the room, resting briefly on her. She couldn't tell if he was pleased or not, but since no expression crossed his face, she thought she had done well.

Leith cleared her throat. "I've started cleaning up."

J'Qhir nodded. "Corru hasss returned to the ssship."

Leith looked at Rohm'dh who remained a respectful distance behind J'Qhir. She had assumed all Zi were as tall and broad as J'Qhir, but Rohm'dh was not much taller than she and not much broader. Leith bit her lip. It was one of a thousand questions she suddenly needed to ask J'Qhir but couldn't. Later, when Rohm'dh wasn't near.

"We need to dessstroy everything," J'Qhir said. "We cannot leave anything behind that could posssibly one day affect the development of thisss planet."

"The quickest, most efficient way would be to burn it. I have a laserlight," Drew offered and pulled one from his pocket.

"We have one, too," Leith said. She stared at the dozen baskets they had spent many tedious hours laboring over. Hers had improved from the first lopsided attempt to those that were almost as well made as J'Qhir's. She crossed the cave and snatched up the misshapen basket. Patiently, J'Qhir had sat by her side, directing her clumsy fingers.

She surveyed the rest of the baskets which held their supplies and represented weeks of work. She heard Drew change the setting on his laserlight and whirled to face him.

"No, Drew!"

"Thessse thingsss mussst be dessstroyed," J'Qhir said softly.

"I know. I mean—" She broke off and swallowed hard. "Drew, is there a packing skid on the ship?"

He nodded. "The *Starfire* is equipped with a couple of small ones."

"We worked too hard to just destroy all of this. I want to take it with me. Would you get one of the skids from the ship, please?"

"Sure," Drew said and left the cave.

Leith wished she could think of a way to get rid of the other Zi for a few moments, but he seemed intent on remaining by J'Qhir's side

"Wassste not, want not," J'Qhir commented.

Leith's eyes met his. "What?"

"Another of your human sssayingsss."

192

"Y-Yes," Leith agreed. "Yes, it seems a shame to waste the food."

But it wasn't the reason she wanted to take it with her. She would freeze-dry the food and save it for later. She imagined preparing a meal with what they had collected and savoring the memories along with the flavors.

Drew returned with the packing skid, and they quickly loaded it. All in all, it was a pitifully small amount, and she wondered how they had ever hoped to survive a winter. As she and Drew packed, J'Qhir spread dirt over the fire and scattered the stones.

J'Qhir remembered the calendar on the wall. He took the laserlight from Drew and burned away the marks. She dared not look at him as the laser passed over the circled date some four Standard weeks before. She felt foolish for the sentimental feelings that rose within her over scratchings on a cave wall. When all were gone and she looked over the empty cave, she felt as if she had lost something precious.

She felt J'Qhir's eyes on her then, and she glanced at him briefly. She smiled, but he only watched her a moment, his saurian eyes bright, before turning to Drew and handing him the laserlight. The moment was gone before she could react.

The cave was now as J'Qhir had found it, nothing to mark their passage. Only memories were left. Leith looked back once as they left the cave for the final time.

Aboard the *Starfire,* Leith and J'Qhir were outfitted with thermosuits, lightweight jumpsuits with environmental regulators adjustable by the individual. Leith added the blankets to the packing skid, and Drew stored it in the small hold.

Leith surveyed the interior of the ship, dismayed to find that she had been correct. The upper deck—bridge, galley, and sleeping quarters—was one open area. Only the cramped facilities were enclosed for privacy. She and J'Qhir would never have a moment without being under Rohm'dh's scrutiny. And neither of them would have any reason to visit the lower deck, especially at the same time.

"I've put a call through to your parents on LinkNet, as well as a call to the Galactic Police, but I don't know when they'll go through," Drew told her. "According to the report on ENet, the transmitter station in this sector has malfunctioned. They're trying to re-route communications, but it could be Standard days."

Leith sighed. The emergency channel, ENet, could only be used in the case of life-threatening situations. Since nothing threatened them at the moment, in fact, all threats had been removed, they would be heavily penalized if they used the channel.

After a brief discussion, they decided to return to Arreis, where it had all began. The nearest planet was Artilia, but the Artilians did not like off-worlders. Arreis and Artilia were in the same system, yet had little to do with one another. Neutrality was all they had in common. Arreis had become the trading bastion of this sector, where all were welcome and the GP had no authority. The Artilians, on the other hand, discouraged visitors except for a limited number allowed to observe an indigenous phenomenon called the Penelaape Arcs. The privileged tourists paid well for the opportunity.

During a meal of "real" food, Drew prompted Leith. "Tell us what happened."

She related the series of events, beginning with her father's illness, which led to her temporary command of McClure Shipping, up until J'Qhir heard the *Starfire* land. She omitted J'Qhir's attempt at the Zi failure ritual and their intimacy. "It took some adjusting, but water and food were plentiful. I think we would have survived, barring a fatal illness or accident, especially when we moved to warmer climes nearer the equator in the spring. Now, how did you three get together?"

"I think Corru ought to begin the story." Drew motioned to Corru. Feathers ruffling, the Paxian declined with a tilt of his head. Corru was, Leith observed, a quiet being although she didn't know if this was a trait of the Paxians in general or Corru in particular. He had said little at their initial meeting, other than to keep the participants focused.

"As I understand it," Drew began, "when Corru left you outside the tavern on Arreis, he was followed and attacked in an alley."

"Were they human?" Leith interrupted, directing her question to Corru.

"Yes," he confirmed.

"Steve set it up," Leith explained. "Just before we left the tavern, he stopped short and I ran into him. He nodded toward a group of humans sitting at a table in the far corner."

"We thought as much. Anyway, they meant to leave him for dead, but the Paxians are tougher than they look. Shortly afterward, he was found and security rushed him to a med unit. Unfortunately, he was in a coma until a few weeks ago. By the time he regained consciousness, the story of the Warrior's and your disappearance was old news. It was several days before he learned what had happened. Corru knows the Warrior well and didn't believe the story Steve had concocted, even though almost everyone else in the galaxy did. He returned to Arreis to start his own investigation. That's where he met Lieutenant Rohm'dh."

Everyone turned to the smaller Zi. His saurian eyes blinked rapidly at the sudden attention. "Beg forgivenesss, mine Terran Ssstandard isss not well. Continue?"

Leith shivered inwardly. It was strange to hear the sibilant speech coming from someone other than J'Qhir.

Drew shrugged and continued. "Rohm'dh refused to believe the Warrior would disgrace his position or his people by denouncing his government, kidnapping a human, or any of the other things Steve made it look like he'd done. At the risk to his own position within the Zi Force, and if I understand correctly, much greater risk to his clan's position in Zi society, he made enough noise that the Council authorized him to investigate what happened on Arreis."

"Elder M'Bat`h give authorize," Rohm'dh clarified.

Leith noticed how J'Qhir's eyes widened as if he were surprised M'Bat`h, the Elder who had been his father-in-law and always opposed him, would care if he were found and the truth known. Leith wanted to point out that M'Bat`h might not like him, might even hold him accountable for T`hirz's death in some irrational way as J'Qhir believed, but M'Bat`h also knew J'Qhir and knew he'd never do anything dishonorable.

"Corru and Rohm'dh ran into one another on Arreis and compared notes. Still, they had no proof, only speculation. They would have gone to Cameron, but Corru knew of his illness, so they had to settle for me."

"Drew!"

He laughed and chucked her chin. "Cameron had his suspicions all along. Truth to tell, so did I. Although neither of us really suspected Steve. If we had, I might have checked the encoded log of the *Catherine McClure* sooner."

"Surely, Steve had the foresight to change the log." Leith shook her head. "He's crazy, but he's not stupid."

"No, Steve isn't stupid, but he is farking crazy if he ever thought this scheme would work. Too many variables, like Corru surviving the attack and Rohm'dh's faith in the Warrior and a nice feature of the latest starships. I don't know if he never knew about it or forgot about it or assumed his plan was so brilliant no one would ever doubt him. The primary log is the normal log every ship has. It can be easily altered if one knows how. But the newest ships have an auxiliary log. The encryption code is virtually impossible to break. Most encryptions are broken within days of release to the public. This has been on the market six Standard months and no one has broken it yet."

Leith shook her head. "Steve stays on top of new developments. We were supposed to take one of the older ships, but there was a mix-up and it was leased out the morning before we left. Steve was furious. He tried to recall several of the older ships, but none of them could be returned in time. The *Catherine McClure* was the only one available large enough to hold the cargo. If he already had his plans in place and contacted the Crucians, he had to take the chance."

"Well, it was one of several mistakes he made and the most damaging. Everything else was pure conjecture, but this was concrete proof against him. The log clearly indicated the trip to Paradise when he said he'd left Arreis only after he'd been given clearance and returned straight to Earth. We decided he had to have left you two on that planet."

Drew went on to detail their trip to Paradise, but Leith stopped listening. The food she had eaten had tasted wonderful, but it didn't seem to be settling well on her stomach and threatened to come back up. She tried to draw in deep, even breaths, and after a few moments the nausea passed.

Corru had wrapped himself in his voluminous wings and appeared to be meditating. Drew, J'Qhir, and Rohm'dh had gravitated toward the bridge consoles. Drew happily explained

197

the meanings of all the buttons, dials, and lights while J'Qhir and Rohm'dh listened intently. Leith drew near them and watched a while.

She was all too aware of J'Qhir, how close she was to him in the confining quarters, yet how far away she was in that she could not touch him or speak to him the way she wanted. When J'Qhir never once looked her way, she sighed softly, and started to walk away. At her movement, J'Qhir turned toward her. His amber eyes blinked once, but otherwise his expression did not change as he returned his attention to Drew.

Leith calmly walked away from them, but inside she was inconsolable. She maintained a steady pace until she reached the bunks. With careful, deliberate movements, she climbed the ladder and lowered the bunk at the top of the tier of three. After crawling onto the mattress, she pulled the curtain for a modicum of privacy.

She didn't give in to the hollow sobs that threatened to shake her body, but tears filled her eyes and overflowed. She wiped them away as quickly as they fell, dampening her fingers and the thin pillow beneath her head.

Another wave of nausea rippled through her, as if her stomach rebelled against the food she'd eaten. She decided it was the sudden change in diet as well as emotional stress. She swallowed hard and closed her eyes, waiting for the ill feeling to go away.

Leith slept and a couple of hours later when Drew woke her the nausea had gone. Her eyes felt swollen and grainy, and Drew asked her how she was feeling.

"I'm fine," she assured him. "Have the calls gone through yet?"

He shook his head. "If it takes much longer, we'll have you back on Earth and you can tell your parents in person that you're alive before the call ever gets through to them."

"How long before we reach Arreis?" Leith asked as she descended the ladder. As she stepped off the last rung, a mild wave of nausea hit her. Drew had his back to her and couldn't see her. She clung to the ladder and closed her eyes until it passed.

"Another eight Standard hours. The *Starfire* could make it in less time, but I'd rather not push her. Nothing beats a Rover in short bursts, but it's better to keep her at a moderate speed over long distances."

Leith nodded and followed Drew toward the bridge. J'Qhir and Rohm'dh were still studying the control panels. Corru hadn't moved from his meditation. Leith sat and pulled a viewer into place. With nothing else to do, she could catch up on news of the past two months. The ship's library would have past news accounts in its backlog. Perhaps later they all could watch a vid together.

She had viewed several weeks' worth of news when J'Qhir called out, "Captain Garrissson."

Leith looked up from the viewer and warmed at the sound of his voice. She wished she could sit with him, as they had atop the hill, watching the starscape slip by on the large viewer above the control consoles. Her body ached for some physical touch from him and the closeness they couldn't demonstrate in front of Rohm'dh. If only he wasn't here. But if not for Rohm'dh, Drew might very well have put off Corru or ignored his own concern. She couldn't wish Rohm'dh hadn't become involved, but she could wish that Drew had brought a larger ship.

"It's another ship, Stellar class. According to the I.D. imprint, the ship is the *Brimstone.* It's within hailing distance,"

Drew commented as he examined the readouts. "I'll contact them and see if they've managed to get a call through on LinkNet."

Drew punched buttons on the comm panel and spoke clearly, identifying himself and the *Starfire*. He waited a few moments and when no response came, repeated the hail.

Starfire and *Brimstone*...a shiver ran up her spine at the ominous connotation.

Finally, communication opened between the two ships and Drew punched one more button. The large viewer flickered, went black, then a face appeared onscreen.

J'Qhir was the first to react. "Hancock!"

Chapter 12

Leith froze as the life-sized image of Steve Hancock fuzzed then cleared to crystal sharp resolution. She felt as if he were actually present on the Rover, once again looming over her, demanding her complete attention. She pushed the small viewer out of her way and started to rise, but she realized there was nowhere to run as well as no reason. He was aboard the other ship, not the *Starfire*.

She held her breath and tried to steady her nerves as Steve looked at each of them in turn. His gaze rested on Drew.

"Well, Captain Garrison, you managed to find them. Maybe you're not the dorgian pilot I've always said you were." His dark eyes lit on Corru, who had unfurled his wings and stood. "The Paxian is still alive, I see. Tsk, tsk. I knew I should have taken care of you personally."

Drew scowled. "Give it up, Steve. As you can see, it didn't work. I've already contacted the GPs—"

"I don't think so, Captain. LinkNet is still jammed in this sector because of a blown transmitter. They don't expect it to be up and running for another twelve Standard hours. Don't try to bluff, Drew. You're no good at it. Remember who always won at Martian poker."

Drew's face flushed red. "We always suspected you cheated, Steve, but no one could ever prove it."

Steve laughed. "Sure, blame me for your lack of skill. Ah, Leith..." He turned his eyes on her and the humor left them. "Sorry your vacation was cut short. Did you enjoy yourself?"

Even though she was separated from J'Qhir by several meters, she sensed him tense as Steve addressed her. Before Leith could frame a suitable caustic reply, J'Qhir spoke, drawing Steve's attention away from her.

"Your plan hasss failed, Hancock."

Steve cut his eyes to J'Qhir, then to the smaller Zi, and back again to J'Qhir. "Two Reps with one stroke. I consider this my lucky day."

"What the hell—" Drew suddenly shouted and lunged at the control panel, frantically punching buttons. "Are you insane?"

Steve's frenetic laughter answered Drew's question. His image winked out to be replaced with the radar scan. Leith saw the blip that represented the *Starfire* and the slightly larger blip of Steve's ship...and the torpedo pulse that traveled between them. Steve had fired at them!

"Defense shields are powering up, but they might not reach max before it hits," Drew shouted. "Harness up and hang on!"

Leith barely had time to snap the harness in place before the *Starfire* pitched to starboard upon impact. Neither J'Qhir nor Rohm'dh had harnessed up, but both remained in their seats. She glanced at Corru who had returned to his seat, the harness secure over his shoulders.

"Dammit! The bastard knows what he's doing." Drew's fingers flew over the controls. "I opened the SOS beacon, but the torpedo demolished that section before the shields hit max."

"Can it be repaired?" J'Qhir asked, snapping his harness in place.

Drew shook his head. "I don't know. Damage is extensive. Here comes another one. Besides, we won't get a chance to make repairs if he keeps throwing torpedoes at us."

This time, the *Starfire* rocked to port.

Drew examined the readouts. "Shields are holding at one hundred percent, but a few more hits, and they'll start to deteriorate. I'm going to try to outrun him, but it's a Stellar class ship and he'll catch up before we can reach the nearest port."

Leith closed her eyes. She thought being rescued meant being safe, but she hadn't counted on Steve's desperation or tenacity.

It was over, wasn't it? A Rover couldn't outrun a Stellar, and the smaller ship wasn't outfitted for battle. Its main defenses were the powerful shields and ability to gain high speeds at short distances. Rovers weren't built for deep space exploration and great distances. She watched as Drew fired back at the *Brimstone*, but the torpedo pulses were like mosquitoes buzzing around a human—annoying but hardly lethal.

She listened as J'Qhir made suggestions for defensive maneuvers. Drew put them into action, avoiding the next three torpedoes. Leith knew Drew was an excellent pilot, but he had never been in a real battle. Simulations were not the same as actual wartime experiences. Drew wisely turned the helm over to J'Qhir's console. The wait, if only in seconds, of J'Qhir having to explain a tactical maneuver could mean life or death for them.

All of this only delayed the inevitable. Leith opened her eyes and reconfigured the viewer in front of her to display the same readings as the control panel. According to the readouts, the *Brimstone* would catch up to them and erode the defense shields long before they reached the safety of a planet, just as Drew predicted. Steve had already cut off their path to Arreis, and they headed in another direction. Before Leith could determine the nearest planet, a salvo of torpedoes hit and Leith rolled with the ship.

"His system is computing your maneuvers," Drew explained, "and anticipating the next move before firing."

J'Qhir nodded. Leith could only see the back of his head, but she could imagine the grim determination on his face as he concentrated.

They were going to die. The worst part was Steve would probably get away with it. The only beings who knew his plans were on this ship. Once they were dead, Steve could concoct a plausible story. He probably already had an alibi in place for this time period.

Leith released the harness and stood. Everyone's attention was on the viewer or controls. Even Corru didn't notice as she slipped to the back of the ship. The next salvo of torpedoes hit and Leith, clinging to the edge of a bunk, remained on her feet.

"Shields at ninety-four percent," Drew announced.

Leith pushed the button to open the tube door. On a ship as small as a Rover there was no lift, only a ladder between the two decks. She swung onto the rungs and placed the insides of her booted feet firmly against the outsides of the ladder, then slid all the way down. Steve chose this moment to send another salvo against them. Slightly off balance from her rapid descent, what few seconds she had saved were wasted as she fell against the bulkhead. Her hold on the ladder prevented her from going down.

The secondary control room was to her immediate left. She sat in the lone chair and snapped the harness in place.

The room was barely larger than the facilities, yet the ship could be operated from here if the main bridge were damaged or destroyed. Leith had taken the required basic flight courses in school. She could fly a ship the size of the Rover, but since she wasn't here to take over command, her eyes bypassed the flight controls and settled on the communications panel.

Leith had decided if they were destined to die by Steve's hand, the universe would still learn of his treachery as well as the truth concerning the Zi-Crucian conflict. Leith took a few moments to gather her thoughts, pressed the record button, and began to speak into the microphone.

Fifteen Standard minutes and two torpedo salvos later, she turned off the recorder. She hadn't explained the situation as eloquently as J'Qhir since she lacked the passion of the oppressed, but she tried to remember his words and repeated as much as she could.

Unfortunately, message beacons couldn't penetrate the defense shields. With shields up, they were essentially cut off from all communications, but she had seen a trick used in a vid last summer and hoped it was based on reality. If not, her only hope was the survival of the black box. She had inserted her recording in with the continual stream of the ship's data. A ship could be blown to stardust, but the black box usually survived. A wry smile crossed her lips as she thought of the old joke, if the black box was indestructible, why didn't they make the ship out of the same material? She had never heard a satisfactory answer to the question.

And then it occurred to her how many things she would never learn or do. Her life would end here and now. She thought of her parents and tears filled her eyes. She would never see them again. They already thought she was dead, but then they would learn she had been alive and rescued only to succumb to Steve's drive for vengeance. They would have to grieve all over again. She wished she could somehow spare her parents, but the only way was to delete her recording. In this instance, the salvation of an entire species was more important.

She thought of J'Qhir, of their differences both physical and cultural. She regretted only that she had never told him she loved him. Until this moment, she had believed she couldn't truly love him. Because of their differences, yes, she had to admit that, but also because they had known each other for such a short time. Love, she believed, a deep and abiding love developed over time, aged like fine wine, and withstood the test of time as well as hardships. Until now, she thought their physical intimacy was the result of their situation, nothing more. Two abandoned souls reaching out to one another rather than face the empty loneliness of a lifetime.

In these last few moments of her life, she realized with crystal clarity, she loved J'Qhir. With the realization came the resolve to tell him before they died. When she finished here, she would return to the upper deck. She would stand behind him and lay her hands on his broad shoulders, to have a connection to him when the end came. She would wait for a moment in between attacks, when she wouldn't be a distraction. She would share with him one last kiss and tell him that she loved him. The action would shock Rohm'dh, but she didn't care and she hoped J'Qhir didn't either. She didn't think her declaration of love would mean much to J'Qhir because he had never spoken of love in any context, but it would give her the strength to face whatever lay beyond death.

Leith wiped the blurring tears from her eyes and glanced at the readouts. Shields were at seventy-nine percent. She remembered from the battle simulation course that with standard torpedo pulses shields lost five to seven percent with each hit until they reached sixty percent. After that, percentage loss was geometrical and the chances of shield recovery were slim and none.

Leith prepared the message for general dispersal and pushed the send button. Under normal conditions, the send light would flash green and automatically spew the message into all subspace frequencies. With the defense shields up, a flashing red light warned the message wasn't going through. The trick was in the torpedo pulses. Upon impact, the shields disintegrated for a few nanoseconds, then rebuilt. At the point of disintegration, the message would deploy.

Leith watched the panels. For every ten salvos the *Brimstone* tossed at them, only one scored a hit due to J'Qhir and Rohm'dh's expertise. If not for them, the *Starfire* would have been blasted to stardust long ago. As each salvo grew closer, Leith kept her eyes on the send indicator and braced herself. When at last a torpedo hit, the indicator light briefly turned green then resumed its annoying red flashing.

Satisfied, Leith released the harness and stood. She would leave the message to be deployed as many times as possible before the destruction of the *Starfire*. She had no hope that someone would receive the message in time to save them. Subspace communication was excruciatingly slow, but the message would eventually be heard and the word spread.

Leith hurried to J'Qhir's side. She was inside the tube and halfway up the ladder when the next salvo hit. Unprepared, the force knocked her backwards off the ladder. She crashed into the bulkhead and fell to the deck. Pain ripped through her head as stars burst across her eyes. When the lights faded, blackness consumed her and she lost consciousness.

Leith opened her eyes to find Drew perched at her side on a bottom bunk. He held a coldpack to the side of her head. She saw movement at the edge of her vision and turned, much too quickly, but caught a glimpse of J'Qhir as he paced back and forth between the sleeping area and bridge. She brushed Drew's hand away.

"Are we—" She stopped short and bit her lip. She had almost asked, *Are we dead?*, but she didn't believe the afterlife would be eternity aboard a Rover. Somehow they had survived. Somehow the *Starfire* had outrun or out-maneuvered the *Brimstone*. Somehow the danger was past because Drew was too calm.

At the sound of her voice, J'Qhir had stopped pacing. He hovered near, but not too close, just out of range of her sight.

"We're safe," Drew assured her and tried to replace the coldpack, but she pushed him away again. "You have a concussion. How are you feeling?"

"I'm fine," she said a little too loudly and started to sit up.

Drew placed his hands on her shoulders and forced her to lie back again. She didn't argue. The Rover had begun to spin around her, and the pounding in her head increased.

"The med said you shouldn't move."

"What med?" As far as she knew, there had been no med aboard the Rover unless he had been hiding in the hold.

"From the Artilian ship that's towing us in."

"Artilian?"

"By the time it was all over, we were closer to Artilia than Arreis anyway. The Artilian ship picked up one of the messages you sent and came to help. The *Starfire* took a beating, so they're towing us to Artilia." Drew tightened the hand he'd left on one shoulder. "Steve's dead."

Relief flooded through her. "I hate to say it, but I'm glad. How did it happen?"

"It was amazing, Leith. The shields were all but gone, and the *Brimstone* had almost caught up to us. We were bombarded with torpedo salvos. Steve made the mistake of following too closely. J'Qhir kept turning in ever tightening circles until he suddenly switchbacked and the *Brimstone* followed along, getting caught in its own crossfire. I still don't know how J'Qhir did it. Anyway, Steve was blown to stardust along with the ship."

"Steve is insane, but he's not stupid," Leith said uneasily. She'd said the same thing earlier when Drew told them about the auxiliary log encoded in the *Catherine McClure*. It was one thing for him to ignore something he had no control over and hope for the best, but quite another to blindly get caught in a maneuver, however complex. Steve was a better pilot than that.

"Maybe one of his dorgs was actually at the helm," Drew suggested.

"Maybe," Leith agreed. She hardly knew Carter or Phillips, but neither was a pilot. They were crewmembers hired by the job and had worked for McClure Shipping on and off for years. Drifters, who would never settle down in one place and hired on any ship that would take them, were said to be starkissed, always lured into space by the promise of the stars. Then Leith remembered another reason one could be called starkissed…if one loved an alien. She liked this definition much better.

If Steve had let one of them navigate while he blithely manned the weapons console, it was possible he was too caught up in the certain destruction of the *Starfire* to notice the tricky maneuver.

Leith let Steve slide from her mind. He was gone and it was for the best. She tried once more to sit up, to see J'Qhir, but Drew wouldn't allow it.

"The med examined you and said you should be fine, but he was firm in saying you shouldn't get up until we reach Artilia where he can scan you thoroughly."

Leith reluctantly settled back down.

"We didn't know why you were in the hold." Drew leaned in and lowered his voice. "The big guy brought you up the ladder. How he did it with that injury of his, I don't know."

Leith closed her eyes. The one chance when they could have had a few moments of privacy and she had to be unconscious.

"I know you're tired, Leith, but the med said if you came to, you shouldn't go back to sleep. And I should look for signs of sluggishness, incoherence, and disorientation. You don't seem to be suffering from any of those."

She opened her eyes to appease Drew. "I'm not sleepy."

"Good. Anyway, we had no idea why you were on the lower deck until the Artilian ship came along and informed us of the message you sent out. Our communications are gone except for subspace transmission. We docked with their ship and they sent their med over. He didn't want to move you over to their ship then have to move you again when we reach Artilia."

"I saw it in a vid." Leith explained what she had done. "I didn't know if it would work, but when the torpedo hit, the light turned green."

"Well, according to the Artilians, they're not the only ones who picked it up. Every major planet in this sector is sending a media team to Artilia."

"What! They can't do that!" Leith exploded then shrank back into her pillow. "Artilia has strict controls about who they let on their world."

"It's part of the standard treaty with the Galactic Alliance. If they become involved in an interstellar incident, no matter how tangential their involvement or how inconsequential the incident, they have to allow the Alliance Board, the GPs, and any media representatives from any Alliance members on their world. When Steve included the Zi, he created the interstellar incident to end all interstellar incidents."

"What are you saying?" Leith asked warily.

"I didn't have a chance to tell you before, but when Steve made it appear a Zi had rebelled, it brought Zi to the attention of the galaxy. The Alliance Board was on the verge of a full-scale investigation into the Zi-Crucian conflict when Corru, Rohm'dh, and I put the pieces together. Now that your little message has gone out over LinkNet—"

"LinkNet! I thought the transmitter was down in this sector."

"Oh, didn't I tell you? It's been repaired."

"No, you didn't tell me," Leith said dryly. "Just how long have I been unconscious?"

"Only a few Standard hours. We should be reaching Artilia soon."

"All of this has happened in just a few hours? It sounds like I've been out for days."

Drew shrugged. "You know how the media jumps on things. Once your message went out on LinkNet there was no way to stop them. They'll claim media rights and overrun Artilia within Standard days. The Alliance hasn't made an official announcement yet, but speculation is the board will reconvene on Artilia within a Standard week to negotiate with the Zi delegates about Zi joining the Galactic Alliance."

"We were supposed to go to Arreis," Leith groaned. "The Arreisans wouldn't mind all the attention."

"It might not have mattered anyway. You know negotiation sites are normally picked at random among the neutral worlds. It could have been Artilia as easily as any of them."

"Nura will kill me."

"Nura won't kill you." Drew laughed. "She'll love all the excitement. She told me once how she wished Artilia would open up more."

Leith didn't think Nura meant like this. Nura had roomed with Leith during her year on Earth. The Artilians, while not as reclusive as the Zi, kept contact with others to a minimum. Nura had been granted a year to continue her studies elsewhere and she chose Earth. Leith had met Nura her first day at the university. Not an outgoing person herself, Leith had felt sorry for the pale Artilian who seemed to wither in the sultry heat of late summer.

Somehow, the two had become fast friends. Probably, Leith decided, because neither of them was demanding as a friend. Nura readily accepted Leith's offer to share quarters. At the end of her year, Nura was genuinely reluctant to leave. At the same time, she was anxious to return home to her family. Since then, they had kept in touch regularly.

"You're right. Nura won't mind, but Artilia will ban me from this sector."

"None of this is your fault."

"Isn't it? If I'd only realized how far Steve would go to get what he wanted. If I'd only been paying attention to what was going on around me, I might have stopped him."

"None of us knew," Drew pointed out. "Hell, Cameron was closer to him than any of us before his illness, and he never suspected Steve had any ulterior motives."

"J'Qhir suggested that Steve caused Dad's illness, maybe even meant to kill him."

"After we started putting the pieces together, Corru and I discussed the possibility. Cameron's illness was too much of a coincidence. Steve was off-Earth as much as the rest of us. He could have obtained the Snow Fever virus anywhere."

A thin beep sounded from the bridge.

"That's the Artilian ship. We're probably ready to land." Drew stood. "Rest, but don't sleep until the med has a chance to examine you. Captain's orders."

Leith put on a stern face and saluted him. "Aye, aye, sir."

Drew flashed her his boyish grin and hurried to the bridge.

Leith eased over as far as she could and craned her neck, but she still only saw part of J'Qhir. He hovered near out of concern for her, she knew. If only he would take a few steps closer so she could beckon him to her. If she called out, Rohm'dh would hear.

At the thought of his name, the smaller Zi passed by the end of the bunk tiers, and Leith heard the door to the facilities slide open then close. Taking advantage of the situation, J'Qhir stepped into the sleeping area.

"You are all right?" he asked as he moved toward her. He stopped a few paces away from the bunk and looked down at her, amber eyes unblinking.

"I am somewhere in the middle," she said and smiled a little.

"I am glad you are not all left," he said softly.

She wanted to hold out her arms to him and have him hold her close as he had done so many times before. He kept the distance between them deliberately, and she had to respect his decision no matter how much it hurt.

"Drew told me what you did. About Steve. Thank you."

"It wasss my pleasssure," he said with no trace of humor.

"I wish I could have seen it. It's a relief to know he's truly gone and can do us no more harm." She rubbed her hands over her face and looked up at him. "J'Qhir—"

The door to the facilities opened and closed, and J'Qhir stepped back a pace. He was withdrawing again. They had wasted their few precious moments in idle chatter when they could have used the time more wisely. Maybe neither of them wanted to hear what the other had to say.

Leith closed her eyes against the sight of him and heard his quiet footfalls as he left the sleeping area without saying another word.

Chapter 13

Artilia

Settled in the spacious guesthouse in the capital city of Katasa~ri, the first thing Leith did was take a bubble bath and wash her hair with shampoo. After soaking until the water cooled, she dressed in a white robe of cloth as soft as well-washed Terran cotton. She carried a tea tray and handheld viewer outside through the double doors where delicate lacey wickerwork chairs and table furnished the terrace. A light breeze blew over her damp skin and began to dry her hair. She sat and poured a cup of steaming tea.

They had arrived in the middle of the deep purple Artilian night and were carried to the medical facility. She and J'Qhir were taken to different areas, and she hadn't seen him since. After a thorough examination and treatment, she was allowed to sleep the remainder of the night.

When she awoke, the bump on her head had all but disappeared. She and Drew, who had slept in a comfortable chair in her room, were escorted to a guesthouse in the visitor section of the city. Drew told her that J'Qhir had been released during the night and he and Rohm'dh were in this guesthouse as well. Drew also informed her that Corru had left Artilia already and sent her his regards.

The thin sunlight of Artilia reminded her of Paradise, and she closed her eyes. She wanted to go back, just for a few days, so she and J'Qhir could have the opportunity to sort through their options and make a decision before being thrown back into civilization.

Leith opened her eyes and sipped the sweet tea as she logged onto LinkNet. The link took awhile, but after the initial connection, transmission was instantaneous.

"Leith, sweetheart, how are you?"

"Hi, Mom." She spent ten minutes reassuring Catherine McClure that she was fine. "How's Dad?"

"He's right here and recovering splendidly. He's tired of staying in bed, but it's what the doctor ordered. He wants to talk to you."

The picture jiggled, showing ceiling then floor, as Catherine handed over the viewer. Leith spent another ten minutes convincing Cameron McClure she was unharmed.

"Warrior J'Qhir took very good care of me." She found it strange to speak his name so calmly.

"I never doubted he had," Cameron said confidently. "As soon as we heard that you were with the Commander—"

"Warrior," Leith corrected.

Cameron grinned. "So he told you about that, eh."

"Yes. J'Qhir explained everything."

"J'Qhir?"

Warmth crept into her face at the slip. The blush might show up on the viewer, but Leith met her father's eyes. "We were the only two people on the entire planet. We thought we would be there for the rest of our lives. We became friends and dropped the formality."

One of Cameron's eyebrows arched, then he smiled. "I can understand that."

The raised eyebrow conveyed he had never, ever considered the possibility...but the smile told her more than a thousand words ever could—he approved. Leith relaxed a little. If her father wasn't concerned then maybe she had no reason to be anxious.

The view on the screen bounced wildly. Leith heard furtive whisperings, but couldn't catch what either of them said. Suddenly, Catherine's worried face reappeared.

"Leith? Are you *all right?*"

Her mother didn't miss a nuance. "Yes, Mother."

"You don't call me *Mother* unless you're upset."

"I've just returned to civilization from being stranded on a deserted planet and was almost blown to stardust by someone whom I once considered a harmless dorgian. I would say *upset* doesn't quite cover it."

"Hmmm..." Catherine expressed her skepticism, but Leith wasn't going to discuss everything right then.

Cameron snatched the viewer back. "We're sorry about Steve. We had no idea—"

"Neither did I. I'm sorry, too, because I wasn't there for you and you had to depend on Steve."

Cameron shook his head and waved away her apology. "We've always understood that McClure Shipping didn't interest you. We wanted it to be different, but we knew you had to follow your own course. We felt you might come around some day and if you didn't, that was all right too."

Leith had to change the subject. "I'll be glad when all this is over. The media has jumped all over it and has laid siege to Artilia."

"That's good, Leith. The truth has finally come out. Commander—excuse me, Warrior J'Qhir never said much about the situation with Crux, but I always felt there was more to it than the Crucians were telling." He frowned. "I tried talking to some of the members of the Board, but no one wanted to listen since Zi always flatly refused any offer of Alliance assistance. And I couldn't harass anyone face-to-face since I've been sentenced to bed."

"Since everything has come out into the open, I think they'll listen and accept." Leith shook her head. "I just hope the media focuses on Zi as a whole and not J'Qhir. He will be extremely uncomfortable with the attention."

"Leith, you know they will. You're a target as well. The message you sent has made every major newspaper and news program on Earth. It has spread to every major planet, too."

Leith groaned. "I never wanted that. I would come home right now, but I won't abandon J'Qhir to face the media alone. I'll catch the first Earth-bound ship as soon as the media conference is over."

Catherine's face appeared beside Cameron's. "You're coming home?"

"Of course." Leith blinked. "Where else would I go?"

Cameron poked Catherine. "Your mother is afraid you might have been starkissed."

Leith laughed. She had been starkissed, but not the way her parents meant. "No chance of that. I've had enough interstellar travel to last the rest of my life. I can't wait to see you again. Dad, you need to rest and so do I. I'll talk to you again tomorrow. I love you both!"

Leith closed the connection. She started to call the house steward to find out which room J'Qhir occupied but hesitated. This wasn't Paradise and they weren't alone anymore. She wasn't sure how he would react to the intrusion. She'd wait. Let him come to her. Let him construct some semblance of a proper Zi courtship...if that was what he wanted.

She left the terrace doors open, the warm breeze stirring the gauzy curtains. She stretched across the bed and slept until a knock on the door woke her hours later.

The air had grown chilly, and the evening sun slanted at a low angle across the terrace. The knocking sounded again. Leith jumped from the bed, ran her hands through her hair, and straightened her robe. She opened the door...and her heart fell into the pit of her belly.

"You're not dressed?" Drew greeted her. "It's time for dinner and I'm starved."

"I-I was asleep. Come on in."

In the dressing room stocked with a variety of clothes, Leith chose a floor-length cream-colored dress that gathered at the shoulders and formed angel-wing sleeves. A wide bronze belt fastened at her waist, bronze sandals to match. She left her hair long and loose. She thought she looked pale and touched her face with only a little of the cosmetics from the well-stocked dressing room.

"I'm ready."

"You're not like other women." Drew laughed. "I expected to wait for hours."

She punched him lightly on the shoulder.

As they walked down the hall, she asked, "Do you know which room J'Qhir is in? Maybe he and Rohm'dh haven't gone down yet."

"He's gone, Leith."

The finality of the word stopped her. "What do you mean, gone?"

Drew shrugged. "He's left the guesthouse."

"Left? Why?"

"Let's go to the dining room, and I'll tell you what I know."

Several tables filled the area, all empty. With J'Qhir and Rohm'dh gone, Leith and Drew were the only guests. They chose a table by the open patio doors. Sunlight faded rapidly and stars began to twinkle in the dark lavender sky. They made their choices from the menu.

"Hykaisian paow steak." Drew's eyes widened. "I thought the Artilians were strict vegetarians."

"They are, but they cater to their guests."

"But paow steak is illegal."

"Artilia is neutral, remember." Neutrality meant a planet reaped the benefits, but wasn't obliged to obey all the rules.

Leith didn't recognize half the dishes so she chose Terran beef stew, bread, and iced tea.

"Tell me, Drew."

"I went to get J'Qhir and Rohm'dh. I thought all of us could escort you to dinner. The steward said they left earlier in the day. His exact words, 'It was requested they be moved'."

"Did the steward say where?"

"He didn't offer the information. I asked because I knew you'd want to know. He said he couldn't divulge the location. But, Leith, the way he worded it doesn't mean J'Qhir made the request."

"Rohm'dh wouldn't. J'Qhir is his superior. Who else?"

"You know a Zi ship arrived not long after we landed. It came from Arreis. They were still investigating the situation." Drew laughed. "Investigating is too strong a word. The Zi really don't know how to function among others. According to what I heard, they were hanging around hoping someone would come to them. Anyway, maybe someone from the ship made the request."

"Maybe," Leith conceded. "But J'Qhir, as the Warrior, answers to no one except the Council of Elders."

"Unless the ship received orders directly from the Council."

Leith nodded. "They want to isolate him, keep him from being influenced by off-worlders. And he would go along with it. Duty, obligation, responsibility..." Words of honor that turned to ashes in her mouth. J'Qhir placed them above all else and rightly so. Except that he now placed them above her as well.

"Many worlds do that, Leith. They keep contact with others to a minimum, to keep from diluting their own cultures. Even Artilia does it to a great extent. Not every culture wants theirs to become a melting pot like our own."

She understood the concept well enough, but now it hit her on a personal level. While dressing, she had decided to find a way to be alone with him, entice him to her suite, make love to him all night long in a real bed with soft sheets and pillows. Tomorrow, over a breakfast that did not consist of food they had gathered or killed themselves, they would discuss their future and make their decisions. No, it wasn't the proper courtship she had envisioned earlier in the day. But she had expected him to come to her without being prodded. When he didn't, seduction was the only way she knew to force him to choose. Hadn't she feared he would choose Zi and his position as Warrior over her all along?

By leaving, J'Qhir had made his choice. There was no future. He hadn't even said good-bye.

Leith's eyes burned. She stood. "I'm sorry, Drew. I-I don't feel well."

"I'll have your food sent up to you," Drew offered as she ran from the room. She reached the stairs as hot tears scalded her cheeks.

Drew knew her well enough not to come after her. If only J'Qhir had known her well enough to come to her!

In her suite, Leith changed into a warmer robe. She scrubbed her face free of cosmetics and tears. She propped herself in bed with a viewer and tried to reach Nura. As Chief Servitor of Security, Nura could find out to which guesthouse he had been moved. She was told again and again, "Servitor Nura is unavailable at this time."

When her food arrived, she uncovered the stew, but she wasn't really hungry. Instead, she found a channel showing Terran programming and watched an old vid from a century ago. The actors were long dead and the plot rehashed, but it kept her from thinking about what she had planned to do in this bed this night. She fell asleep before the vid was half over.

✻ ✻ ✻

A beep on the viewer woke her the next morning. She punched the button.

"Ready for breakfast?" Drew asked cheerfully.

She stared at him sleepily. "Is food all you can think about?"

"I'm starved."

"You're not starved, especially if you finished off that paow steak last night."

"I did. It was delicious, pink and bloody, just the way I like it."

Leith's stomach roiled and she covered her mouth.

"What's wrong?"

"Nothing, I'm fine."

"I'll come by and get you in ten minutes."

"I'll meet you downstairs, Drew. I wouldn't want you to waste away to nothing while waiting on me."

Drew laughed as his image disappeared.

Leith lay still for a while, letting her stomach calm. When she thought she could move without retching, she slowly got out of bed. As she passed the food tray, she stopped to replace the cover. Lumps of meat and vegetables floated in a greasy broth. She rushed to the facilities and emptied her stomach in the waste receptacle.

The transition from Paradise to civilization wasn't agreeing with her. Maybe her system wasn't compatible with Artilia, although she'd never heard of other humans having problems. And she'd felt queasy on board the *Starfire* before ever reaching Artilia. Stress. Leaving Paradise, anxiety over her relationship with J'Qhir, the conference with them on interstellar display... Nerves.

Leith made another call to Nura and was once more told the Servitor was unavailable. She left a message that it was an emergency, for Servitor Nura to get in touch with her as soon as possible.

She dressed in a loose pale blue tunic and trousers and joined Drew downstairs. He had ordered a Terran breakfast she had often craved in the past two months—eggs, sausage and gravy, biscuits, and hash browns. This morning, Leith's stomach churned at the sight and smell of it. She ordered tea and plain toast.

"The conference is tomorrow evening," Drew said and drained the last of his coffee. "That leaves a day and a half for sightseeing. I'd like to visit the Penelaape Arcs. How does that sound to you?"

"I can't get in touch with Nura. I'm going to stay here and keep trying."

Leith didn't think the Artilians would appreciate her raiding all the guesthouses till she found J'Qhir. Certainly, J'Qhir wouldn't relish the attention. On the other hand, he knew exactly where she was. Surely, he could have found a moment to call her and explain. To say good-bye, at the very least. If he wanted to. Unless he just wanted to make a clean break of it. Damn, all she needed was a few moments with him, just to find out. Guessing what was going through his Zi mind was useless.

A server brought her tea and toast.

"You're not eating much, Leith. Are you ill?"

"I don't know. I don't think Artilia is agreeing with me." No need to mention she'd had the same symptoms aboard the *Starfire*. Maybe she had picked up a virus on Paradise. As soon as the media conference was over, she'd see a doctor.

"You look pale. Do you want me to stay with you while you wait for Nura to call?"

"No thanks, Drew. I'd rather be alone. You do your sight-seeing."

"If you're sure. If you need anything, just call. I'll be carrying a beeper with me." Drew wiped his mouth with a napkin, then stood. "Just think, Leith, people pay small fortunes to visit Artilia and the Arcs, and we're getting the royal treatment for free."

She told him to enjoy himself, then sat for a while sipping tea and nibbling toast. The bland food settled her stomach, and she felt better. She only hoped she could hold out until after the conference.

✳ ✳ ✳

Penelaape Arcs of myriad sizes shimmered in bright metallic hues as Leith walked among them. The graceful arches sensed her unrest and responded. She drew a deep breath and felt some of her fear and trepidation ease. The Arcs of Artilia were known galaxy-wide for their calming effects. Beings traveled from far away to spend time in the public parks.

Leith chose a cluster of small Arcs, in pale shades of pinks and blues and dusky lavender. Their glossy surfaces trembled as she drew near. Leith thought her alien emotions might traumatize them, but she had been assured the Arcs in this private garden would be all right.

She knelt in the sandy soil lightly covered with silvery-green moss and touched each Arc in turn.

"Thank you," she whispered, "for allowing me here."

One Arc shuddered violently. Not the tallest, largest, nor brightest, but the "leader" of this little group. She could leave and return in an hour or a day, and find the Arcs in this garden completely rearranged. She might find another small cluster, which might or might not include any of these and this leader might not be a leader at all.

Even the Artilians didn't know how the Arcs functioned, what they were made of, or how group leaders were chosen. No one knew how or why the Arcs moved from one position to another. They did so when completely unobserved. One park had been kept under surveillance for decades, with hidden recording equipment. None of the Arcs moved until the equipment malfunctioned, and the Arcs rearranged themselves once more. The Artilians then decreed no park should ever be secretly watched again.

"Leith!"

The Arcs, recognizing the voice, shivered pleasantly. Leith stood, brushed dry sand from her ankle-length tunic, and straightened to greet her friend. Nura hadn't changed since their days at the university. If anything she was more beautiful. Long silky white hair flowed freely around her shoulders, and her eyes were clear, celestial blue. Her skin was as translucent as starlight. The tunic she wore was white and sparkled in the pale Artilian sunlight.

"Leith, I'm so glad you thought to call me. I would have been heart-broken if you hadn't contacted me."

"Nura, it's good to see you." Leith threw her arms around her friend. "I've been trying to reach you for two days. Yesterday, I finally told them it was an emergency. I know you're busy, but I wanted to see you before the conference." Leith had anxiously waited for Nura to return her call, but it came only a Standard hour before. Since it was only a few Standard hours until the conference, Leith saw no reason to try to track down J'Qhir now. She would see him then.

"I'm so sorry, Leith. I was away from Katasa~ri on business. And frankly, Artilians don't consider off-worlder emergencies *real* emergencies. Artilians feel that most others, especially humans, are much too emotional and tend to 'make mountains out of molehills'." Nura laughed at the Terran phrase. "It feels good to use your idioms again and actually have someone know what I'm talking about."

The Arcs around them shimmered. "They like you, Leith."

"I like them, too. I've thanked them for allowing me here. Please let them know how grateful I am."

Nura's eyes twinkled. "They know. Sometimes I think they hold the knowledge of the universe. Come, Leith, let's walk."

Leith fell into step beside her friend, and Nura hooked her arm around Leith's.

"You've had quite an adventure," Nura observed.

"More than enough for one lifetime." Leith related an abbreviated version of the story.

"Stranded on a planet with a Zi!" Nura led them to a bench beneath a huge Arc.

"Well, you were always pestering me to get out and see more of the universe."

"Artilians do not pester," Nura denied sternly, then laughed. "I miss those days at the university. I wish I could have stayed longer, but I must be grateful for the year I was allowed. Now, tell me about your Zi."

Your Zi... Suddenly, Leith blinked back tears that burned to escape. "He— He isn't *my* Zi. We were both in the wrong place at the wrong time—"

"Leith, my friend. You cannot hide your feelings from me. You know that. Now, tell me about *your* Zi."

"His name is J'Qhir and he is the Warrior, chosen by his people to serve and protect. And..." Leith blinked back more tears. "I love him."

The words sounded strange when spoken aloud to someone else.

"How does J'Qhir feel about you?"

"I don't know!" she cried out. The large Arc over them shuddered. "I'm sorry. I'm distressing the Arcs. Should we go somewhere else? I don't want to hurt them."

"You won't. They thrive on distress. They absorb it and in doing so give you relief. You can't hurt them, Leith. Don't worry so."

Leith shook her head. "There were so many people—the media, tourists, gawkers."

"I wish you had called ahead from the ship and asked for me. A distress call from a crippled ship is different. They would have had to let me know. I could have made arrangements for your arrival to be more private."

"I wish I'd thought of it. I didn't realize that most of the messages I deployed had been intercepted and half the galaxy would be waiting for us."

"The Officials had no choice but to let them in. Media rights, you know. It's in the Treaty, but Artilia never realized what that could mean. Nothing like this has ever happened on Artilia before."

"When Drew told me it was an Artilian ship that reached us and towed us in, I told him it would be a problem for your planet and your people wouldn't like it."

"They don't," Nura confirmed. "But I'm glad we'll be exposed to more off-worlders. We allow tourists to visit the Arcs, but under controlled circumstances. There is no way to completely control this situation. I think it will do us good."

Leith grinned. "Radical as ever. What does everyone else think?"

Nura shrugged. "Some agree, some don't. So no changes are made. As always. Now, you effectively managed to change the subject, but I'm changing it back. Finish telling me about J'Qhir."

"Nothing more to tell."

"Leith," she said sternly then sighed. "Oh, very well. Have it your own way."

Leith looked at her helplessly. "I don't know how he feels. What happened on Paradise seems to have nothing to do with reality. And the reality is he is going back to Zi and I am going back to Earth."

"Have you talked to him?" Nura asked.

"I haven't had a moment alone with him since Drew and the others arrived on Paradise. Because of Rohm'dh, I had to treat him distantly. I left it up to J'Qhir how he wanted to handle it in front of another Zi. He never said or did anything to indicate that we were anything other than cordial acquaintances."

"Do you realize he may have taken his cue from you? Perhaps he thought you wanted it that way."

"I thought about it, but I didn't have any other choice. We had never taken the time to explore 'what if'. What if we're rescued? What happens between us then? It had to be J'Qhir's move, if we acted like lovers. It wasn't my place to bring attention to something he might not want known at the time."

"I understand, but J'Qhir is Zi and may not."

Nura, as always, had a way of reaching the heart of the matter, and Leith knew her friend was right. J'Qhir wasn't human, and she shouldn't expect him to react as a human would. His entire thought process was so different than her own.

Still, she stubbornly clung to the notion that if he truly loved her, he would instinctively know what needed to be done. He had told her that her instincts were good. Weren't his a thousand times better? She refused to believe he didn't know he should come to her and tell her what he meant to do.

"Well, you'd think he would have taken a few moments to find out." Leith frowned. "He left the guesthouse before I knew about it. He never tried to get in touch with me. It was the reason I kept trying to reach you, to find out where he had been moved. It's too late now. Only a few hours until the conference."

"I could arrange for you two to be alone—"

"No!" Leith vehemently cut her off. "J'Qhir has made his choice and I have to live with it."

"Very well," Nura conceded. "Will you stay here a while after the conference is over? You may use the guesthouse as long as you like. When this spectacle is over and everything has returned to normal, Artilia is a tranquil place. I would so enjoy spending time with you again."

"I'd like to, but I need to get back to Earth. Dad is ill and although he's recovering, I would like to see him and Mom. I've been away too long."

"Of course. Perhaps later, you'll come visit me. Promise that you will."

"I promise," Leith said and meant it, but she knew it would be a long time before she ever wanted to travel in space again.

A server appeared with a tray of tea and delicacies. Leith sipped the hot tea and chose a pink confection. The sweet, creamy morsel melted in her mouth, blending perfectly with a sip of the unsweetened tea. She waited a moment but neither caused the nausea to return. Suddenly, she missed the taste of cone nuts and fresh water and set aside the slender cup.

"Is it not to your liking? I can have something else brought."

"No, it's wonderful."

"To be perfectly honest," Nura's voice lowered conspiratorially, "I have Terran cocoa and chocolate chip cookies. I have them smuggled in every so often from that little cafe near the university."

Leith laughed. "Keep your stash. When I'm back home, I'll have Terran food again."

"Now, what are you going to do about J'Qhir?"

Leith sighed. She should have known Nura wouldn't allow the subject to be dropped. "Nothing. As I said, J'Qhir has made his choice. If he wishes to continue the relationship, then it's up to him to come to me."

"Leith, you're giving him every reason in the galaxy *not* to come to you."

"Exactly. If he does, then I'll know he truly wants me, that he doesn't come to me out of his overblown sense of duty or honor or whatever the hell it is the Zi feel." Leith regained her composure and said more softly, "I won't let him see me as an obligation, and that's exactly what he'll do if I go to him now."

Nura nodded. "I see your point. But what if he doesn't, Leith? What if he doesn't think *you* care?"

"If he cares, then he will come to me and ask me if I care. His duty should allow him that much."

"I don't know," Nura said softly. "He is, after all, male."

❋ ❋ ❋

Later, Leith walked with her friend through the garden to the waiting aircar.

"You're welcome to stay as long as you like," Nura offered. "Meditating with the Arcs can help."

"They've helped enormously as it is. I do feel better, calmer. I need to return to the guesthouse and get ready for the conference."

"I wish you'd change your mind about staying afterwards. And I wish I could ask you to stay with me, but I live in my parents' home. They find humans emotionally unstable."

Leith smiled. "I really need to get home and see my parents. The guesthouse is very comfortable. I wouldn't want to cause you any more trouble than I already have."

"No trouble, Leith. You are my friend. Artilians, too, know the meaning of obligation. On Earth, you took me in and helped me more than you'll ever know. Whatever I can do while you're here will never begin to repay what I owe."

"Nonsense. You've done more for me than I can ever repay. But we are friends, and friends don't keep score."

"You're right."

"Will you be at the conference tonight?"

"And miss meeting your Zi? Never! Besides," she added with a laugh, "I am Chief Servitor of Security. I have to be there. You know, the Zi Tri-Council of Elders is in Katasa~ri. They arrived from their ship this afternoon."

Leith felt a chill skip down her spine. J'Qhir would never do anything to go against the Council.

"You were always so careful in the giving of your emotions," Nura said. "As if the other person had to prove him or herself worthy."

"What?" Bewildered, Leith puzzled over her friend's words. "Why would you think that? I always felt lucky you chose me to be your friend."

"And I would have done anything to be your friend. You have no idea you're so hard to reach? No matter. I am sorry that you're having difficulty with the male to whom you finally gave your heart."

Leith nodded in agreement, but the implications of Nura's observation made her blink. They said their farewells, and Leith got in the open aircar. As it carried her from Nura's family's estate and through the streets of Katasa~ri at a leisurely pace, she pondered what Nura had said.

Had she really seemed so unreachable? Could Khris and even Steve have been right—to a degree? In the end, was her testing of J'Qhir and his motives merely a way to keep him at a distance and protect her own heart?

Until that moment, she had come to the decision not to attend the conference. If J'Qhir didn't want her, there was no need to torture herself by being near him but unable to be with him. On the other hand, it would be her last chance to see him. Perhaps he hadn't had an opportunity to contact her because of the Council's arrival. She'd give him the benefit of doubt and confront him with her presence, reminding him of what they'd shared.

She stared up into the lavender sky and sighed. Either way, she'd find out tonight.

Chapter 14

"Leith!"

Everyone called her name except the one she wanted to hear.

As she turned to greet Drew, one of her sandals caught against the floor and nearly sent her sprawling. Drew threw an arm around her shoulders to steady her, and Leith smiled at him gratefully.

"These shoes are catching on everything. Maybe I ought to go barefoot like the Biian monks," she whispered as several of the robed and hooded Biians passed by.

"Sorry I'm late. I lost track of the time checking on the Rover. The repairs are almost finished." He looked around at the crowded Hall. "This has turned into a big event."

"I don't understand how so many arrived so quickly. It's only been a few days and half the galaxy is here."

Drew nodded toward a group headed toward them, and his arm tightened around her. "Media reporters, headed our way."

Leith leaned her head close to his. "What could they possibly want with us?"

"Not us. You. Haven't you listened to any of the reports on LinkNet? You're a hero."

"Me? Oh, no—"

"You opened communications with a people that has always been incommunicado. That's news."

"But I didn't do anything. I just told the story that J'Qhir told me. Please make them go away, Drew."

"I can't. Besides, you spent six weeks on a planet alone with a Zi. No, not just any Zi, but the Warrior of Zi. They want to know what that was like."

"No! Drew, please, I can't. Get me away. *Now!*"

"I'll do what I can. There are enough people here to hide behind." Drew steered her past a group of dignitaries. The reporters trailed close behind, and Leith felt as if she were being chased by the horde of flyers all over again. Except these creatures carried cams instead of stingers and were far more dangerous.

Past the dignitaries, around the refreshment tables, Leith came face-to-face with—

"Leith..."

Finally, she heard her name spoken the way she longed to hear. She wanted to fling herself into his arms. He would make them all go away. He would protect her with his life...

As was his duty.

Did she dare show the least bit of intimacy with the Council of Elders and a horde of reporters surrounding them, watching their every move? She could not chance hurting him in any way.

"Commander," she murmured and nodded slightly. Then embarrassment burned her face. She wished she could sink into the polished stone floor under her feet. Why had she reverted to *Commander*? She should have called him Warrior. She couldn't look him in the eyes. She couldn't bear to see what she had done to him by using the word that had no meaning for him.

"Msss. McClure," he rasped, each syllable precision cut.

The frenzied horde clamored for a picture of them together.

When she finally raised her head to see if he wanted to comply, she saw nothing in his exotic amber eyes. The black slits were narrow, but he only casually gazed at her. There was nothing in his eyes or on his face to indicate she held any special meaning for him whatsoever.

She'd done it all wrong. In trying to protect him, she'd given him the impression that she wanted this cold formality between them. She had fouled it up beyond all repair.

Stiffly, he held out his arm to her and she saw that he had removed his glove. The cool Artilian temperature must be uncomfortable for him. The three Zi behind him frowned and one muttered gutturally. J'Qhir replied sharply and briefly in his own language.

Leith looked at his hand, a hand that had held her breast but didn't know what to do with it...a hand that had explored her intimately and knew exactly what to do. She laid her fingers over his. Their eyes met again, his unblinking. Then she turned and smiled for the cams. Lights flashed and their images were instantly transported over a hundred LinkNet channels to over a thousand worlds.

Questions were thrown at them, so many, so quickly, she couldn't understand one from another. All the while, her fingers lay lightly upon his and his trembled beneath hers. She attributed it to the chill in the room. She wanted to squeeze his fingers, to let him know somehow that what she had said was wrong, but she was too scared to move and afraid whatever she did he would misinterpret again.

Then his hand was gone from hers.

She looked around to find him disappearing into the throng, trailing behind the Council. She reached for Drew.

"Get me out of here now," she whispered between gritted teeth.

Drew hustled her past the reporters, beyond dignitaries and ambassadors. They threaded their way through a sea of beings until Drew stopped short. Two Artilian watchers, who acted as security, stood beside an unmarked door. While Drew spoke to one, Leith frantically searched the floor. No sign of J'Qhir or any of the Zi. Where had they taken him? What would they do to him? Would the Council consider their hands touching a transgression? Would they *punish* J'Qhir for allowing, even encouraging, the picture taking?

As the reporters descended once again, Drew grabbed Leith's arm and pulled her through the door. They walked down a corridor and Drew opened a door to one side.

"The security guard said you will be unmolested here— that's the word he used. Do you want something, Leith? Something to eat or drink?"

The thought of food made her sick, but she agreed to water and Drew left to get some.

The room was small, its walls colored a soothing pale blue, with muted lighting. The only furnishings were a table and several chairs and a divan. Leith paced a few minutes, then burst into tears and collapsed on the divan.

She had to get control of herself before Drew returned. Oh, what had she done! She should not have called him Commander at that moment. She should have said his name in answer to his using her own. But she was frightened of how the Council of Elders might retaliate if they suspected something improper between them. Of course, she would choose the wrong thing to do.

It would always be so. Why would she ever think she could be competent in anything she did or said? She had failed as she had failed in so many things before. Except in loving him with all her heart and soul.

Perhaps she should perform the Zi failure ritual that she had stopped J'Qhir from carrying out.

Slowly, the door opened. Leith hastily wiped at her eyes. She wished she didn't have to face Drew in this condition, but if he hadn't figured it out by now, he never would. She looked up to find a hooded Biian monk closing the door behind him.

"I-I'm sorry," she stammered, "but you have the wrong room."

Biian monks took their vows of silence so seriously they had their vocal chords surgically altered so they wouldn't utter a sound. This monk shook his head negatively so that his whole body moved from side to side.

"This is my room. If you'll go back to the watchers, they'll give you—"

"I have the right room, Leith," a familiar voice said from the depths of the cowl, then he lifted his hands and drew back the folds of cloth around his head.

"*Steve!*" Leith choked on the name. "How— You're dead. J'Qhir blew your ship to stardust."

"I was never aboard that ship," Steve explained. "I created the illusion of being there. I was on another ship, transmitting my image to your ship via the *Brimstone*. The Rep blew Carter and Phillips to stardust, not me."

Leith made a dash for the door, but Steve caught her and held a Blaser to her neck.

"Blasting you this close, I'll lose a few atoms but don't think I won't do it."

"What are you doing, Steve?"

"Revenge for everything you and the Rep have cost me. I can't get to the Rep, but killing you and his unholy spawn will be enough."

It took a moment for the meaning of his words to sink in, but they still didn't make much sense. "His *what?* What are you talking about?"

"Oh, didn't you know? When Carter scanned the *Starfire,* it read six lifeforms. Drew, the two Reps, the birdman, and you. That left one unaccounted for. The only answer is you're carrying his half-breed bastard. Let me be the first to congratulate you," he snarled.

A child! Leith would have dropped to her knees if Steve hadn't been holding onto her. A child...she thought numbly as Steve pulled out another robe. Woodenly, she allowed him to slip the sleeves over her arms and draw up the hood.

Not stress or nerves. It explained her nausea and why her monthly cycle was overdue. Stress or malnutrition or excessive physical strain—she'd come up with a dozen sensible reasons. And the one, burning in the back of her mind, the one she thought impossible because of their physiological differences, the creation of a child, was the answer.

Steve jabbed her with the Blaser again, pressing the heavy material into her neck.

"Drew will be back any minute."

"No, he won't. I've taken care of him."

"You didn't—"

"No, I didn't. I left an emergency message for him to contact McClure Shipping. It will take him a while to get a free line because of the media."

She had to stall for time. *Where there's life, there's hope,* J'Qhir had reminded her so long ago when Steve had incarcerated them on the *Catherine McClure*. If she had only herself to consider, she wouldn't go with Steve and dare him to blast her where she stood. She'd lost J'Qhir to his dedication and her own incompetence, she would have nothing more to lose.

Except now she knew she carried a baby—J'Qhir's child—and she couldn't risk that life. Even if the probability factor was high that Steve had lied for his own malicious purposes, the baby, however slight the chance of its existence, came first.

"What are you going to do with me? Whatever it is, you can't get away with it."

"I'm going to kill you, Leith, for the universe to see. I don't intend to get away with it. Everything is spoiled now. All I can do is make sure the Rep suffers."

"But why?"

"Why not?" Steve opened the door and checked to see if the corridor was clear. He pushed her through the door. "Remember, Leith, I have the Blaser on you at all times. And if you make me use it, I will take as many Artilians as I can as well."

Leith allowed herself to be herded along. *Where there's life, there's hope.* Maybe Steve would exact his revenge in front of the universe, but Leith felt that every moment alive was one moment closer to rescue. Drew had to be alive, tricked as Steve said. Drew would be her salvation somehow.

Steve pushed her through the door at the other end of the corridor, into a dimly lit back hallway.

Hurry, Drew, Leith thought as Steve led her deeper behind the Great Hall.

✽ ✽ ✽

The Council of Elders led J'Qhir away from the unrelenting reporters, the flashing cams, and Leith. He had wanted to twine his fingers around hers and take her with him. Find a place where they could be alone. So many things he wanted to ask her, tell her, do to her.

Now was not the time. The three Council Elders of the Bh'rin'gha, disgruntled by his seeming disregard for the situation, despised him for bringing such garish attention to Zi—as if he had a choice in the matter. They acted as if he engineered this entire plot to put himself and his people in the spotlight. Sss't!

The Zi were now forced to *mingle* with other-worlders, and the Council of three felt this was an atrocity committed against their people in general and themselves in particular. The Zi did not mingle socially, politically, or personally.

Only half-listening to Elder M'bat'h awkwardly answer a question posed by an Elder from the Lha'awh Council, J'Qhir maneuvered his body around, positioning himself where he could see the greater part of the Hall. In doing so, he turned his leg wrong and the familiar dull throb started up once again. He eased most of his weight to the other leg.

His amber eyes flicked over the crowd of beings in search of one in particular. He could not find her now. The same group of reporters had rallied around a side door, guarded by two Artilians. Had she gone in there?

Suddenly, he was aware the Elder of Lha'awh as well as the three Elders of Bh'rin'gha had turned their attention to him. They watched him expectantly, as if they awaited his profound answer.

He had no inkling what they had asked of him.

Bowing slightly, he murmured in Zi, "Beg forgiveness..."

Bodies pressed close to him as he threaded his way toward the door. He walked slowly, mindful not to aggravate his injury. What he really wanted to do was charge through, find Leith, and leave all this unpleasantness behind.

Would she come with him? Did she want to be with him again? Some of the questions he needed to ask but didn't know how. Deserted on a planet, no one but the two of them, was one thing. Now, they were back in the middle of civilization. She could return to her Earth and continue the life she regretted leaving behind. Perhaps she had no desire to ever be with him again.

Could he bear it if her answer was no?

By the time he had progressed halfway across the room, the reporters had dispersed, looking for a new target. He steadily made his way toward the door, careful to avoid any of them. If they caught him alone, they would try to pry knowledge out of him. Or admission of something. Hadn't some of the questions he'd heard before the Elders led him away aimed at delving into what sort of relationship he and Leith had maintained during their stay on Paradise? How could they inquire into a situation of such a delicate nature?

They could not *know*, but they suspected the truth. Did the Elders suspect also? Was leading him away at that moment to keep him from admitting the truth? Did they truly expect him to lay bare his privacy, and Leith's as well, before strangers eager for a hint of scandal?

Yet, he could not speak falsely. Truth was a tenet of his culture and position, but he also could not deny what passed between Leith and him. He would not dishonor what they had shared.

Two of the reporters caught sight of him, just as he approached the Artilian guards. He tilted his head, indicating the beings now heading toward him. He spoke in Terran Standard. "Isss there sssomeplace..."

The Artilian nodded his understanding. "These are privacy rooms. When you enter the corridor, the second room on the right is empty."

J'Qhir bowed his head in gratitude. The other guard had opened the door, and he slipped inside as the reporters, now joined by a few others, were stopped by the guards. The door slid shut behind him.

Sweet silence.

He leaned back against the door, relieving his bad knee of all pressure. The dull throb lessened only slightly. The medical technician had been correct on several counts. He should have brought a walking staff with him, and he should have rested the knee a few days longer before attempting any length of time on his feet. He would need surgery after all.

J'Qhir had declined surgery because recovery would have kept him bedridden. He would have missed the conference...and seeing Leith. The technician had supplied him with a staff he discarded before entering the Hall. The Council had looked upon its use with contempt. Physical impairment in one Zi, however temporary, could be construed by others as a sign of weakness in Zi as a whole.

He hissed and pushed away from the door. Leith was in one of these rooms, but which one? Unless he pounded on each in turn, he had no way of knowing. He disliked the thought of invading anyone else's privacy, but he knew no other way. He could stand in the corridor until Leith emerged, but she might not return to the Hall until time for the conference, which was over a Standard hour away. His knee would not allow him to stand that length of time.

He limped a few steps toward the first door on the right. Fresh sparks of pain shot up his thigh. One thoughtless twist had completely undone two Standard days of rest and medication.

J'Qhir took a few more halting steps and raised his fist to knock when another door, the third on the left, opened. Drew Garrison emerged, and J'Qhir quickly dropped his hand.

"Warrior," Garrison acknowledged him with a nod and smile, but briskly walked past him and disappeared through the door at the end of the corridor.

At least he would not embarrass himself and his people. He now knew which one contained Leith. He was almost even with the second rooms when the corridor door opened once again. A Biian monk, robed and cowled, stepped inside. The monk paused stiffly when he became aware of J'Qhir's presence.

J'Qhir said nothing since Biian monks did not speak. Patiently, he waited for the monk to find his appointed room. Before the monk could move, once again the corridor door opened and the Council of Elders of the Bh'rin'gha filed in. The monk swiftly stepped aside, then halted again.

Damnation! J'Qhir swore silently in Terran Standard. Although cursing and its religious connotations meant nothing to him, or any Zi, Leith had explained the concept. Although J'Qhir could not conceive an omnipotent being manipulating all of life, he thought if any gods existed, they now created an elaborate joke at his expense.

The Elders charged past the monk without giving him a second glance. J'Qhir looked longingly at the third door on the left, then opened the one he had been assigned, the second door on the right. The Elders marched in behind him.

J'Qhir let his bulk fall heavily onto the divan, a laserblast of pain shooting from knee to hip. He closed his eyes against the pacing of Elder M'bat`h, the nervousness of Elder S`huhfh, and the affected indifference of Elder P`hi`in.

"Warrior, how dare you disgrace the Bh'rin'gha?" M'bat`h growled.

"My knee painsss me," he said...in Terran Standard.

His eyes slid open to gauge their reaction. M'bat`h scowled furiously, his crested brow raised to a point. S`huhfh's eyes were as wide as they could get, his mouth a small circular shape. P`hi`in smirked, his talons tapping together.

P`hi`in, he decided, was the most dangerous after all.

"My knee hurts," he repeated in Zi. He could not explain how most of his thoughts came to him in Terran Standard now. It was all he had spoken for the six weeks he had been on Paradise...except for the times he had murmured Zi words of longing into Leith's ear after their lovemaking. His first reaction was to speak Terran Standard so that Leith would understand.

But Leith wasn't here.

She was across the corridor, one room down. He had been within minutes of seeing her, holding her, if it was what she wanted. Kissing her *there* and *there* and *there*, if she would allow it.

"—have to uphold the dignity of Bh'rin'gha," M'bat`h snapped.

"Yes, Elder," he muttered although he had only a vague notion of what M'bat`h had said. "I know my duty. I know my obligations. I have been exposed to the position of the Warrior almost as long as you have been a Council Elder. My father taught me well." He broke off, having lost the impetus of the anger with which he had begun. He did not want to argue. He certainly did not intend to be chastised for a marginal transgression, at worst.

"Perhaps Warrior J'Qhir is not well enough—" S`huhfh began.

"If the Warrior suffers debilitated health then the Council is obligated to appoint someone in his place." P`hi`in looked quite pleased at the prospect. "You have no issue, do you?"

"You know as well as anyone here that my lifemate died before bearing young, Elder," J'Qhir snapped.

M'bat`h hissed and turned away from them.

J'Qhir regretted the sharpness of his tone. T`hirz had been M'bat`h's daughter, and although she had died many years ago, he must still feel the loss. P`hi`in was well aware of this.

P`hi`in shrugged. "You have been repeatedly exposed to many new experiences on your off-world journeys. The temptation—"

"Enough!" J'Qhir cut off the accusation before it could be spoken. P`hi`in came too close to the truth and the possibility. *If* it were at all possible for Zi and human to procreate... No, their physiologies were similar, but much too different. Surely, Leith would have told him if it were so.

"I have done nothing to bring dishonor to me or my people." In truth, he had not. He had found comfort and companionship with the only being on an entire planet. He'd had no logical reason to assume they would ever be rescued. How could he? Hancock had carefully engineered and executed his plans to ensure no one could find them. His plot had been flawed, but how could J'Qhir foresee those circumstances. *Always be prepared; always expect the unexpected.* If he had adhered to this tenet, would he have done anything differently?

"My health is not debilitated, only my knee." He continued brusquely, "Surgery and a short period of recovery will remedy it."

"Of course, Warrior J'Qhir." S'huhfh attempted to defuse the situation. "Let there be no more talk of appointing another Warrior. The one we have is quite capable of handling the position."

J'Qhir bowed his head in gratitude at S'huhfh. If only he knew what Leith would answer, he would damn all three to Terran hell and walk away. If Leith wanted no more to do with him, then his status as Warrior, as empty as it had become, was all he had. He could not jeopardize it until he knew how Leith felt.

"He must also uphold our tradition of honor and dignity," M'bat'h growled fiercely. "Leaving in the middle of a conversation with a Lha'awh Council member is not dignified."

"Nor is writhing in pain, Elder," J'Qhir pointed out. He decided he'd taken enough harassment from them all. If he could make them leave, he still had time to talk to Leith. "I came in here to rest before the conference. Beg forgiveness, Council, but—"

A sharp tap at the door startled them all. J'Qhir hissed inwardly. Another delay. Always something to keep him and Leith apart. According to her, some things were meant to be. She called it "fate". Perhaps their fate was *not* to be together, other than little moments spent near one another, yet unable to connect.

M'bat'h scowled and nodded at S'huhfh who scurried to open the door. One of two Artilian guardsmen stood just outside, quite embarrassed.

"I do beg your pardon, but someone insists on speaking with one of you. He says it's an emerg—"

"Warrior." Drew Garrison brushed past the Artilian. "Leith has disappeared."

J'Qhir lurched to his feet. "What?"

Garrison explained in a rush. "I left Leith in one of the other rooms. When we met in the hallway earlier, I was on my way to get her some water. I was approached with an urgent message to contact McClure Shipping. When I finally got through, no one there had sent a message at all. I hurried back to the room and...Leith's gone. The guards say she never came back into the Great Hall."

"Ssshe isss not here asss you can sssee." P'hi'in had stood and now swept the room with his hand.

Garrison ignored him and looked at J'Qhir. "She wouldn't have returned to the Hall. She was tired of the media and wanted to rest before the conference. She wouldn't have chanced going back in there."

"Did you check the other roomsss?"

Garrison nodded in the direction of the guardsmen. "They wouldn't let me. They didn't want to let me in here, but I told them it would cause an interstellar incident if you weren't informed."

"Alert her ambasssador," M'bat'h snapped. "Now, leave usss. Do not interrupt usss again."

J'Qhir was already limping out of the room. "Which roomsss are occupied?"

"These are *privacy* rooms—" one of the Artilians began.

Pushing him aside, J'Qhir crossed to the door opposite and pounded on it with a heavy fist.

"You can't—"

"Garrissson. Sssee that the Artilian sssecurity isss informed. Now."

"You got it." Garrison solidly clamped his hand on the second Artilian's shoulder and led him away.

The door slid open beneath J'Qhir's fist, and a frail Danid peered out at him. He stepped into the room and saw it was otherwise empty.

The wide-eyed Danid shook his tentacles. "F-First th-the B-Biian, n-now th-the Z-Zi!"

"A Biian monk?" J'Qhir questioned.

"I-Is th-there a-any o-other k-kind?" the Danid sneered.

"What did the monk want?"

"S-Same a-as y-you. L-Looked a-around a-and l-left."

J'Qhir whirled on the guard, but nearly collided with M'bat`h instead. The Elder blocked the doorway.

"Warrior, what are you doing?" M'bat`h snarled in Zi.

"My duty."

"How is this your duty? Your responsibility is first and foremost to your people, not some inconsequential alien female."

Inconsequential? Never. Alien? Leith had not been *alien* to him in a long time. Female? Most definitely... J'Qhir suppressed a smile.

"This female is not alien to me." In defiance he stepped past the Elder. "My duty is to protect and she is within the realm of my protection. My responsibility has not ended because we are on another world. This is what being the Warrior means to me."

His fierce determination silenced M'bat`h.

"How many othersss?" he demanded of the guardsman.

"Two." He pointed them out.

A group of Peridots crawled over one room. The other was empty.

"The Biian monk should be here," the Artilian declared. "He didn't leave past us."

J'Qhir systematically searched the empty rooms. When finished, he faced the door at the opposite end of the corridor.

"Isss this a privacy room alssso?"

"No. It leads to storage rooms, the food preparation center, and the emergency stairwell. These areas are not open to the public."

J'Qhir jerked open the door then felt a restraining hand on his arm. The pressure was so light, he thought for a moment Leith touched him.

"Warrior. I am Security Servitor Nura. Let my people do their job."

"Nura. Msss. McClure'sss friend."

"Yes. You are Warrior J'Qhir."

It was not a question, J'Qhir decided as Servitor Nura's pale blue eyes delved into his. Her smile was friendly as if they knew one another. Leith must have told her about him. Had Leith confided in her completely? Perhaps, perhaps not. It did not matter.

"I've already closed off the Great Hall. The watchers will search for our friend." Her voice lowered so only he could hear. "I know you are in pain, but there is nothing to be done right now."

At first he thought she must have sensed the terrible ache in his chest. Then he realized she meant the throbbing of his injury. The intensity of his search had driven everything from his mind except his desire to find Leith safe. During his search, he had twisted his limb again and now he was aware of pain rolling in burning waves to his hip.

He had never felt more useless in his life.

Servitor Nura listened intently as the watcher relayed information in the liquid tones of Artilian. Nura fired off orders and the watcher disappeared.

"Please come with me, Warrior. Until the watchers have gathered information, there is nothing either of us can do."

J'Qhir nodded his assent.

As Nura led him through the door, M'bat`h barged down the corridor. "Where are you going?"

J'Qhir refused to show disrespect by speaking Zi in front of one who did not know the language.

"I am going with Ssservitor Nura," he said in Terran Standard. "I will return when Msss. McClure hasss been found."

He bowed stiffly and followed Nura through the door.

Chapter 15

J'Qhir propped his leg upon a stool and absently massaged his swollen knee. Nura, as she insisted he call her, left him in her chambers while she attended to matters. One matter, he noted as he watched the large viewer mounted on the wall, was explaining to the assembly in the Hall that the conference had been delayed indefinitely for reasons she could not divulge at this time. No one was allowed to leave or enter the building or grounds until further notice. He muted the sound.

The Biian monk. If not for the monk, everyone would think Leith had wandered off somewhere to be alone. Garrison had said the media reporters upset her. He had sensed her unease when their images had been recorded earlier.

At that time, she had called him Commander. He approved of the way she kept formality between them in the presence of others. It was the Zi way. He didn't completely understand why she used Commander when she knew it was not his title. Perhaps she had used it for so long prior to their use of birth names, that it slipped out before she thought. He could tell she was nervous and upset. He tried to be as supportive as he could, but there were too many others surrounding them, waiting to pounce—the Council as well as the reporters.

He should have spoken to her sooner, but he had never found an appropriate time. Others were always near during their rescue and onboard the small ship. When they landed on Artilia, Leith and he had been taken to the medical facility immediately. He had refused treatment other than a mild medication to suppress pain. Leith remained behind, but he had been sent to a guesthouse.

Good food, a comfortable bed, and the medicine put him to sleep until Rohm'dh awakened him late the next day. The Council had arrived with orders for them to report to the ship at once. He would have ignored the command anyway, unwilling to leave without speaking to Leith, but his injury had worsened so that he could not walk without excruciating pain. Instead, he allowed them to transfer him to the medical facility.

When he declined surgery, the technician injected him with other medication and suggested he stay off his feet a few days if he wanted to be ambulatory for the conference. He readily complied because it would delay a meeting with the Council.

At his release, only a few hours before the conference, a technician had given him a syringe containing a powerful pain suppressant to be used if the pain became unbearable. Injected directly into the knee, the drug would alleviate the pain for a Standard hour, long enough for him to reach the medical facility. Although one thoughtless twist then another had aggravated the pain, it hadn't intensified enough to use the syringe yet.

He watched images flash across the wall viewer. Somehow he and Leith had been thrust into the roles of heroes. How that came about, he did not know. He had never felt like a hero at any point in his life, now least of all. Once again he had failed Leith and could not atone for the failure. He had promised her that he would never perform the ritual of failure and he would keep that promise.

The picture he and Leith posed for caught his attention. If only he could go back to that moment. Rewriting history, he would resist the Elders leading him away. He would never have let Leith go. He would have asked her the question he had asked several times before, but this time he would explain the meaning. He would hold his breath until she gave her answer. The Biian monk would never have come near her.

The Biian monk was not a real Biian monk. Whoever he was, he used the cowled robes to shield his true identity. If J'Qhir had not known Hancock died in the destruction of the *Brimstone*, he would be the logical choice. If not Hancock then one of the others who had helped him with his plans carried out the vendetta.

Apparently, the reporters were mystified by the latest developments. In order to keep their viewers from switching channels, they replayed earlier transmissions.

J'Qhir grimaced as he watched himself limp clumsily into the Hall. He followed along behind the Council of Elders in the manner of a trained pet. The Elders refused to speak with the reporters, and J'Qhir, taking their lead, shook his head. With nothing to gain from the stoic Zi, they moved on.

Other ambassadors from other worlds, members of the Galactic Alliance Board, entered. Some preened before the cams, some spoke hesitantly, and others were as unresponsive as he and the Council had been.

Then Leith entered the Hall. She nervously twisted her hands in the delicate material of her silvery tunic. She kept her head bowed so that her lustrous hair fell over her shoulders and hid her features. He craved the full sight of them and was rewarded when she stopped and turned slightly to greet Garrison with a fond smile. Her head dipped close to his and her lips moved.

Garrison slipped an arm around her protectively and something snapped and spasmed in J'Qhir's chest, making it difficult for him to breathe. Once again, he rewrote history. *He* should have been there to meet her, not Garrison. *He* should have protected her from the reporters.

Instead, he had allowed the Council to intimidate him, to make him think that at this point in time his relationship with Leith was not his most important concern. How could he have allowed his *duty* and *obligation* to cloud his judgment? The conference would go on without him. Zi would survive without him, if need be. He would survive without the title of Warrior. He didn't think he would survive without Leith.

Why could he not still be stranded on Paradise with Leith where life was much simpler?

No...he would not rewrite the history of their rescue even if he could, but he didn't completely understand why returning to civilization complicated everything.

His eyes flicked toward the images on the wall viewer. Now there were scenes of the crowded Hall, and he searched for another glimpse of her. When he saw himself hobble across the room, he knew she had already gone into the privacy room. He picked up the pad, to find another channel that showed earlier scenes.

Before he could key the pad, the scene cut off abruptly. A female reporter stood outside the Great Hall, a brisk breeze ruffling her pale yellow hair. She spoke frantically to the cam. J'Qhir fumbled with the pad and finally found the mute button.

"...of the Artilian government has given no official word on who the jumpers are or what they hope to accomplish at this time. It has been speculated that it is a protest against admitting Zi and Crux into the Galactic Alliance. Yet, no one offers any explanation why Biian monks would be against—"

J'Qhir lurched to his feet. Having forgotten his knee, the joint gave way and he crashed to the floor. The thick, soft carpeting did little to cushion his fall. A supernova of pain exploded underneath his kneecap and he almost blacked out. He lay on his side and cradled his leg, clenching his teeth. He tried to focus on the wall viewer, but his eyes refused to adjust.

"...not a Biian monk at all. Leith McClure, heir to Earth-based McClure Shipping, is being held hostage. No one has identified the kidnapper..."

He shook his head and concentrated on the wall viewer. A cam panned up the face of the building and zoomed in on one of the figures. Dressed in monk's robes, the cowl fallen away, her long brown hair fluttered in the stiff wind.

"Leith..." he moaned.

In a blinding haze, he reached into his pocket for the syringe. He flicked the cap off and jammed the end against the side of his knee. The pain quickly eased until he felt nothing. The cessation of pain did not lure him from his purpose.

A Standard hour was more than enough time to kill whomever had dared touch Leith.

❄ ❄ ❄

Wispy lavender clouds drifted lazily across the deep violet night sky as Leith peered through the opening of the domed roof of the Great Hall. Five of the seven small moons of Artilia, visible in various lunar phases, cast enough light to see clearly.

Steve had moved them ever upward through the complex until he at last found the utility stairway to the roof hatch. Leith hadn't been able to prod him into telling her what he planned. All of her questions had been answered with silence. The only time he spoke was to snap orders when she slowed or hesitated.

Now, Steve roughly grabbed her arm and pulled her through the hatch. She fell to her hands and knees on the coarse roofing as he slammed the cover shut. Leith sat back on her heels and watched him aim the Blaser. He fired off a series of short bursts, completely sealing the hatch cover and latch.

"That should get someone's attention," he said and strode to the edge where the dome curved away.

Leith carefully stood. "What are we doing up here?"

When he didn't answer, Leith looked around the flat apex of the circular roof. On two sides, the dome dropped about seven meters to flat roofs covering the wings of the Great Hall. At the other two sides, the front entrance and the rear of the complex, there was an additional fifteen-meter drop. Leith might survive a tumble to one of the flat roofs, but she would die—and her child with her—if she fell toward the front or rear.

Then she noticed the maintenance ladders, no more than rungs constructed to blend in with the corrugated roof design, leading off in the four directions down the slope of the dome. Leith glanced at Steve, but he was still searching for signs that the Blaser blasts had drawn attention.

Leith gathered up the long robe. As she took a step, one of her flimsy sandals caught on the gritty roofing and sent her sprawling. She put out her arms and landed hard, her hands scraping across the roof. The sudden jolt of pain brought tears to her eyes and made her cry out, but she crawled toward the edge. She had just reached for the top rung when Steve grasped her from behind and slung her back toward the center.

"Not that easy," he sneered and aimed the Blaser at her.

Leith searched for a way to stop him or at least delay him until help could arrive. They would have to either force the hatch open or come from one of the other roofs by way of the ladders. Either way Steve would hear and see them. It would give him time to do whatever he planned to do.

"What do you want, Steve?" Leith repeated the question she had asked him the last time he held her at Blaserpoint.

"Right now, I just want it to end, but not without a show for them." He angled the Blaser to the front of the building.

"It doesn't have to be this way. It's not too late if you stop now." Leith spoke the cliched words, but she had no hope they would sway him.

"It's been too late for a while. There's Carter, Wiley, and Phillips. I caused all their deaths. And the two Biian monks whose robes we wear. They're dead. One more doesn't matter. Two more, counting the child you carry." He pulled her to her feet and forced her to the edge, his arm tight around her middle. "They can execute me as easily for seven as for five. Or give me life in a penal colony and I'd rather die. This way, I make sure I die."

Leith's cowl had fallen back and she raked the hair out of her eyes. She looked down into the wide expanse of front lawns and parking areas. A crowd had gathered, many of them media reporters. She couldn't distinguish anyone in particular at this distance, but she could see the ones with arms raised, focusing their cams. They would be able to hear everything as well as see them as if they were only a few paces away. By law, they couldn't transmit the audio portion of what they recorded. A group of Arcs, several larger than any she had seen and almost as tall as the building minus the dome roof, glistened in the pale moonlight.

Was J'Qhir in the crowd? Or somewhere inside watching them on a viewer? Did he still feel it was his duty to protect her? She hoped not. Steve would kill him instantly if he somehow made it onto the roof.

"Why do you have to take me with you?" Asking questions should prolong his final action. "I never encouraged you, Steve. I never—"

"I know!" he snapped. "You *never*. You never had any interest in McClure Shipping, but when Cameron became ill he chose you to take his place. You never had a clue, but I had to answer to you."

"That's not my fault, Steve. That was Dad's decision."

"You could have turned it down."

"How could I?" Leith cried out. "He asked me to do it. How could I tell him no again? I had told him no so many times before. I never considered myself in charge, Steve. I never would have managed if not for you."

"It's too late for that," he growled into her ear. "Too late for everything. I didn't fall in love with you, Leith, but you and me—Cameron's daughter and his protege—couldn't have been more perfect. It would have secured my future at McClure Shipping, only you wouldn't go along."

"Why couldn't you be happy the way things were?" Leith shot back. "Dad let you run the company the way you wanted—"

"No, he didn't."

A loud pop sounded behind them, and Steve turned.

"They're breaking through the hatch!" Leith allowed a small glimmer of hope to fill her. If she could keep him distracted a little longer. "They're almost here, Steve. Please throw away the Blaser."

Instead he aimed the Blaser at the hatch and resealed the cracks with short bursts.

"The metal won't hold much longer," he observed, then turned back to face the crowd with Leith. "Cameron shot down every suggestion I ever made to expand McClure Shipping. We should have had an office and fleet of ships on every major planet in the galaxy, but Cameron wouldn't hear of it. He wanted to keep the company small. He didn't want it to get bigger than one or two could manage. Cameron has no *vision*."

Steve had let the Blaser drift away from her and, without planning the move, she lunged for it. Steve jerked back and she fell into his arm. The force knocked the weapon from his hand. They teetered on the edge as it clattered down the side of the dome, disappearing over the far edge.

Steve pulled them back at the last moment. "You know," he said, and she could feel him shaking against her. "All I ever wanted was to be part of your family. I thought if I could do that then Cameron would take me seriously."

Leith tried to wriggle free as he wrapped both arms around her, but he held her tightly and she couldn't move. *Where there's life, there's hope.* As long as she was alive, there was always a chance. Leith clung to the thought like a lifeline. She heard another loud sound from the hatch. They could break through at any moment before Steve made them jump. If only she could keep him talking.

"What were your plans for McClure—" She broke off when she heard the intense hiss, and Steve was yanked backward. Instinctively, she pulled away from Steve who held her a moment longer. With a feral growl, he suddenly released her. The rebound sent her over the edge and she turned, trying to gain her footing. Once again the sandal caught, tripping her, and she dropped to the dome side on her stomach. She hardly dared to breathe to keep from sliding down the curvature.

J'Qhir stood, his arms around Steve the same way Steve had held her. J'Qhir's amber eyes widened as he realized her precarious position. When Steve brought his leg up, Leith knew his intention.

"*J'Qhir!*" she screamed out in warning, but he didn't have time to react before Steve drove his heel back into J'Qhir's injured knee. J'Qhir roared in pain and broke the hold. Steve turned and kicked J'Qhir's knee again.

The effort of shouting sent Leith sliding down the side of the dome. She spread her limbs to slow her slide, but each movement made her descend faster until her feet were dangling over the bottom edge of the dome. The robe caught on an uneven edge and she stopped momentarily. The maintenance ladders were too far away and any movement to reach them would send her plummeting to her death. If she could stay where she was until J'Qhir subdued Steve once and for all, she would be safe. Leith had no doubt about the outcome. J'Qhir would succeed.

Leith's gaze was riveted to the top of the dome, expecting J'Qhir to appear any moment. Instead, both appeared, each with a hold on the other. J'Qhir's face twisted in agony, but he did not lessen his grip as Steve once more struck his knee.

Twice more Steve managed to drive his foot into J'Qhir's knee and finally J'Qhir collapsed, landing on his good knee, the other leg turned out to the side at an unnatural angle. Steve prepared for one final blow to send J'Qhir to his death, but just as Steve's foot connected, J'Qhir threw himself into Steve and both went over the edge.

Horrified, Leith reached for J'Qhir although she knew it was impossible to save him. She heard the material rip and felt it give. All three sailed from the roof at the same time, and Steve's scream rent the air but ended abruptly.

Leith closed her eyes. She expected her life to flash across her mind's eye. She also expected fear to kill her before she

261

could hit the ground. Neither happened. Calm flowed through her as she floated downward as light as a feather. She felt something soft and warm and pliable beneath her aching fingers, and it cocooned her whole body. She slipped ever downward, the soft shroud moving with her until she at last gently spilled onto the carpet of grass.

When Leith opened her eyes, a wild-eyed group of spectators, many with cams recording her undignified sprawl, formed a wide circle around her. Drew broke through the ranks with Nura just behind.

"Leith, are you hurt?" Drew knelt on one side of her as Nura moved to the other. Nura spoke quietly into the communicator at her chest and issued orders before dropping beside Leith.

"No, I-I don't think so." Now that she was safe and still, she could feel all the aches and pains from her ordeal. Her hands stung, and she looked down at the raw and bleeding scrapes from heel to fingertip.

"J'Qhir!" she cried out and tried to rise. Drew and Nura held her down, and she didn't have the strength to fight them.

"He's fine," Nura said softly.

"Are you sure?"

She nodded. "He survived the fall the same way you did. The Arcs."

A team of watchers arrived and started breaking up the crowd. They allowed a med unit through.

"And Steve?"

"Steve's dead. For real, this time," Drew said with no regret.

As the med unit started to prepare the anti-grav stretcher, Leith protested. "I don't need—"

"Let them take you in, away from everyone," Nura suggested. "It will be easier this way."

Leith nodded reluctantly.

Inside, meds bandaged her hands and tended the other minor lacerations she'd received. She asked Drew to contact her parents and let them know everything was fine. Soon, she was in a change of clean clothes and settled in Nura's office, a cup of hot Terran cocoa in her hands.

Her hands were covered in skinseal and felt clumsy. Carefully, she lifted the handleless cup to her mouth and sipped. "How is J'Qhir?"

Nura sat beside her on the sofa and sipped her own cocoa. "The meds have him sedated while they work on his knee. The joint is shattered."

Leith frowned and set the cup aside. She had seen J'Qhir in terrible pain from just walking, it must have been unbearable when Steve continued attacking that one spot.

"They will do what they can, of course, to mend the injury and relieve his discomfort when he awakens. The Council has refused to agree to replacement surgery which the meds recommend. Without it, he will never be completely well. But of course, J'Qhir can make that decision later."

Leith nodded. "When can I see him?"

"After surgery. You can be with him a short time without the Council's knowledge, but he won't be conscious."

Leith leaned back against the soft pillow. "What happened out there?"

Nura laughed. "I think you should tell me."

"Why didn't all three of us die?"

"The Arcs," Nura said simply.

"I know, but why did they save J'Qhir and me and not Steve?"

"Many will say you and J'Qhir landed on the Arcs in such a way that they cushioned your fall. Unfortunately, Steve didn't. They will say you and J'Qhir were lucky and Steve wasn't. There are others who will say the Arcs pick and choose whom they save."

"And what do you say?"

Nura smiled enigmatically. "I say it's best left up to the individual to choose which to believe."

Leith reached for her cup and took another sip of cocoa. "Being absorbed by the Arc was a strange sensation."

"Absorbed? Leith, as far as we could see, you slid along the curve almost like your sliding playground equipment on Earth. You were never inside the Arc."

"But that's what it felt like, as if I were safely inside, out of harm's way."

"An illusion to make you feel safe so you wouldn't panic," Nura suggested, and it was as good an explanation as any.

Drew entered, his long dark hair coming loose from its fastening at his neck. "I can't get a connection on LinkNet," he said in exasperation. "The media reporters have jammed the transmitter again. But the good news is the Rover has been repaired."

Before Leith could say anything, a barely audible chime sounded through Nura's communication pin. She answered in the soft, soothing tones of Artilian and exchanged a few words with the voice on the other end. When she signed off, she looked at Leith.

"J'Qhir is out of surgery."

"Can you make the arrangements now, please?"

"Done. We'll give them time to get him settled, then visit while the meds are speaking with the Council."

A while later, another soft chime sounded and Nura told Leith they could go now. Nura led her to a lift that moved them swiftly through the complex to the med section. After walking through a few corridors, Nura keyed a door open and waited for Leith to enter. The door closed behind her and she was alone with J'Qhir.

He lay on a firm bed, his breathing strong and steady. She walked to his side and lightly ran her fingers along his crest.

"I know you can't hear me," she whispered. "But there is so much I want to tell you when you awaken. I want to tell you I love you and I want to explain what love is. I want to tell you about our child, a child we didn't think was possible to create, but we did anyway. I want to thank you for coming to my rescue and giving your life for me. Because of the Arcs you didn't die, but you didn't know that would happen. I can tell you all that tomorrow, can't I? Rest, J'Qhir, and tomorrow we will talk."

Leith remained at his side until Nura came for her. She kissed his cheek, crest, and mouth. She rubbed her forehead against his crest, then followed Nura from the room.

She and Drew bade Nura good night and boarded the aircar that returned them to their guesthouse. Leith slept through the rest of the night and late the next morning.

As soon as she finished showering, she turned on the viewer and ordered breakfast, plain toast and tea, brought to her room. She ate as she listened to all the news channels repeating the events of the previous evening. One reporter explained how the conference had been postponed indefinitely because of the sudden departure of the Zi Tri-Council from Artilia. He went on to explain the political ramifications to Zi and what it might mean to their admission to the Galactic Alliance.

Leith forgot her food as she switched channels again and again, hoping that particular reporter had been given erroneous information. If the Tri-Council had left Artilia, so had J'Qhir. To her dismay, several other reporters repeated the same story.

Leith tried to get in touch with Nura, but once again she was told the Servitor was unavailable. Frustrated, she switched the viewer to a local Artilian channel that was fortunately subtitled in Terran Standard. As she waited for a newscast, she tried to get in touch with Drew, but he wasn't in his room or the dining area.

A Standard hour later, a knock sounded at her door. She ran to it and keyed it open to Drew. He took one look at her stricken face and shook his head.

"It's true, they've gone." He stepped inside and closed the door. "I knew when I heard the reports this morning that you'd want to know for sure. I've been asking around. The Zi ship left during the night. I don't think they realize what an insult this is to the Alliance Board."

"And J'Qhir?" Leith asked in a small voice.

"I'm sorry, Leith. He's gone, too."

Leith fought the tears that burned her eyes and found the viewer on the bed where she'd dropped it. She left a message for Nura, thanking her for everything. She walked past Drew and opened the door. "I'm ready to go."

"Where?" he asked warily.

"Where else? Earth."

Chapter 16

Earth

July 2308 TST

Leith leaned over the countertop as the Peridot crawled underneath, out of her line of vision.

"I understand your needs, sir," she began and sincerely hoped the being was indeed a male. With the Peridot, it was difficult to make the distinction. "But none of our early model Galaxians can accommodate your physical requirements."

The Peridot crawled over her feet, and Leith suppressed the urge to grab something and swat him away.

"While I'm aware the older Galaxians are within your budget, the newer models do include alternate control systems." Leith sighed in relief as the Peridot moved back into view. He stopped long enough to look up at her beseechingly, the only way to describe the expression on his countenance. "Of course, we value you as a customer. We'll lease you a new Galaxian at the same rate as an older model. McClure Shipping strives to..."

As she spoke the Peridot crawled to the outer door and exited.

"...keep our customers happy," she finished the spiel to an empty room.

Leith sank into a chair that automatically conformed to her expanding curves and filled out the leasing contract as she sipped a chocolate milkshake. When the forms were completed and a copy sent to the Peridot's office, she leaned back and absently rubbed her distended belly.

On her return to Earth, Leith had decided to do what her parents always wanted and become part of the family business instead of hiding behind a computer console at the university. She thought time might have changed her, but she found dealing with the customers as tedious as when she had worked at the office during school breaks.

She wasn't suited to the faux cheerfulness she had to adopt when confronting the customers in person or on the viewer. She allowed them to walk all over her literally as well as figuratively. She was miserable...but she couldn't lay all the blame on McClure Shipping.

The child within kicked fiercely and Leith closed her eyes. She was only a little over four months along, but she felt huge and ungainly. Dr. Val Mitchel, her xeno-obstetrician, thought she might carry only seven months. Other human-alien hybrids were not uncommon, but Dr. Mitchel could only hypothesize since human-Zi crossbreeding had never occurred before.

Information trickled out of Zi. Leith gathered every word of it, bits and pieces of the language, the culture, the geography of the planet, even medical procedures. She had spent six weeks alone with a Zi, but she still knew so little.

Even less information came through that would help Leith and her child. Dr. Mitchel had requested obstetric information in the name of research, but the Zi were slow in responding. As long as they were both healthy, Leith wouldn't let the doctor reveal the real reason for her interest. She didn't want anyone on Zi to know unless it was absolutely necessary.

If everything went well, in as little as three months she could be holding her child—hers and J'Qhir's.

She regretted not having the chance to tell him she loved him aboard the *Starfire*, even if the words held no meaning for him. She wished she had made a greater effort to let him know her feelings during their stay on Artilia. But what she had told Nura was true. Ultimately, the decision was up to J'Qhir.

He had made his choice, and she had to abide by it. If only he had cared enough, felt *obligated* enough to say good-bye. Perhaps a clean break was easier, but it sure as hell couldn't hurt less than if he'd confronted her and said, "*I do not want you.*"

Not that she believed for an instant he didn't want her. They had discovered passionate pleasure together. J'Qhir, who never knew pleasure could be a part of the mating ritual, had enjoyed it as much as she had. No, he chose to return to the rigid moral code of Zi. He chose his *duty* and *responsibility* to his people over his own personal happiness.

Shouldn't she love him all the more for his choice? Shouldn't she respect his decision and be proud of his integrity? She shook her head and wiped at the tears. She couldn't feel any of those things because she was, after all, only human. She could let the ache in her heart make her bitter or she could do something about it. She hadn't wanted his duty and responsibility to bring him to her, but he had a right to know.

Leith leaned over to the console and connected to LinkNet. It was time to contact J'Qhir and tell him about the child they had miraculously conceived. Looking back, they shouldn't have taken the chance, but neither of them thought creating a life between them was possible. She located the number of the

Galactic Alliance offices on Earth. A temporary liaison had been appointed to Zi and she would start there.

Three hours later, she was only a little closer to contacting J'Qhir. After being shuffled through half a dozen offices and then told she would have to wait six Standard months before a request of contact with the Alliance-Zi office would even be considered, she used her clout and notoriety and reminded them of who she was. This got her as far as an under-secretary who sniffed as he informed her the liaison was unreachable at the moment. Then he surprised her by lowering his voice, as if he were sharing a confidence, and said, "The Warrior is not on Zi at this time. He is expected to return in two Standard weeks. The liaison should be in his office at that time as well. You can try again then."

Leith had thanked him and broken the connection.

Now, two Standard weeks seemed an impossibly long time. She had anticipated hearing his sibilant speech, watching subtle expressions only she could interpret cross his face. She wouldn't have given him the news over the viewer but asked to meet with him. She supposed it would have taken longer than two Standard weeks to make all the arrangements...if he agreed. It frightened her to think he might never want to see her again.

The outer door opened. Most customers conducted business through LinkNet, but some, like the Peridot, preferred doing so in person. A few insisted on retaining hard copies so the contracts were printed on plastisheets. Occasionally, customers requested natural materials, such as paper made from wood pulp. She hoped it wasn't a Hykaisite who only signed in blood. She was not in the mood to watch one rip his skin open with a jagged knife and bellow out the ritual conclusion to the transaction.

Leith stood, sucked in her stomach, and straightened her dress. The loose, flowing garment hid her condition well enough. She wasn't ashamed of her pregnancy, but it wasn't something she cared to discuss with virtual strangers. Tears came too easily these days.

"Leith, darling," Catherine McClure called out.

Leith relaxed and turned to face her parents. Cameron McClure sat in an anti-grav wheelchair, the bottom floating a few centimeters off the floor.

"Dad!" Leith hurried around the counter, kissed her father and hugged her mother. "What are you doing up and around? Isn't it a couple of months early?"

"My tormentors have released me from my horizontal confinement," Cameron laughed. He looked better than when she had first returned from Artilia, but he was still too pale and thin. "How's my grandson?"

"Granddaughter!" Catherine corrected.

Leith smiled at their never-ending argument. They had taken the news of their grandchild and its paternal heritage better than she expected. She kept them informed of everything Dr. Mitchel told her. They knew the risks.

"He or she is doing well. He's moving around a lot and hurts me when he kicks, but Dr. Mitchel says everything looks good right now."

"That sounds encouraging, Leith," Catherine said.

Cameron nodded toward the other console. "Where's Tasha?"

"I gave her the day off." At her father's frown, she continued, "It's been slow the past few days. Tasha kept mentioning all the things she needed to do."

"You look tired," Catherine observed and felt her forehead. "Are you sure you're all right?"

"I am tired, but I'm fine. Don't worry about me. I would tell you if anything was wrong."

"I hope so, Leith. Naturally, your father and I are concerned."

Leith glanced at Cameron who had steered his chair toward the console. "I know, but you and Dad have enough problems without me."

Catherine smiled toward her husband. "The worst is over. Now, we have to get through recovery. Your father begins therapy three times a week at the hospital. The sessions will last a few hours, and I've decided to spend them here at the office instead of waiting uselessly at the hospital."

"Have the doctors said how long before he'll be walking?"

"Another six months, at least. He has decided he will be walking in six weeks. You know how hard-headed he can be."

Leith smiled and nodded. "It's that positive attitude that's gotten him through so far."

"True enough. One doctor told me about some cases of the Fever where it took two years for the patients to get to the point where he is now. But they had become very despondent over their condition. Your father has never lost faith he'll recover."

"Leith! What's this?" Cameron shouted from the console.

"What, Dad?" Leith asked, knowing what he had found.

"The Peridot contract. Did he give you that old story about financial straits?"

"Well, yes—" A blush of embarrassment infused Leith's face.

"That Peridot has more credits than all of our other clients combined," Cam snorted. "Tasha would have known how to deal with him."

Leith shook her head. "I'm sorry, I didn't realize—"

"Cam, please," Catherine admonished.

Cameron scowled and turned back to the viewer.

"It's all right," Catherine said soothingly. "We didn't expect you to be an expert overnight."

"No, it's not all right." Leith moved over to the large window and looked out over the city of Memphis sprawled beneath. The sparkling ribbon of the Mississippi River ran lazily beneath the M-shaped bridge. She could see two of the three steel and glass pyramids built in the last few centuries. She lay her forehead against the cool glass. "I knew the Peridot was bluffing me, but I didn't want to argue with him."

"Cam has been doing this for over twenty years, and he's known the Peridot longer than that. It comes with time and experience."

Leith heard the disapproving sounds her father made as he looked over other files. She sighed. "Meanwhile, McClure Shipping goes belly up because I can't say no."

"It's not as bad as all that. Cam will make it up on the next contract with the Peridot."

The outer door opened again, and Leith turned to find Drew sauntering in.

"Are we ready yet?"

"Ready for what?" Leith asked.

"Drew!" Catherine snapped. "I haven't had a chance to ask her yet."

"Ask me what?"

Drew kissed Leith on the cheek and shrugged. "Oops."

"What is going on?"

Catherine frowned at Drew. "Your father and Drew are taking us to lunch. I have some errands to run afterwards."

Leith looked back and forth between them and knew her mother's annoyance at Drew meant there was more to it than lunch and shopping. "Will one of you please tell me what is going on?"

Cameron steered around the counter and joined them. "Your mother needs a few hours away from me. Drew agreed to join us or your mother wouldn't go."

"Well, what am I, chopped paow steak? Not that I mind Drew having lunch with us, but I'll be with you."

"We thought you might have some things to do this afternoon, too," Cameron said. "I shut down the console. Since Tasha isn't here, we'll just close the office for the afternoon."

"No, we won't. I don't have anything else to do so I'll come back here."

"Well, darling, you never know what might pop up," Catherine said. "Now, are we all ready?"

Leith meekly followed along as they shut the office and left the building. Drew drove them to a restaurant not far away, and they enjoyed a leisurely lunch. Every time Leith tried to ask questions, either her father or mother turned the conversation in another direction. Finally, she gave up. They would tell her in their own time.

At last, Catherine got up and kissed Leith's cheek. Leith watched the gentle kiss and subtle touches her parents shared before her mother left. It was difficult to believe they had been married for almost twenty-five years. They acted like newlyweds. It was the kind of relationship Leith always wanted and probably the main reason she had never taken casual lovers. She wanted a deep, lasting relationship like her parents had.

What she yearned for with J'Qhir.

Tears burned her eyes as she looked at her father. "Is there something you haven't told me about your condition? Is that what this is all about?"

"Of course not, Leith," he said, but he sounded tired. "We haven't been keeping anything from you about my condition. Besides, your mother wouldn't have left if there was anything to tell you."

Leith nodded. "All right, then. Are you ready to go home, Dad? You've done quite a bit for your first day out."

"I'm fine. Actually, I was thinking of a walk in the park, if you two don't mind."

"What about Mom?"

"She'll meet us there later."

Leith sat quietly in the vehicle while Drew drove them to the park, found a parking space, and helped Cameron out. Beads of perspiration broke out on her skin immediately. In late July, in the mid-south, the heat and humidity was almost unbearable. By the time they entered the park, she felt as if she were wrapped in a layer of damp cloth.

"Are you sure you're up to this?" Leith asked. "We can do this another time, when the humidity isn't as high. The air's no cooler beneath the trees."

"I'm fine."

Leith glanced around the park, wondering what this was all about. Very few beings were out and about in this heat. A group of young Peridots crawled over the play area. Two Hykaisites performed battle exercises to a small group of interested humans. A few others walked here and there under the shade of the huge, sprawling trees.

Leith stopped when she saw the robed being standing a dozen meters away. His long, dark gray robe had blended so well within the shadows she had missed him the first time her gaze swept the park. Her heart thudded erratically. J'Qhir.

She glanced down at her father.

Cameron smiled. "It's up to you whether you want to see him or not."

She looked at J'Qhir again and said stupidly, "I already see him. Why didn't you tell me?"

Cameron cleared his throat. "J'Qhir explained that this is the way it's done, according to custom. I saw nothing wrong with it as long as he understood that if you turned around and walked away, then no one would stop you. It's up to you."

"Why couldn't Mom be here?"

"According to their custom, only male family members are allowed and the meeting place must be neutral ground. I told him Drew was like a member of the family and he agreed."

"And the purpose? I can't believe everyone went to all this trouble just for him to say hello."

"That's for you and J'Qhir to discuss."

Cameron would say no more.

It was what she had dreamed of, J'Qhir coming to her. She took one step then another and as she approached him, he turned away from her and moved deeper into the trees. She noticed he still walked with a limp.

She drew in a deep breath and followed along behind.

※ ※ ※

J'Qhir was all too aware of Leith's delicate stride behind him. When he first saw her as she entered the park, he could barely restrain himself from rushing to her and embarrassing himself into self-imposed exile. He wanted to hold her and kiss her *there* and *there* and *there*, carry her away to lovemake with her until their bodies ached sweetly with the spending of their passion, as Leith called it.

Passion, a wondrous Terran word. The Zi equivalent did not lend itself to such a meaning. He was passionate in his desire to save Zi, but he was also passionate in his desire for Leith. The two feelings were distinctly different. The Zi word did not extend to the intense physical need and longing he had for Leith.

The pattern of her walk was different, as if her center of balance had been altered. Did she reel with emotion at seeing him again? And which emotion? Excitement or displeasure? Each could cause the same response. She had not smiled when she found him beneath the tree. She had not appeared angry, but she had not seemed happy either. He knew well her happiness from their time on Paradise.

He had wandered through the park earlier and learned the many paths. Cameron had explained few others would be about because of the heat. The air here was damper than that of Zi, but he was quite comfortable even with the formal robe. Today, he was not the Warrior and gladly left his war attire behind.

Leith's steps quickened and she drew nearer. "J'Qhir..."

He stopped at the sound of her voice, as he should. For him, the bonding ritual had begun.

"Do you have to walk so fast? I can barely keep up." She glanced around the dense foliage. "Where are we going?"

"We are there," he said without turning to her.

She was silent a moment, not comprehending then discarding as unimportant. "J'Qhir, it's good to see you again. I tried to get in touch with you, but I was told you had left Zi."

Something swelled within his chest.

"I don't know what my parents have told you—"

"Cameron hasss told me all that I need to know. We have been communicating sssince my return to Zi."

"Oh."

Did he detect disappointment in that one small sound? Why should contact with her father disturb her? Of course, she didn't completely understand the bonding ritual. Perhaps he should have allowed Cameron to explain the process, but he wanted her reaction—good, bad, or indifferent—to be uncontrolled by forethought. It was critical to his peace of mind that she answer spontaneously.

Even so, he must diverge from the proper script. The demands the Council arbitrarily placed upon his position changed the procedure.

"The Council—" he began then cleared his throat. "The Council hasss decreed the Warrior mussst be bound. They have chosssen a lifemate for me."

Leith made a very small, strangled sound—he barely heard it—but when he turned, her face was as noncommittal as before.

"I told them I would not bind with one they chossse. I would choossse my own."

"And...have you?"

"Yesss. If ssshe will agree."

"She would be a fool not to." Liquid shone in her eyes, but she quickly blinked it away.

"*Nhi'a`aqh'fi johl meh' pohlas`h,*" he said in Zi. *I will build a lair for us.* He stopped and inhaled, in preparation of repeating the words in Terran Standard.

"*Ehl, whaz ghajh dhi'i`i nhehw.*" Leith shocked him by responding in Zi. *Yes, that would be most proper.* Her voice shook as she carefully enunciated the unfamiliar words, and this time liquid filled her eyes and overflowed.

"Leith...do you know what you sssay?"

"Yes. I know."

"Do you know what it meansss?"

She nodded and her lustrous brown hair fell over her shoulders. He resisted the urge to touch the filaments. He should not touch her at all until the bonding ritual was completed.

"For life," he explained anyway. "Forever and alwaysss."

"Forever and always," she repeated with a smile, yet liquid continued to spill from her eyes.

J'Qhir almost returned the smile, but thought better of it. Even though she had assured him numerous times he wasn't frightful when he smiled, he suspected she was only being kind.

"I know," she said breathlessly, "it is not your way to be demonstrative in a public place, but it is the custom of my people to seal a promise with a kiss."

He hesitated. His fingers ached to touch her, to run through her hair, to strip the thin fabric from her body and feel her liquid heat. Her presence and his improper thoughts poised him on the verge of release.

"It isss not proper we touch at all." But even as he spoke he moved toward her. His large hands framed her pale face. Her natural scent filled his nostrils as he bowed his head to hers.

Their mouths met briefly, her warm moistness almost his undoing. He could allow no more and withdrew.

"J'Qhir, we have done much more than touch," she reminded him, her voice soft and husky.

"I want to do thisss in the mossst proper way."

Leith sighed and nodded. Her own words had come back to haunt her. She didn't want to stand here exchanging words, she wanted to place her arms around him and have him hold her as he had so many nights before. She had asked it of J'Qhir the first time they had made love and it was only fair that she concede to his request.

"We leave for Zi in one Ssstandard week. Thisss ssshould be enough time for you to prepare. I have made arrangementsss for you to ssstay in the lair of Rohm'dh. You do remember him?"

Leith hesitated. Everything was happening too fast and not at all as she had hoped. She was thrilled he had come and asked her one more time, but she had wanted him to come on his own because he wanted her. Not because he felt obligation toward the child she carried. When he said Cameron had told him all that he needed to know, she thought her heart might burst from the disappointment. Of course, Cameron had told him of her pregnancy. He was her father and would do everything to protect her and the child.

J'Qhir watched her expectantly, saurian eyes unblinking. Cameron might not have told him about the complications and the risks. Or J'Qhir didn't understand how fragile their child was at this point.

"Of course, I remember him." She wrinkled her brow as she looked up at him. "But you expect me to go to Zi?"

He stiffened visibly. She saw every muscle go rigid and his jaw clench into knots. "Temporarily," he said coldly, "if that isss what you wisssh."

"J'Qhir. I can't go to Zi now. Perhaps we should talk more before we consider ourselves bound to one another." When his only response was the narrowing of his eyeslits, she continued. "I mean, I thought you understood...that my father had explained—"

"We are already bound, Leith," he said sharply. He hadn't listened to what she was doing a poor job of trying to say. He only heard what he interpreted as rejection. "Asss sssoon asss you ssspoke the proper resssponssse, we were irrevocably bound. You sssealed it with your kisss."

"I know! I don't mean—"

"We go to Zi." He inhaled a hissing breath. "It will take time to build our lair. Usssually, one Zi year which isss lesss than a Sssstandard year. The wood mussst be harvesssted from the mountainsss. Sssince I have no clossse male clanssmember, Rohm'dh hasss agreed to accompany me. While we collect the materialsss and consssstruct the lair, you will ssstay with hisss clan to learn—"

"J'Qhir! Are you saying you'll build the house yourself?" Her voice rose in pitch, but she could not control it. The incredulity of what he suggested overwhelmed her. "And I won't see you for a year?"

"It isss our way, Leith." He shook his head and turned his back to her, but not before she glimpsed the disappointment in his eyes. "I ssshould have made that more clear."

"I understand. But you have to understand, I can't—"

"When our lair isss finisssshed and you and I have ssslept beneath itsss roof for three consssecutive nightsss," he cut her off as if she hadn't spoken, "then we will be formally bound for

281

life. It doesss not matter if we ssshare the sssame blanket. It will be done. Then, Leith, you may go wherever in the galaxy you wisssh."

Leith flinched at the harshness of the last of his words. The Zi did not swear, but he had, in effect, told her she could go to hell. Leith drew in a deep, shuddering breath. If he was willing to be separated from her for a year and equally willing to let her go, then he couldn't know about the child! She had assumed her father told him about her condition, but what if he hadn't?

She placed her hands on his rigid back and laid her head on his shoulder blade. He didn't move away from her, but neither did he yield to her touch. Instead of *trying* to explain, she whispered, "I-I thought you would want to be with me when your child is born."

More tears filled her eyes and spilled over. She felt him grow pliant beneath her hands. Through the watery blur, she saw him turn and face her, but she couldn't tell if he was displeased or not. She blinked and rubbed at her eyes, but before she could see him clearly, he swept her up into his arms. Limping, he carried her deeper into the trees, until he found a stone bench encircled by hedges to ensure their privacy. He sat, but he kept her bundled against him. His head rested against hers.

"I want nothing more than to go to Zi with you or wherever you go. I want nothing more than to be with you." She slipped her arms around his neck and hugged him.

"Leith...Leith..." he murmured into her hair and held her tighter. "Why did you not tell me?"

"It was why I tried to get in touch with you. I finally decided you should know." She paused and then told him what had hurt her for so long. "You left, J'Qhir, you left without saying good-bye."

"Leith, there wasss no need to bid you farewell. I never intended to leave Artilia without ssspeaking with you. During the ssstruggle with Hancock, my knee wasss broken."

"I know. The Council wouldn't let them replace the joint. Why haven't you had this done?"

"I promisssed you I would not perform the ritual of failure. Thisss injury I will carry the ressst of my life asss my atonement."

"No, J'Qhir—"

"Leith, it isss not open to debate. You will allow me thisss." Briefly, he touched his crest to her forehead and continued. "Afterwardsss, I wasss ssedated for sssurgery. While I wasss ssstill unconsssciousss, the Council took it upon themssselvesss to transssport me to Zi."

Fresh tears filled her eyes and she hugged him closer. "I-I didn't know they had taken you without your consent. I assumed—well, I assumed the worst. I'm sorry."

"No, I ssshould beg forgivenesss from you. I let the Council control my actionsss and, in thisss inssstance, I ssshould not have. You are too important to me."

Leith laughed. "We're a fine pair, aren't we? I would trust you with my life, but I couldn't bring myself to completely trust you with my heart. And you—"

"Yesss, I. I did not trusssst you enough to undersssstand you truly meant you *could* not go to Zi, not that you *would* not."

Leith grew solemn. "Our baby. I can't go anywhere. I need to stay near Dr. Mitchel. She doesn't know…"

"Doesssn't know what?" he prompted gently.

"J'Qhir, she doesn't know if I can carry the baby full-term. She says every day I go without any major problems, the chances get better. But she's only guessing. She hasn't had much success getting obstetric information out of Zi, but then I wouldn't let her tell them the real reason either."

J'Qhir removed his arm from underneath her knees, and his hand hovered over her mid-section. "May I?"

"You never have to ask permission to touch me." She guided his hand to rest atop her swollen abdomen.

"Thisss changesss many thingsss."

Leith pressed her forehead to his cheek. "Can you tell me this is all right?"

"Oh, yesss, it isss very right."

She closed her eyes. "But it is not done. Will your people ever understand? Will the Council?"

"It doesss not matter. If they exile me, I will gladly go to be with you. I have ssserved my people and done my duty to my father'sss memory. I have given them enough." Tenderly, he ran his hand over her belly. "I am ssshamed, but I admit I kept our relationsssship a sssecret becaussse I did not know how you felt. I wanted to dissscover what you wanted before I jeopardized my posssition. If I could not have you, then I would have the title of Warrior, poor sssubsssstitute that it isss."

"It makes sense, J'Qhir. It's nothing to be ashamed of."

"I have done more to ssshame mysssself." He drew in a sharp breath. "Do you remember on Paradisss, how many timesss I ssspoke to you, 'I will build a lair for usss'."

Leith groaned and opened her eyes. "I didn't know what you were asking, J'Qhir. I didn't know the significance of the words."

"I know."

"And if I had, I don't think I would have answered differently. We barely knew one another. Even though we never thought we would be rescued, I don't think either of us ever gave up hope. How could we have made promises to one another that we might regret if we were rescued?"

"I underssstand, Leith. But you mussst underssstand, lovemaking to you wasss forbidden to me unlesss we were bound. The firssst time I sssaid the wordsss, I only meant we needed sssshelter. I sssspoke them before I realized what I wasss sssaying."

"Yet you didn't stop asking, using those words." Quickly, she pressed her lips against his cheek, so very glad she could touch him. She was afraid he might start that proper nonsense again and forbid her to touch him.

"Yesss, the wordsss ssseemed right. We were the only two beingsss on the entire planet. We did not know if we would ever leave. I had reacted to you physsssically from the moment I met you. By the time we had sssettled in the cave, all I could think of wasss *rhi'ina'a*." He paused and looked thoughtful. "I do believe it isss becaussse of your never-ending cycle."

"It has ended now that I'm pregnant."

"Ssss, and sssstill I want you. The theory isss flawed."

"I think you have finally broken free of all the rules that oppress you. If you are told enough times that you can't feel, then you don't feel. If you are pressured into not experiencing passion, then you won't experience it. On Paradise, you let down your guard and threw away all the rules and regulations that have always governed how you think and feel and react."

"I think you are correct." He looked at her thoughtfully. "Do you remember the day when you returned to the cave unexpectedly, when I performed—?"

"Yes, I remember," she interrupted quickly, unwilling for him to mention that insane Zi ritual again.

"Do you remember what I asssked of you?"

"Yes..." Her voice trailed off.

"I sssaid I would build a lair for usss."

"You know, that's really not a question—" she began.

"Sss't. But it requiresss a ressssponsssse. Do you remember what you sssaid?"

She nodded and traced a path around his tympanum. He brushed her fingers away.

"I cannot think when you do that."

"Good! And I remember what I said. 'Yes, J'Qhir, you do that.' Or something to that effect."

He said nothing more and waited, his amber eyes expectant.

Leith sat up straight in his lap. "Does that mean—"

"Yesss, Leith. Asss far asss I wasss concerned we were bound at that moment. We ssspent three conssssecutive nightsss together under one roof."

She let her arms fall away from him and drew back. "Why didn't you tell me?"

"You didn't know what you were sssaying. How could I bind you when you didn't know the meaning of the wordsss? Yet, it made the sssituation acceptable for me. I knew we would join eventually, and I could not have done ssso under any other conditionsss."

"You made me feel guilty."

"It isss for that I am ssshamed, but I wanted you to realize the gravity of what we did."

"I knew the seriousness of the decision without that. J'Qhir, it was an important step for me also."

He nodded. "Yesss, I came to undersssstand that, but by then it wasss too late to explain and not caussse hard feelingsss. I do beg forgivenesss for the sssubterfuge."

"What if I had said no today?"

"Then I would have returned to Zi."

"You would have become bound to the female the Council chose for you?"

"No, Leith. I am bound to you."

"But what about me?"

"The lawsss of Zi do not apply to off-worldersss."

Leith tried to assimilate his logic but failed. "If Zi law doesn't apply to me, then how can we be bound at all?"

"If you accept the lawsss of Zi then they apply to you," J'Qhir explained with the patience of a saint. "By anssswering in Zi and ressssponding in the posssitive, you indicated you underssstand and accept the lawsss of Zi."

"I see. You would never have told me that we had become lifemates on Paradise."

"No." He laid his crest against her forehead and gently rubbed back and forth. "Pleassse tell me about our child."

She told him everything, of the risks involved. "Dr. Mitchel is monitoring me closely. She's as anxious to see this baby born as I am but for different reasons."

"I am in awe of thisss life we have created. Truly, Leith, I had no idea we could procreate or I would never have put you at risssk. If we had not been ressscued...sss't! Even here, with your advanced technology, you are in danger." He pulled away from her. "If thisss child comesss at the expenssse of your life—"

"Shhh." She pressed her hand to his mouth. "Dr. Mitchel doesn't think it will come to that. She doesn't think he will do me any harm."

"He?"

"Well, we don't know. With your hidden equipment, there's no way to tell. J'Qhir, would you mind if your child has hair?"

He ran his fingers through her long locks. "*Ssshe* will have your hair. Why would I mind?"

"He or she will be a part of us both." She hesitated, then whispered, "There is something I have wanted to tell you for a long time...I love you, J'Qhir."

He thought a moment. "You do not mean lovemaking, do you?"

"No. Love is the emotion I feel for you. Do the Zi love? Can you love?"

"We have no word for love. We ressspect and we honor and we have obligation and duty, but we do not love." He paused. "Yet, if love meansss I ache when we are apart and I am filled with joy when you are near and I want you more than anything in the galaxy then yesss, I love you, Leith."

Leith sighed happily, pressing her mouth to his. She made a mental note to tell her mother she had indeed been starkissed.

About the Author

Lanette Curington, who also writes as Lani Aames, was born and raised in west Tennessee and resides there with her husband, two daughters, and a clowder of cats. She is the author of the critically acclaimed futuristic romance, Starkissed, her first release with Samhain Publishing. As Lani Aames, she writes erotic romance and is multi-published in a variety of sub-genres, including Master of Disaster, also available from Samhain Publishing. For the latest information, visit her author websites www.lanettecurington.com and www.laniaames.com.

Look for these titles by
Lanette Curington

Now Available:

Master of Disaster (writing as Lani Aames)

A sexy alien with secrets to hide, an irresistible reporter determined to expose the truth; when resistance succumbs to temptation, they are forced to pay…

The Price of Discovery
© 2006 Jordanna Kay

On the hunt for a juicy story and a promotion, Erin Price is determined to prove she can move beyond her past mistakes. An eerie Victorian house in the middle of nowhere and a sexy stranger hiding secrets could be her ticket to success. Racing against time and a competing journalist, Erin breaks every rule to be near the stranger. When she discovers the truth, she'll be forced to decide if her career is more important than her heart.

Drakor has nothing but contempt for Earth after his best friend disappeared on the planet during a previous assignment. When his family accepts a critical mission to find a cure for bone crippling disease at home, Drakor is forced to return to the planet he despises. As his birthday nears, Drakor is losing time to find his life-mate. Will his encounters with a nosy reporter change his opinion of Earth and is his deep attraction to her proof that his true life-mate is human? When a series of failures force Drakor to take his family and run, will he leave behind the only person he can ever love?

Available now in ebook and print from Samhain Publishing.

Enjoy the following excerpt from The Price of Discovery...

Erin wiped her palms on Drakor's shirt and tested the door at the end of the hall. The room she snuck in earlier. It was unlocked! She slipped inside and quickly closed the door behind her, locking it.

This room too was darkened by the shadows of the moon. If only she could have gone home and gotten her flashlight. Now, she'd have to poke around in the dark. There had to be something in this massive bookshelf to her left. She already knew that nothing was on the other side of the room other than a bed. This must have been his parents' bedroom. It seemed creepy to be in here when they only died two days ago. But still she had work to do and she couldn't let anything stand in her way.

She went closer to the screen on the desk. It looked similar to a computer monitor, but much flatter and shinier. Erin reached out to touch it when a sound startled her from behind.

Had someone come in? She locked the door, she was sure of it.

Erin tried to ignore the galloping of her heart and slowly turned to face the dark corner of the room. She could see nothing against that shadowed wall but then a figure stepped forward.

"So this is the real Erin."

Her breath stilled but her heart jumped for an entirely different reason. Drakor.

But how did he get in here? Or was he in here all along? There was no sense in lying like she tried to with Brundor. Drakor knew what she did for a living and why she was here.

She folded her arms under her breasts, suddenly very aware of her bare legs and his scent on her collar. "And? What of it?"

He took another step forward and Erin had to muffle the intake of breath in her dry throat. The glow from the window lit up his bare chest, narrowed waist, and arms, casting shadows along the hard lines of his muscles. He wore a pair of shorts, unbuttoned but zipped, and nothing else.

Drakor leaned one hand against the shelves near her. "I never imagined you would use my sisters to get what you want."

Erin tilted her head, trying to not be tempted by the allure of his body.

He moved closer still and Erin backed up until her butt hit the edge of the desk. Drakor put an arm on either side of her head, blocking an escape.

Erin stared up at him, wanting to run from him but knowing she could not. Not when he was this close. Not when shivers coursed through her body in the anticipation of his next move. She licked her lips but couldn't control the deep yearning crashing through her blood. He held her spellbound, intoxicated by his raw sexuality.

Drakor leaned toward her face, stopping just inches from her lips. "You and I are playing this game, but only one of us can win."

Why couldn't she respond to him with some witty comment? One glance into those mysterious eyes made her heart skip a beat. His heady, masculine presence enveloped her so completely that all logical thought emptied from her brain.

Erin muttered something unintelligible and lifted her chin a little. Damn it, why didn't he kiss her?

A hot hand clamped down on her thigh and Erin gasped. Her pulse rocketed. She could see one corner of his lips curl as he slid a knee between her legs. "What do you hope to find, Erin?"

She tried to answer but her mouth was too dry to even swallow. If only he would kiss her...

hot
stuff

Discover Samhain!